SALKEHATCHIE SOUP

SALKEHATCHIE SOUP

A SOUTH CAROLINA STORY

by KEN BURGER

EVENING
POST
PUBLISHING CO.
Charleston, S. C.

This novel is a work of fiction. Any reference to historical events; to real people, living or dead; or to real locales are intended only to give the fiction a setting in historical reality. Other names, characters, places and incidents either are the product of the author's imagination or are used fictitiously, and their resemblance, if any, to real-life counterparts is entirely coincidental.

Published by
Evening Post Books
134 Columbus Street
Charleston, South Carolina 29403

Copyright © 2012 by Ken Burger
All rights reserved.
First edition

Editors: John M. Burbage/Holly Holladay
Designer: Gill Guerry
Cover and interior photos: Henry Gillam
Author portrait: Bonnie Grossman

First printing 2012
Printed in the United States of America

A CIP catalog record for this book has been applied
for from the Library of Congress.

ISBN: 978-1-929647-13-2

To my wife,
Bonnie, the love
of my life

ACKNOWLEDGMENTS

You don't write books by yourself. You do it with the aid of a hundred people, maybe more, who populate your life and provide the bits and pieces you cobble together into a readable tale.

They are the storytellers, jokesters, accomplices, roommates, classmates, and everyday livers of life who say the damnedest things when you just happen to be around, listening.

Among those are my good friend Andy Solomon, who sits on my dock and makes me laugh a lot. And Billy Love, an amateur sociologist and city councilman from Gaffney, who always provides a unique perspective on the world.

Another unindicted co-conspirator is Ephraim Ulmer, an Allendale boy who survived our childhood to become an unwitting carrier of all things humorous.

And I cannot tell you, although I tried, how many raunchy, hilarious, untellable things I heard from my buddies in the "Down The River Gang" that camps each October on the Savannah River and stirs old stories into the Frogmore Stew when we're away from polite company.

The same goes for my lifelong friends, Hall Boylston, Chuck Brewer, Buddy Gillam and Bill Kearse, who compete with me each year for the coveted Tin Cup, a trophy that has a golfer on top for no apparent reason. Buddy Gillam also contributed most of the photography for this book.

Then there are guys like John White, the park ranger at Rivers Bridge Battlefield, who walked me through the cypress knees in the Salkehatchie Swamp that stand as eternal tombstones to soldiers, blue and gray, who fell in a fitful, fruitless, fight over a lost cause.

And a hearty thanks and deep appreciation to Francis Fleming Chavous, who preserves our heritage through her devotion to an arts program called Salkehatchie Stew, a title I bypassed to spare them being fictionalized unfairly.

Of course, this book would not be the same without Carl Gooding, who in real life is a character unlike any other behind the Pine Curtain. And while I briefly considered using a fictional name for this larger-than-life radio personality, it just didn't seem right to disguise a man with such talent. He is, indeed, the King of the Salkehatchie.

Another tip of the hat goes to Tommy McQueeney, a fellow writer, who allowed me to peek into his stories about golfing legend Henry Picard, where I extracted a few nuggets I otherwise would not have known. And I must mention Sammy Fretwell of *The State* newspaper in Columbia who shared some of his reporting on the toxic waste buried in our beautiful state.

Then there is Hugh Thompson Jr., the real-life chopper pilot who stopped the killing at My Lai, only to watch in exasperation as his superiors tried to cover it all up.

I must mention Lawton O'Cain, of Estill, who gives Sherman tours through the brushy backwaters along the Savannah River, where the Devil Himself invaded our state and left it burning in the latter days of the Civil War.

And I cannot forget that winter day I flew in a small plane with pilot Mark DiBiasi over the length and breadth of the mysterious, meandering, Salkehatchie River, clearly seeing it for the first time, despite growing up in its swallows. Or the time spent with author and historian Jack Bass, who just happens to be as funny as he is smart.

As always, thanks to John Burbage, publisher of Evening Post Books, who makes this endeavor possible. A special thanks to Holly Holladay of Evening Post Books, who not only edited this book but also allowed me to use her beautiful name for the female lead.

And last but not least, my wife Bonnie Grossman, who not only lets me chase these silly dreams but also reads and edits the outcome with loving care.

To everyone who has allowed me to pursue my passion, I say thanks, from the bottom of my heart.

Spartanburg

Greenville

South Carolina

Columbia

Savannah River

Aiken

Williston

Lake Marion

Barnwell

Bamberg

Lake Moultrie

Salkehatchie River

Groton

Cooper R.

Edisto R.

Charleston

Sullivan's Island

Beaufort

Atlantic Ocean

Savannah

Hilton Head Island

CHAPTER 1

O rrie Adger waded knee-deep into the downstream tug of the Salkehatchie River, a bottle of Wild Turkey in one hand, a 1-iron in the other. When the cold water engulfed his testicles, he screamed skyward, cursing God in heaven for everything that came to mind.

"You do-nothing, holier-than-thou, beyond-understanding, life-everlasting son of a bitch," he swore loudly, swaying as his golf shoes sank in the mucky matter and stirred up silt as he staggered, one foot in front of the other, trying to keep his balance.

"Where have you fucking been? What can…I do…now? How could you…?"

As if on cue, an unearthly darkness swept away a slip of sunlight that seeped through the canopy of tree branches hanging over the narrow stream, the temperature dropped dramatically, and a deep, far-away rumble vibrated through Orrie's spine.

That's when he felt a presence and turned quickly to see if anyone was standing behind him. Assured that he was alone, Orrie hesitated, then unleashed another unholy tirade.

"I don't care what they say," he screamed, taking another slug from the bottle and waving the 1-iron for effect. "I think you're a fucking phony. A figment of everybody's frightened imagination. A goddamned…."

The lightning struck so fast it ionized electrons in the air, sucking the words out of Orrie's mouth, making him gasp as he fell back on his butt in the dark water.

"Shit," he said, using the golf club as a cane to regain his footing, still managing to keep the whiskey bottle above water. This was, after all, the worst day of his life, an existence that had seen its share of highs and lows.

CHAPTER 2

Not yet 30, Orrie Adger had been a has-been half his life, most of which was predicated on a single moment that caught the golf world by surprise. It happened close by, at Palmetto Golf Club in Aiken, one of the storied shrines he grew up playing when he was considered a phenom.

Raised on Butler Island, a pristine slip of sand outside Charleston, South Carolina, Orrie couldn't remember when he didn't have a golf club in his hand. Nor could he remember a time when he wasn't good.

As the only child of the island's owners, Tom and Jeannie Adger, he had full run of Butler's three manicured golf courses and access to the pros who played there. Once an exclusive treatment center for drunks, Butler Island rose in golf prominence after Orrie's father leveraged his soul to oil-rich Kuwaiti developers. First came the tourists. Then a PGA tournament. Then the Ryder Cup.

Before Orrie was old enough to carry his own bag, renowned golf course designer Pete Dye had molded the signature course, Butler Bay, into an iconic piece of golfing lore. This put Orrie inside the ropes when the PGA Tour came to call every April, the week after the Masters in Augusta. Not only did he have autographed pictures with players like Arnold Palmer and Jack Nicklaus, he had a swing both men admired.

That's because Orrie was suckled on the milk of golf purity, privately taught from an early age by Henry Picard, a Charleston resident who won the Masters in '38 and followed it with a PGA Championship in '39.

Around town, Mr. Picard was the quiet, unassuming, retired pro at the Country Club of Charleston. But to those who really knew golf, those who understood the swing, the old man was the real thing, a unique blend of art and science.

Picard, almost forgotten by the time Orrie came along, liked the gangly rich kid whose mother dropped him off on Wednesday afternoons at an old par-three course on nearby Johns Island. Somewhere in the boy's sinewy structure he sensed a rare athleticism, the kind that could make the kid a gift to the game.

So Picard passed along his secret of golf, the Morrison Method, a technique he'd learned as a young pro in Pennsylvania. Rather than putting the torque of the golf swing on the hips and knees, the old man taught Orrie to roll his feet when he swung. It not only reduced the wear and tear on his body, it produced more power.

"I call Mr. Picard every time I win something," Orrie was quoted in *The Charleston Courier* after capturing the Azalea Amateur Tournament at age 14. "He makes golf seem easy."

To Orrie it was. The game that maddened millions came to him like walking down steps. He could do it without thinking. Without a care. Without a doubt, he could maneuver the golf ball right or left or low or high or long or short by willing it from his brain to his beautiful hands. That's what Mr. Picard called them. Beautiful. The kind of hands that steer ships through storms, make metal bend against its will, defy gravity and other forces of nature without explanation.

Orrie always called him Mr. Picard because it was the only name that seemed to fit the distinguished old pro who wore white, long-sleeved cotton shirts and a tie, even in the depths of sweltering South Carolina summers.

And his teaching methods were just as dignified. Instead of high-fives and atta-boys when you got something right, Mr. Picard would simply look at his student and say, "Thank you," for not wasting his time.

All of which hurled Orrie into the competitive arena early, a place where he thrived, believing he could win, no matter what. Partly because of Mr. Picard. But also because of Butterbean Green, one of the top caddies at Butler Bay, and Orrie's best friend since childhood.

When Butterbean was on his bag, Orrie knew he could do anything, anytime, anywhere. Because Butterbean said so. And Butterbean knew more about golf than anybody he'd ever known. Even Mr. Picard. Which is why white people overlooked Butterbean's peculiar ways. Like going barefoot so he could read the greens with his feet. And always wearing sunglasses, telling people he was blind as Ray Charles.

So it was that Butterbean was at Orrie's side that fateful day at Palmetto, when the sun's last rays tipped the tallest pines, and a gaggle of golf enthusiasts trailed him and Chris Patton around the clubhouse loop of the last three holes.

"He's the biggest golfer I've ever seen," Orrie, then 15 years old, told *The Aiken Standard* going into the final round. "But the bigger they come, you know, the harder they fall on you."

He'd get better with his media quotes, but young Orrie would never be closer to God than on that July afternoon when Patton, a 300-pound, 18-year-old golfer from Fountain Inn, was the crowd favorite to win another junior title. His huge size and monster drives kept people chasing him down the fairways, wanting him to win so they could say they were there when he did.

But Orrie had other ideas. He could see Patton sweating profusely when they stood on the 10th tee, their 28th hole of the two-round final. The heat was in the big boy's head, and there wasn't a breeze for 40 miles.

After Orrie drained a 20-footer for birdie on 17, he was tied with Patton as they walked to the back tee on 18, a short par-4, uphill to the clubhouse.

With the honors, Orrie stepped to the box, calmly pushed his tee into the soft earth, and rocked back on his heels. Holding his driver out in front of him, using it like a sight on a rifle, he stepped around, addressed the ball, and thought of Mr. Picard. Orrie felt the club come back straight and slow, kept his eye on the Titleist with the two black dots under the number 1, knew when the club reached a perfect parallel at the top of his swing, then started to unfold the left side of his body toward the target.

He was just beginning to roll his feet when a spectator sitting on a golf umbrella lost his balance and fell against a woman standing next to him, just on the edge of Orrie's peripheral vision. That's when Orrie's left knee buckled. The ball shot to the right in a hurry, headed for an ancient oak towering over a fairway sand trap that had double bogey written all over it.

The man who tumbled froze when he caught himself, but it was too late. The crowd turned and stared at the exact place where Orrie's concentration had shattered like glass on a tile floor.

But the murmur in the gallery did not keep Orrie from doing his job. Despite its errant path, Orrie intently followed his ball's flight, losing it for a moment as it entered the leafy edge of the trees. Then he leaned forward, listening, straining to hear if it hit anything.

The ominous "conk" echoed solemnly through the forest, followed by a serene silence. Orrie's ball hit something dead center, and soon everyone would see it bouncing straight back toward them, coming to rest in the rough, behind another gigantic tree.

Orrie stepped back, caught his breath, tried not to stare at the man with the umbrella chair, and watched Patton pound his drive down the middle for an easy sand wedge to the green.

Unfazed, Butterbean snatched up Orrie's bag and headed for the woods, walking straight to where he heard the Titleist hit the tree.

"What's it look like?" Butterbean quizzed Orrie, who was starting to feel the pressure, knowing his dream was slipping away.

"It's clean," Orrie reported, having been trained to tell his caddie everything he needed to know. "It's sitting up, Butterbean. Mostly scrub brush and hardpan. But it's dead behind that big oak. I got no shot. I'll have to punch out."

Butterbean Green licked his forefinger and held it up, hoping for a hint of breeze, but there was none. The kid was good enough to hammer a big slice out of the rough, get the ball back in play, but the driving range loomed left and was big trouble. Under this much pressure, he wondered if a 15-year-old could pull it off. Then he made the call of his caddying career.

"Piss on it," Butterbean said.

"What?"

"Piss on it," Butterbean whispered between his teeth. "Piss all over it and in front of it, 'specially in front. Do it now 'fo' Mr. Tom gets here."

Never doubting Butterbean's word, Orrie unzipped his pants, turned his back to the crowd and urinated all over his golf ball.

"Don't forget to piss on the ground in front of it," Butterbean said, smiling and waving to the crowd he heard chatting across the fairway. Just as Orrie was tucking it back in, Tom Moore, Palmetto's club pro, emerged on the scene to provide a ruling.

"Think we's got a problem here, boss man," Butterbean said, hearing Tom rustle through the shrubbery.

"What's that?" Tom Moore asked, looking at Orrie's lie.

"Casual water," Butterbean said matter-of-factly.

"Casual water?" Tom exclaimed. "It hasn't rained in a month of Sundays. How could you have a wet lie?"

"I ain't rightly know myself," Butterbean said. "But we's got it. Check it for your own self."

Reluctantly, Tom asked Orrie to address the ball, and to his surprise, the boy's shoes caused the ground to squeeze forth fluid, invoking the casual water rule 12-25-1, Official Rules of Golf: "A temporary accumulation of water on the golf course that is not a water hazard and that is visible before or after the player takes a stance. Player may drop a club length no closer to the hole to gain relief."

Shrugging his shoulders, Tom said, "Well, the water table is kind of high around here," and gave Orrie a free drop out of the wet area, no closer to the green, providing the boy a slender sight line to the flag.

"Here," Butterbean said, handing Orrie a club. "You so far back it gone take everything you got to get up dis hill to dat back pin. Now, take dis 1-iron, choke 'im down, put it a scooch back in your stance, keep da club face close, take dead-ass aim at dat flag, then knock that sucker in and let's go home."

Orrie Adger looked even younger than his 15 years when Maxie Roberts of *The State Sentinel* snapped the picture, just as he finished his follow through. In years to come, that photo would become part of South Carolina golf history. There was Orrie, young and beautiful, gazing out of the shady trees toward a sun-splashed green where gallery members were just starting to raise their arms in disbelief.

Off to the left, slightly out of focus, was Chris Patton, leaning on his putter. While waiting for the ruling, he'd pitched up to four feet, and was eager to knock in a birdie for the win.

When Orrie's shot hit the green, some thought it might have been too much club; 1-irons don't check up, and this one was steaming to the back of the green where the flag was tucked on a gentle, up-hill pin placement.

In those few seconds it took the Titleist to roll its way toward the pin, for the people to draw a deep breath, and for Chris Patton to suddenly realize he'd been robbed, Orrie's young life would change forever.

As Orrie's ball clanged against the flagstick and dropped in for an eagle, the gallery went wild, screaming and yelling. The reality of defeat caused Patton to let his putter fall quietly to the green.

"I think it went in!" Orrie shouted to Butterbean, who calmly took the club from his player's hand, wiped the face with a towel, and said, "Of course it went in, son. Even a blind man can see dat!"

That was the high point of Orrie Adger's life. From there it was all downhill. From treachery to tragedy, to the very last flicker of his dream; to small-town oblivion; to reckless abandon, to that fateful moment in the Salkehatchie swamp where he and God were having it out for the very last time.

Stunned by the shock wave from the lighting strike, Orrie struggled to his feet, still knee-deep in the muddy water, with fresh rain slapping his face. He looked up and shouted, "You missed me, you overrated sumbitch! You missed me! Trevino was right; even you can't hit a fucking 1-iron."

CHAPTER 3

Fifteen years after Orrie's miracle golf shot, another South Carolinian, Brumby McLean, stared out the window of the Senate Press Gallery in Washington, D.C., as an early November snowfall obscured his view of Union Station.

It was in moments like this that Brumby, raised in the same geographic area but a few demographic rungs below Orrie Adger, pinched himself, hardly believing he was there at all.

Growing up, he certainly had no idea he would be walking among giants. But here he was, sitting in his small cubicle, tapping out a feature story on U.S. Senator Strom Thurmond's plans for the Millennium Celebration, literally shoulder to shoulder with some of the nation's best journalists.

To his left was Reuters. To his right the Associated Press. Down a few windows was Helen Dewar of *The Washington Post.* Next to her was Jonathan Fuerbringer of *The New York Times.*

In his time on The Hill he'd come to know these people, talked to them on a daily basis, wore the same press credentials around his neck, rode the same elevators, chased the same senators through the tunnels that connected the Capitol Hill complex.

Barely 30, Brumby was a one-man Washington Bureau for Trinity Press Inc., a consortium of South Carolina weekly newspapers of no particular significance. And while he looked like other reporters, he was an aberration.

He worked for a huckster named Granville Trinity, a former used-car salesman who turned newspaper publisher when he inherited *The Barnwell Bugle* from his late uncle.

While Granville Trinity knew very little about the newspaper business, he quickly fell in love with its profit margins and prestige. That's when he leased Bubba's Used Cars to a guy named Macon Moses, and set up shop in *The Bugle's* back office. There he relished the cash that rolled in from legal classifieds, grocery stores, department stores and a steady stream of full-page ads from Nu-Chem, the nuclear waste company that touted safety and promoted itself as a good citizen by supporting everything from softball teams to bowling leagues.

With the profits, Trinity quickly expanded his empire, stitching together a valuable quilt of newspapers that stretched across the Southwest corner of South Carolina, from Ridgeland to Barnwell, Manning to Batesburg.

This mini-empire gave Trinity a circulation of more than 20,000 and an income that allowed him to join The Confederate Club, a private golf club in North Augusta built by millionaires snubbed by Augusta National.

It was, by all measures, a rowdy boy's club where the only rule was you had to be wearing pants while playing golf. Anything else, including wine, women and loud all-night parties, was perfectly acceptable at Confederate, which suited Trinity's personality to a tee.

In fact, the only thing he liked more than a good poker game in the back bar was the unfounded respect he got from fellow members as a newspaper publisher. At times he felt like E.F. Hutton because when he spoke, some dumb-ass would actually listen.

That led him to start writing a regular op-ed column in all his papers called Trinity Times, a badly composed rant about whatever was on his mind at the time.

But his ultimate brainstorm was creating a Washington Bureau for Trinity Press, a correspondent in the nation's capital who could give his readers something more than the watered-down rewrites of public relations handouts that filled other weeklies.

That opportunity arose during a poker game with Bobby Morris, brother of Billy Morris, a member of Augusta National and owner of *The Augusta Chronicle*. Bobby was the black sheep grazing in the Morris empire that included other Georgia newspapers in Athens and Savannah, as well as *The Jacksonville (Fla.) Times*.

While brother Billy hobnobbed on Magnolia Lane, Bobby boozed it up with the Snake Lady and other bottom feeders along the banks of the swampy Savannah River. His real job was running *The Waynesboro Democrat,* but he was never there. It ran itself into the ground without his expertise.

But despite Bobby's estrangement within the family, he still had the God-given right to sit on the board and was entrusted with what his older brother thought was a harmless committee to run — bureaus and circulation.

Thus it came to pass that Granville Trinity's three aces were bound to beat Bobby Morris' two pair when the car-salesman-turned-publisher upped the bet another $10,000 and everyone else at the table quickly folded.

Bobby, drunk and broke, had the right to fold, but didn't have the ability. That's when Trinity made him an offer he should have refused. Trinity would cover Bobby's bet if he'd put forth one of the *Chronicle*'s coveted Washington Bureau seats as collateral. As an old established newspaper family, the Morrises had three assigned seats in the Capitol. One in the Senate press gallery, two in the House.

True to form, Bobby bet the Senate seat and lost to the aces, giving Granville Trinity something he couldn't buy off the shelf — access to power.

CHAPTER 4

Brumby had just filed his last story for the weekly deadlines when the secretary in the press gallery called his name.

"Brumby, line four."

While the outside world was moving ahead in technology and common sense, the U.S. Congress was still stagnated in the 1940s.

The Senate Press Gallery was on the third floor of the majestic Capitol building, a long, narrow room that ran the length of the east side. With black-and-white tiled floors, small cubicles along the walls, a couple of overstuffed leather sofas, a few overpaid staff members, and a row of telephone booths that ran down the inner wall, it was a throwback to the good old days in newspapering.

Hearing his name, Brumby turned from his laptop, saw the light blinking over the fourth of six phone booths, grabbed his reporter's notebook, stepped inside, closed the folding door, lifted the receiver and said, "Brumby."

The voice on the line was familiar, belonging to Mark Vandenheuvel, Senator Strom Thurmond's press secretary.

"Whatcha doing tonight?" Vandenheuvel said. "There's a South Carolina party down at the Potomac Club. Everybody's going. All the reps, their staff and their interns. Best chance you'll get to Shag with somebody in this town."

Brumby had come to like Vandenheuvel, a Wofford College grad from a good family in Cheraw. His father was a big Republican donor, which is why Mark was working for Strom.

Brumby had learned a lot since he hit town. Mainly, who he could trust and who he couldn't. In his short time on The Hill, he'd been tricked more than once, buying into flimsy story ideas because of free booze and a few cocktail weiners at a party.

Not that his stories mattered that much. Sure, they ran in 11 newspapers, but they were rags. Every day, for instance, he had to walk past the desk of Lee Bandy, the longtime political reporter for the vaunted *State Sentinel* in Columbia, South Carolina's capital city. Bandy had worked on The Hill for 25 years and was the undisputed dean of Southern correspondents.

Fortunately, despite his rapier wit and sarcastic style, Lee Bandy was a kind soul. Few, in fact, knew Bandy was a graduate of Bob Jones University in Greenville, one of the most conservative of the evangelical schools scattered about the South.

Bandy took a liking to Brumby when he learned his father was a Baptist preacher in Kline, a farming community in Bluff County. His old man had even been featured in *The Sentinel*'s Faith and Values section just a year before as a dying breed of "hellfire and brimstone" preachers in the South.

Indeed, Lee Bandy was the only person in Washington that Brumby trusted at all. The veteran reporter took him under his wing, taught him how to get into committee hearings, find reports buried in the archives, understand the budget shenanigans, and make sense of the Senate's arcane rules.

By having lunch once a week with Bandy in the Senate Dining Room, Brumby gained the friendship and respect of other reporters, many of whom came to him when they needed help. Which they did every time South Carolina's senators, Strom Thurmond and Fritz Hollings, opened their mouths.

Brumby quickly became the go to guy for reporters from around the country when they needed an interpreter. Seems none of them could understand a single word spoken by either South Carolina senator, due to their very distinctive southern drawls.

Quite often, after the senators spoke, the other reporters would turn to Brumby and ask, "What the hell did he just say?"

Brumby would laugh and instruct them that, "Strom said he wanted to know the name of that little blonde sitting on the back row," then wait for the snickers about the elder statesman's reputation for philandering.

"And Fritz said he can't believe Strom is still alive," he said, drawing even more laughter from the assembled reporters.

In reality, the two politicians were either talking endlessly about balancing the federal budget or trying to get ill-fated legislation passed to protect the tattered textile industry in the Palmetto State.

But Brumby was way out of his league, and he knew it. He was a poor preacher's kid with two years of college at the University of South Carolina's Salkehatchie campus, a rural outpost of the state's flagship school. The entire college, in fact, was housed in the same building where he went to grammar school. It's where poor people went to college, if they went at all. Brumby stuck it out as long as he could, but he was bored and knew he couldn't afford to move to the main campus in Columbia to finish his degree.

After he dropped out, he tried everything from construction work to sucking out septic tanks. In an area where good jobs are hard to find, his unambitious life changed when he answered an ad in *The Barnwell Bugle*. It simply read, "Are you the curious kind? Do you like to ask questions? Do you like to know what's going on in your community before anyone else? If so, you could be a reporter for *The Barnwell Bugle*. Just call 803-584-2646 and ask for Alice Ann."

That phone call landed him in Granville Trinity's office where the flamboyant entrepreneur gave him a job covering town council and rewriting press releases.

Six months later Trinity stumbled into the office, reeking of cigar smoke and alcohol, and announced, "We now have a Washington Bureau! Anybody want to go?"

Brumby and Alice Ann were the paper's only two employees, so Brumby slowly raised his hand. The next thing he knew he was packing his bags for Washington, D.C., looking for a place to live and applying for credentials at the Senate Press Gallery, compliments of a letter from Bobby Morris assigning one of the *Chronicle's* seats to Trinity Press Inc.

All courtesy of three, liquor-soaked aces. But there was more to the story than a poker game and Granville Trinity's enormous ego.

Twenty-five years earlier, Tatum Trinity, a Citadel graduate, was killed in Vietnam. For Granville Trinity, the death of his only son was a wound that never healed. He tried booze, drugs, women, and wailing in front of the long, black wall in Washington. But nothing made the pain of losing his only son subside. It only made his anger sink deeper and grow darker.

He had raged against Congress, led demonstrations in Columbia, written letters to everybody he could think of, but got no response, not even a simple I'm sorry. So, so, so, so very sorry.

So Trinity was going to get the bastards back, one way or another. And a seat at the table in Washington seemed like a good place to start.

But it didn't take long for Brumby to wish he'd paid more attention in Margaret Tuten's high school civics class. When he arrived in Washington, he hardly knew a congressman from a senator, what they did, or what they were supposed to be doing. Washington, D.C., was a maze of intricate delusions, designed over decades of deceit to hide what actually was happening from the American people.

Brumby, therefore, found it easier and more interesting to write about the people working in the congressional offices. People from back home. Pages. Interns. Administrative assistants. Young people who came and went in the hallways and the underground warrens of Washington, carrying important papers, walking past marble statues, and drinking in the local bars before rotating in a few years back to the real world.

Mark Vandenheuvel started out as one of those, but stayed too long at the fair. He got hooked on the heroin of politics, believed the bullshit, and thought everything his boss did was good for South Carolina, the Republican Party, America, and the world at large.

"I might make it," Brumby said, jotting down the address of the party. "What time?"

"Whenever you get there," Mark answered. "They're bringing in the East Coast Party Band and they'll be playing all night. Should be some nice stuff. Like that gorgeous little intern from Spratt's office. I bet she'll be there."

Brumby's mind immediately went to Holly Holladay's cleavage, a place he hoped no man had gone before. She was 20-something, a graduate of Erskine College where she played volleyball, a striker with amazingly long legs and blonde hair that draped down below her shoulders.

He met her a few weeks earlier when he dropped by John Spratt's office. The

Fifth District Congressman introduced Holly Holladay, a new intern working on environmental issues.

Brumby started to ask Holly to marry him that very moment, but she was wearing an engagement ring on her left hand and a delicate gold cross around her neck, both of which made Brumby an unlikely candidate.

"So, are you coming or not?" Vandenheuvel asked impatiently over the phone.

"Yeah, okay," Brumby said, suddenly interested. "I'll probably drop by."

CHAPTER 5

In years to come, thousands of people claimed they were there that afternoon when Orrie Adger hit the magic 1-iron shot to win the South Carolina Junior Amateur Championship.

But the man who made everyone feel that way was Furman Bisher, the longtime sports columnist for *The Atlanta Journal-Constitution*.

Among the sporting crowd, Bisher was a celestial constant, the North Star, the final word in a regional newspaper that boldly crowed it, "Covers Dixie Like The Dew."

Bisher was already past retirement age, somewhere north of 70, but still in his prime when it came to writing prose about sports in the South. And unlike most sports scribes, Bisher was rich and famous. He owned race horses, flew first class, and married a beautiful blonde he met in Hilton Head who was half his age.

That's because Furman Bisher lived his dreams. He never took the journalistic oath of poverty. He didn't believe it had to be that way. Even told his bosses at the paper that he wasn't going to stay in cheap hotels or travel in steerage just so they could make more money than God.

Nope, Furman Bisher was newspaper royalty because he had the writing chops to back it up. He'd covered every Masters, Super Bowl, Final Four, Kentucky Derby, Rose Bowl and U.S. Open since he came to Atlanta from North Carolina and conquered each story with a flair unlike anyone else.

Not only was he famous, he was fearless. He openly questioned golfers like Snead and Hogan about their club selections. He walked into the clubhouse for lunch at Augusta National like a member, because he felt he was one. He was friends with Arnold Palmer. He played golf with Nicklaus. He knew Bobby Jones in his prime.

Thus it was Furman Bisher, the wordsmith, who played Augusta National that morning, then skipped over the river to have a snort of scotch with his old friend

Tom Moore, and happened to witness Orrin Adger's famous 1-iron shot.

Like a true thoroughbred, Bisher couldn't keep his hands off the keyboard. Before the sun went down, he'd called his copy desk in Atlanta, said he had a column coming out of cycle, and told them to hold a slot on the sports front because this was a story he couldn't wait to tell. Then he sat down at a poker table in the clubhouse and knocked out this lead to his faithful flock of readers:

AIKEN, S.C. — The ultimate beauty of sport is its ability to produce unexpected victory when tragedy seems the only logical outcome.

Such a miracle happened here Sunday afternoon at historic Palmetto Golf Club when a skinny 15-year-old kid named Orrie Adger slew the giant, Chris Patton, with a sling shot to the temple, a 1-iron from the rough that flew like an eagle and lifted this young phenom onto the shoulders of golf history.

Bisher went on to say Patton was unavailable for comment, adding that Goliath had nothing to say after losing to David either.

Then Bisher described Orrie as a prodigy, born to the Bermuda greens of the South Carolina Lowcountry, a student of the immortal Mr. Picard, an apple-cheeked assassin with the swing of an angel who took advice from a blind caddie.

He even quoted Butterbean Green as saying, "I knowed it was in all the way, Mr. Bisher. Soon as I heard it, I knowed it was in. Can't nobody golf no golf ball like young Mr. Orrie. He's natural born."

But it was the next paragraph of Bisher's column that sealed Orrie's fame. When the columnist heard about the "casual water" ruling, he burst out laughing and wrote:

Not only did this promising young buck of Butler Island breeding pull off the shot of the century, he made it possible by bending the game's rules to his favor. On the final hole, under advice from his longtime caddie, Butterbean Green, who happens to be blind, Adger urinated on his golf ball, creating a puddle big enough to get him a free drop and a sight line out of the hellish position he'd put himself in.

It was only natural that the boys on the copy desk in Atlanta loved the story,

26

gave the youngster the nickname Puddles, and wrote the headline that proclaimed, 'Puddles' Pulls Off Magical Shot To Win Sandlapper Title!

The nickname would follow Orrie everywhere he went. But he didn't mind. It matched his easy-going personality, and girls thought it was cute.

So with every tournament he won, his legend grew. With every newspaper tossed from Montgomery to Chattanooga, Columbia to Tallahassee, Orrie "Puddles"Adger became the next Bobby Jones, another Arnold Palmer, a star in the wings, just waiting for greatness to come of age.

Over the next three years Orrie competed in junior tournaments across the South, in Birmingham, Richmond, Columbus and Savannah. In fact, he was playing in a tournament on Hilton Head Island when he got the news about his parents.

Tom and Jeannie Adger's marriage had always been rocky. While they played the happy couple ruling over the Butler Island estate, demons from their past lurked just behind their practiced smiles.

Born of tragic coincidence, their love was haunted. She'd worked for his father, whom they both despised. In the end, no amount of alcohol could douse the flames of hatred that burned in their hearts, mostly for themselves.

When the cops arrived at the family home, they found the walls splattered with blood. Tom's body was crumpled against one wall, Jeannie's against another. Both shot in the chest. Both still clutching pistols.

The Charleston County coroner's first inclination was murder-suicide. He'd seen more than his share in 20 years on the job. But this one was different, and the more he studied the bodies, the clearer the gruesome picture became.

In what must have been a moment of intense insanity, Tom and Jeannie, now in their 40s, drunk as usual, stood face to face, no doubt shouting their disdain and distrust of each other, each holding a .38 revolver, and fired simultaneously.

Instead of a murder-suicide, the coroner declared it a double homicide. In their great, long civil war, civility had finally surrendered.

Almost 18 at the time, Orrie was waiting in the cart barn under the Harbour Town clubhouse, holding his latest trophy when the state trooper found him, told him what happened, and gave him and Butterbean a long, quiet ride back to Butler Island.

There they stayed through the funerals, sitting on the veranda of Butler Bay clubhouse, sipping beer, listening to the surf roll in and out, wondering what to do next.

The answer came all too quickly.

Within a month of his parents' death, a letter arrived from a law firm in New York informing Orrie, the sole heir, that the Kuwaitis had taken full control of Butler Island, and per the legal fine print, he had 30 days to vacate the property or face criminal charges of trespass.

Seems his parents, who'd been in and out of therapy and rehab for years, had borrowed heavily against their share of the island, eventually draining their net worth like the last bottle of Chivas Regal in the men's grill.

This on the eve of Orrie's big plans to play college golf and follow in the footsteps of his hero, Fred Couples.

Orrie got to know the soft-spoken pro golfer when the PGA Tour came to Butler Island for the Carolina Cup each year. He had posters and autographed pictures all over his room. He even learned to walk like Freddie, very nonchalant, almost forgetting he had a golf club in his hand.

And Couples gave Orrie good advice — it's not how well you play the game, it's whether or not you win.

"While the other guy is fist-pumping and high-fiving with the fans," Couples told him. "You should be listening to the grass grow and looking to see if it's leaning toward the setting sun, changing the grain, making your next putt break more than you thought."

While Orrie had always felt a special connection with Couples, it would evolve from hero worship to student over the years as he realized golf wasn't as easy as Fred made it look.

Orrie fully intended to be the next Fred Couples. His dream was to play in the Masters. To walk the pristine fairways at Augusta National, just a hundred miles and a dream to the west of where he lived. To hear the women swoon when he passed by. To live the life of a professional golfer.

And he just might. He had the graceful swing, the emerging good looks, and an easy-going attitude that bordered on arrogance.

He had, in fact, been invited by a member to play the fabled course when he was 15, but turned it down, brashly saying the first time he played at Augusta he wanted it to be because he earned it, not because he knew somebody.

It seemed perfectly logical at the time. All Orrie needed was time to mature. Even Mr. Picard told him that. He said a man plays his best golf when he's a teenager, and his smartest golf when he's middle-aged.

Orrie was inches away from traveling down that long road to Magnolia Lane when his life began to unravel.

As the lawyers came out of the hearing room in downtown Charleston, the family's attorney, Charlton deSaussure of Dingle, Dudley and deSaussure, was ashen-faced.

"They got it all," deSaussure said calmly as he sat down beside Orrie on a wooden bench. "Your parents piled up a lot of debt, Orrie. They assumed they had time to figure a way out of it all, but they didn't. The Kuwaitis foreclosed on their loans and now own the entire island outright."

DeSaussure told him the only thing left to him was the deed to a golf course somewhere in Barnwell County that his grandfather, Frank Finklea, had owned. It was not part of the estate and went undiscovered until they cleaned out his father's roll-top desk.

Just the sound of Frank Finklea's name sent a chill through Orrie's body. It was taboo to speak of the man in his house. His parents avoided all references to that side of the family tree, and seldom mentioned the other.

Orrie had grown up knowing his father's father had a different last name, that he'd been murdered, and that was about it. In school he heard vague references to Frank Finklea in state politics, but never connected the dots. Orrie was playing the best golf of his life on the best golf courses in America. Who cared who his dead granddaddy was?

"Looks like that's where you're going to be living," deSaussure said, trying to get Orrie's attention. "Unless you have other plans."

Orrie sat quietly on the bench outside the courtroom, absorbed the news, then bolted for the door. He did have other plans. He had a full scholarship to Clemson. But all he possessed at that moment was a broken heart, his golf clubs and a beat-up '84 Porsche convertible that had become his trademark. It was pigeon-shit yellow, quite the conversation piece when he pulled up to the bag drops at fancy country clubs around the South. He liked to drive it fast, with his golf bag sticking out from the well behind the bucket seats, his Ping-Eye 2-irons and drivers rattling around as if they were an afterthought to the young boy's talent.

Then he'd ask the cart boys to unload his clubs, send his FootJoys ahead to the men's locker room for shining, and not park his car too close to the Jaguars and Bentleys for fear it might get dinged.

For three years, "Puddles" Adger had been the golden boy of the South. He was written up in *Southern Golf Magazine*, hailed as the next whiz kid, recruited by major colleges, got a blurb in *Sports Illustrated*, and was on the verge of greatness.

In his glove compartment was an acceptance letter from Clemson University, signed, sealed, and delivered by head coach Larry Penley. Full scholarship. He couldn't wait to get there because, suddenly, it was the only place he had left to go.

So he shoved the Porsche into first gear, popped the clutch and swerved out into traffic on Broad Street.

He never saw the city garbage truck.

BOOK 2

CHAPTER 6

Three years later Orrie and Butterbean were sitting in lawn chairs, leaning back against a wall, sharing a joint, swatting away gnats, waiting for the beer man to show up.

Orrie had a full beard, and wore the usual assortment of clothes he found at the Goodwill store in Barnwell — a golf shirt with a faded "Yeaman's Hall Golf Club" logo on the front, a pair of army surplus fatigue pants, Chuck Taylor basketball shoes, and an "Esso Club" visor pulled tight over his long, stringy, blond hair.

Butterbean wore one of his favorite caddie jumpsuits. This one was purple. Orrie said it made him look like James Brown, which made Butterbean smile.

Above them was a hand-painted sign, six feet across and three feet high, that read, "The Healing Springs Baptist Church and Country Club: Pastor, Macon Moses; Head Pro, Orrie Adger; Butterbean Green, In Charge."

Over that sign drooped a tattered Confederate flag, nailed to the bottom of a cross that cast a long shadow down the first fairway at dawn. It was an unusual situation at best, created by a quirk of political fate from the past.

The church/clubhouse sat along a scraggly little creek called the Salkehatchie River, at a bend where artesian water bubbled up on its edges. The local black folk called this spot "Healing Springs," believing the waters contained magical powers to heal what ailed you.

Every day they came down to the river, toting empty milk jugs and Mason jars, filling them with the magic water for baths, cooking, herbal teas, and rubbing on sore and ugly places. It was part of the local culture, the lore, and nothing that Orrie or Butterbean wanted to challenge. All they knew was Orrie's granddaddy, the mysterious Frank Finklea, had come into possession of 1,000 acres of land just outside the Savannah River Plant back in the 1950s. It was a payoff for Finklea's legislative skills in getting the proper clearances and permits for a company called Nu-Chem.

Nu-Chem was a mysterious conglomerate based in Denver with offices in Washington, D.C. Its sole mission, it seemed, was to collect and store nuclear waste materials until proper facilities could be built elsewhere by the federal government.

In reality, it was a dump. Over half the acreage was trenched and turned into a cemetery for nuclear waste. But on the other half of the land, mostly a pine forest, there was an old black church and what was left of an old golf course, which shared the same space.

Orrie and Butterbean didn't know anything about the church until they showed up two years earlier to claim what was left of Orrie's life. That's when they met Macon Moses, a large black man wearing a clerical collar who held in his hand a document signed by Finklea giving his church half of the building, and leaving the other half for the local country club. It was just enough to keep the NAACP and the federal tax vermin away for a while, and Finklea didn't care about consequences down the road.

All of which made for an interesting marriage.

On Sunday mornings, The Right Rev. Macon Moses would open the front doors on the east side of the Lincoln-log building and welcome a few dozen faithful, who filled the six rows of pews in front of the pulpit where he would lead them in a few verses of "The Old Rugged Cross," just to remind them of Jesus' suffering.

So I'll cherish that old rugged cross,
Till my trophies at last I lay down;
I will cling to the old rugged cross,
And exchange it someday for a crown.

After which he would preach the word of God, warn the flock about the wages of sin, sing gospels, stomp his feet, pass the collection plate, invite the sick and afflicted up to be re-baptized in the waters from Healing Springs, then thank everyone for coming, shake everybody's hand and be first on the tee box when the clock struck high noon.

That, according to the document, was when the owners of the country club could officially open the clubhouse on the west side of the building.

The building itself was a rather sturdy structure, a split-log house with a concrete floor and a tin roof that hung out over front porches on both sides. Barely the size of a Boy Scout hut, it was close quarters for religion and rebellion, which agreed to disagree on almost everything.

The Healing Springs Country Club did have one problem. There was only one golf hole. Originally, there had been nine, but the other eight went to seed years ago when the caretaker, a drunk named H.C. Cook, left town with a stripper named Maude.

Orrie and Butterbean were able to save the par-3 that ran from the clubhouse down to the river. It had been the sixth or seventh hole, nobody could remember which.

From the porch, where everybody sat and drank, old timers would point out into the woods and say, "That's where that dang dogleg left used to be; right where that buzzard's circling that dead tree yonder."

It took some imagination to see the old routing, but armed with a half-ass mower and some fertilizer, Butterbean recruited two boys from the church to help him keep one golf hole playable. They cut the grass, and eventually took pride in seeing how fast they could make the Bermuda-grass green roll.

They fashioned their own version of a Stemp Meter using plastic ramps from an old Hot Wheels set. When they let the golf ball roll down the ramp, they would measure how many feet it rolled on the tightly cut grass before it stopped.

"We's got it to 10," Willy and Billy would yell to Butterbean, who supervised the operations from the porch.

"Das good, boys," Butterbean would respond. "Nine too slow, eleben too fast. Come gitcha pay."

The boys would scamper up to the porch where Butterbean carefully counted out eight quarters for each of them, telling them not to spend it all in one place. They'd smile and say "Yessir, Misser Butterbean," but planned to blow it all on cigarettes anyway.

The local rednecks liked coming out to Healing Springs Baptist Church and Country Club to drink and take a chance in the hole-in-one contest. It cost a dollar a shot, with all the money going into a big glass pickle jar. If you made the shot, you got all the money. Then it started over again.

Second prize, everybody joked, was an autographed photo of Orrie "Puddles" Adger hitting that 1-iron shot at Palmetto when he was a kid. It hung unceremoniously and slightly crooked behind the pulpit/bar, next to the famous 1-iron. Orrie would throw darts at the picture when he got really messed up, which was often.

CHAPTER 7

The Salkehatchie was hardly a river at all. In fact, it was barely a creek — a mushy, oozing wet spot dripping down the left groin of South Carolina — a swampy catch basin for raindrops with nowhere else to go.

Only local people knew it existed, or where to find it, because it had a way of disappearing in the sweetgums and willows; too wide to wade across in one spot, hardly a trickle in another.

The Indians called it the Salt Catcher because it slowly meandered through the mucky swampland until it met the brackish water downstream near the small town of Yemassee.

So elusive was the Salkehatchie it confounded Gen. Sherman's troops as they swept up from Savannah en route to capture the capital city of Columbia near the end of the Civil War.

Unlike the mighty Savannah, which required pontoons to ferry the marauding Union troops northward, the Salkehatchie was a muddy slog with 17 separate channels that slowed them down only slightly more than a band of Confederate troops who tried to make a final stand at the Battle of River's Bridge.

It was a cold day in early February 1865, when every Southern soul in the surrounding area sensed the end was near, and knew Sherman's Army was approaching, headed north, hellbent on paying the Palmetto State back for its role in starting the damn war in the first place.

In a 60-mile flanking movement, 20,000 federal troops poured across the Savannah, pillaging as they went, gathering food, killing livestock, and leaving scorched earth behind.

Five thousand were led by Major General Joseph Mower, known to his men as "Fighting Joe." It was Mower's men who waded into the Salkehatchie swamp at Rivers Bridge where they met a desperate Confederate force, barely a thousand lads, who bravely positioned themselves between the invaders and the state capital.

When the smoke cleared and the bodies were counted, 170 Confederates gave their lives to slow Sherman's march by a single day.

On a topographical map, the Salkehatchie swamp looked like an open wound, a gash along an invisible fall line that oozed muck and proved impassable most days, a maze of fallen trees and cypress stumps. Nobody in recent times knew much about the river at all. It was not navigable. It was barely noticeable. Mostly people just spoke of fishing holes along the way, like Cotton Field, Burnt Church, Tractor Bog, and Buford's Bridge.

So when golf balls strayed beyond the slippery slopes of the Salkehatchie, few were ever recovered. They either rolled to the sandy bottom and were swept away by the gentle current, or they plugged in a soupy, sucking grave.

The Rev. Macon Moses always closed his eyes in silent prayer before he stuck a dollar in the pickle jar, teed up his ball, crossed himself like a Catholic, then took dead aim like an atheist.

"Holy shit!" he said as the ball splashed into the muddy water left of the hole.

"Deliver me from this God-forsaken hole, from this unholy game, to a place where golf is unknown except by those who play it in eternal hell," he muttered.

But rather than quit, Moses stuffed a $20 bill in the pickle jar and kept swinging away, always finding a new way of cursing the game each time he failed to make a hole-in-one.

As he kept trying, and cussing, a few white men showed up in a mud-splattered Pathfinder, grabbed some clubs that were leaning against a tree, and waited their turn on the porch.

"Didn't know they let niggers play here," one of them said, spitting tobacco juice into a paper cup and looking up at the Confederate flag as a summer breeze furled it out slowly, left-to-right.

"Must be Tiger Woods," his buddy said, laughing. "Heard he went up to the gates at Augusta National and wanted to play. A guard told him there was a public golf course just a 4-iron away, and he would be welcomed there.

"'But I'm Tiger Woods,' he explained to the guard.

"'In that case,' the guard said, 'it's only an 8-iron away.'"

The boys on the porch snickered and elbowed each other as the reverend stomped off the tee box.

Moses knew all the low-lifes on the porch by name or reputation. Even though he was a man of the cloth, he knew the only cloth some of these rednecks worshipped was that flag that flapped flagrantly above his church.

Moses mentioned bringing it down once when they were arguing about the same issue in Columbia. But his idea was promptly rejected, his life threatened, and he didn't mention it again. The Healing Springs Baptist Church and Country Club had become the hangout for everybody and everything wrong with this forgotten outback of South Carolina, and there was nothing Macon Moses could do about it but pray.

People poured in on Friday afternoons — a line of cars kicking up dust on the road from the highway — parking their trucks, motorcycles and Jeeps wherever they damned well pleased. Inside the old log hut that passed for a church and a clubhouse, the pulpit became a karaoke stage and the pews were pushed up against the wall, turned upside down and used as tables. That's when some good old boy would start plucking away at his guitar and sing an old John Conlee song:

> But these rose colored glasses, that I'm looking through;
> Show only the beauty, 'cause they hide all the truth.
> But they keep me from feeling, so cheated, defeated;
> When reflections in your eyes show me a fool.

It was, on the whole, a seriously sad group of truck drivers and welders who packed the place on weekends, sitting on broken chairs, Coca-Cola crates and beer kegs that encircled a blazing campfire.

On the trunk of an overhanging oak tree were oddly shaped wooden signs that had been nailed up at different times, in descending order, scrawled in red paint.

No Assholes.
No Cops.
No Niggers.
No Women.
No Shit.

The irony of it all was Orrie and Butterbean were not in the golf business at all. It was all a poorly disguised front for their marijuana operation. As fate would have it, Butterbean Green not only knew a great deal about horticulture when it came to Bermuda greens, his green thumb also extended to the cannabis family.

"Irrigation and location," he would often say were the secrets to growing good pot. "My great, great granddaddy used to grow weed on da plantation. How you think we got through slavery? You need just the right touch of water to keep da plant healthy, and a certain amount of secrecy. Pot don't grow good wid people watching."

What went unsaid, and perhaps even lost in the passage from slave days, was that South Carolina's soil was rich in iodine, a substance that further enhanced the illegal weed. That's why Butterbean planted his herb garden the old fashioned way, not in rows where everybody could see it but scattered about in the woods, where only he knew where to look for it — fourth tree down from the creek, turn left, go sixteen steps, then right for twelve steps, then look behind that sweet gum tree. Directions only a blind man could follow.

While most of their clientele worked for the government and couldn't smoke pot due to drug testing, that didn't mean they couldn't transport it. Every Monday morning the truckers would pick up their big rigs in a fenced-off area at Nu-Chem, stuff a big bag of weed under the front seat and head out for places they couldn't even mention to their girlfriends.

Their job was to pick up spent fuel rods and other radioactive garbage from nuclear plants around the country. South Carolina, the land of smiling faces and beautiful places, had sold its soul to the devil, agreeing to store nuclear waste from other states until the federal government figured out what to do with it. This fleet went out every week and returned with its toxic catch.

Once these men delivered their pot to friends on their outbound run, large containers would be strapped to their flatbeds and they'd truck them back home, in the dead of night, followed closely by undercover agents in unmarked cars.

Nobody was supposed to know these midnight riders were cruising through their small towns with everything from reactor parts to peanut-sized pellets that could kill them all and make their hometowns unlivable for 10,000 years.

Most days, people just tried not to think about it. Like today, which happened to be Beer Day at the country club.

"He's late again," Butterbean said, slapping a mosquito and acting like he was looking at a non-existent watch on his left wrist.

"Always is," said Orrie as he pulled the dirty visor down over his eyes. "But he'll be along. He needs us as much as we need him."

That's when Butterbean leaned forward, dropped his head, turned it sideways and said, "He's coming. Maybe two miles away. Be here directly." Butterbean was rightly proud of his hearing. Despite being visually impaired, or maybe because of it, his hearing had developed into a supernatural thing. He told Orrie he had bat eyes.

"You know how dem bats ain't hardly got no eyes, but can see with dey ears?" he said. "Dat's how I does it."

Sure enough, within minutes, they saw the beer truck turn off the highway and come billowing down the dirt road   creating a dust cloud that rolled into the pine trees alongside and disappeared into the darkness of the swamp.

"Glad you made it, Bunk," Orrie said, sucking down the last hit of a joint. Then deciding there might be one more, he hit it again before saying, "We damn near ran out of beer."

This was always the last stop on Bunky Odom's Friday afternoon route because it signaled the end of the work week and the beginning of a high that would last until Monday morning.

"You got the shit?" he asked as he deftly stacked 30 cases of Pabst Blue Ribbon on the porch.

"'Course," Orrie said. "It's in there under the pulpit, like always."

It didn't take Bunky long to retrieve the brown paper bag, open it, shove his nose down inside, and breathe deeply.

"Damn you boys do grow some mighty fine weed," he said. "They love this stuff in the Upstate. I took some up to my cousin at Clemson, and he sold it out before the sun came up the next morning."

Butterbean listened to Bunky inhale the sweet aromas of marijuana, hearing him take the musky essence deep inside his lungs, then allow it to rush back out of his mouth.

"You need to trim dem nose hairs," Butterbean said, causing Bunky to check his nostrils with his index finger. "Ladies don't like no nose hairs."

It took the beer man a second to realize he'd been scammed by a blind man, again, but he laughed as he put some pot in a pipe, lit it quickly, and passed it over to Orrie.

"I'm way ahead of you, Bunk," Orrie said, half staggering. "But if you insist, I'll be your quality control man."

With that Orrie cupped his right hand over the cheap plastic pipe and sucked so hard the bowl lit up like the inside of a volcano. Holding the huge hit and trying not to laugh, Orrie started to spit smoke out of his mouth and nose until it finally poured forth like a mineshaft collapse.

"Yep," he said, grinning and choking. "Smooth."

All three men got stoned and laughed at everything for an hour before Bunky said he had to get the beer truck back to the garage before dark. That's when Orrie stood up to shake his hand and fell off the porch.

"Goddamned leg," he said, grabbing his left knee, writhing in pain. "I oughta sue them damn doctors in Charleston. Guess they never saw one tore up bad as mine."

"Tore up bad" was the unofficial diagnosis after the city garbage truck slammed into Orrie's Porsche on Broad Street, in broad daylight, right in front of the court-house. The result was like that of a rhinoceros running through a spider web. At first they couldn't find Orrie's left leg. It wasn't until an emergency worker smelled the burning flesh that he realized the meat and muscle that once flexed in perfect syncopation, rolling the feet, just like Mr. Picard taught him, were not completely detached.

Butterbean stayed with Orrie the first year he was in the hospital. Even when they sent him up to Duke six times, Butterbean was there, sleeping in his room, listening to him breathe. When the doctors came in for their morning rounds, Butterbean would report Orrie's condition.

"He breathes good all night," Butterbean would say. "'Cept when he dreams 'bout golf. Den he gets fitful. Sounds like he's choking. But den he calms down, and dreams 'bout sumptin else."

They discharged Orrie because he was indigent, and there was nothing else they could do. That's when Butterbean located this place near Barnwell, packed Orrie on the bus, and they came to claim what was left of the Finklea family fortune.

CHAPTER 8

Butterbean hadn't always been blind.

When he was 12 years old he got a job as a helper on Butler Island when they were building Butler Bay, the signature course.

He remembered Mr. Dye, the white man who designed the whole thing. Everybody said he was some kind of genius, but Butterbean said he was more like a child playing in a sandbox.

Butterbean's job was digging holes where the men would stack railroad ties around the edges of sand traps and water hazards. Mr. Dye was always riding around in a golf cart, stopping on hilltops, making sure he could see the ocean. Then he'd stick a little red or green flag in the ground so the workers would know whether to leave the dirt or take it away.

Butterbean's dream was to drive one of those bulldozers that rolled like tanks across the sand dunes. With their blades moving up and down, they reminded him of the big male blue crabs hauled from the tidal creeks, showing off their claws to frighten their enemies.

The big yellow machines, noisy and spewing smoke from their stacks, were like putty knives to Mr. Dye. He'd visualize something, like a fairway sloping left to right, or a putting green with rolling contours, then tell his Mexican workers where to push the dirt and how to smooth it out just so.

This is where Butterbean learned the lesson that would serve him well: Golf courses are all about gravity in general and drainage in particular.

"Rain is the best design tool," he heard Mr. Dye telling a magazine reporter one day. "When it rains, you can see where the water goes. And where the water goes determines where the golf course should go."

Dye started with the natural creeks, the lowest points on the windswept terrain, then found the highest points, knowing where he would put fairways and greens that would shed water.

"Look at Augusta National, one of the most beautiful golf courses in the world," he told the writer. "The entire golf course slopes down from the clubhouse to Rae's Creek, a drop of 175 feet, the same as Niagra Falls. It's a landscaper's delight. That's why Allister McKenzie and Bobby Jones were able to turn a floral nursery into a dreamboat of a golf course."

Building Butler Bay took two years. One to shape the landscape and another for the Bermuda grass to come in full and cover it like lichens on an old oak tree. When it was all done, Butterbean was 14 and old enough to work in the cart barn washing golf carts and searching for treasures the golfers left behind, like watches and rings, loose change and money clips.

When it came to golf, Butterbean learned early that white men with money were crazy. They'd spend all day hitting a ball around in the scorching sun, then spend the night drinking whiskey and talking about hitting a ball around all day in the scorching sun.

Eventually, Butterbean was promoted to the driving range where he got an even better look at the animal known as *golfer*, a loud, colorful, sporadic version of mankind with no particular skills other than opening beer bottles and smoking cigars.

He liked the driving range job because he got to drive the pick-up cart, an ingenious invention that allowed him to gather up balls on the driving range while the crazy golfers were still hitting them.

Protected in a makeshift, wire-mesh cage, Butterbean would drive the cart back and forth across the driving range like a lawn mower, pushing a harrow designed to scoop up golf balls and funnel them into a holding bin. The best part was hearing the balls clang and ping against the outside of the cart while he was driving along in his bubble of safety.

It was considered fun for the golfers to aim for the pick-up cart, hoping to scare the black boy inside, knowing no real harm could come to him. But one Saturday morning, when the driving range was packed with people waiting for tee times, Butterbean made his first run across the wide expanse where hundreds of range balls looked like toadstools after a rainstorm. He'd just about filled the cart when it suddenly stopped. Two golf balls had jammed the tines.

This was the most dangerous time for anyone under fire from a hundred

30-handicappers armed with buckets of range balls. But Butterbean knew what to do.

He carefully pulled a cord inside the cage and raised a white flag. When the wind whipped the two-foot-square sign of surrender, it was a signal to cease fire. The golfers on the range were supposed to stop hitting, allow the cart driver a moment to fix what needed fixing, then fire at will when the flag went back down.

Everybody knew the drill. It was universal.

Butterbean Green waited a full two minutes, long enough for everyone to get the message and for the sound of balls pinging off the cage to stop, like the last kernels of popping corn, before he stepped out to clear the jam.

At the end of the range, however, was a plumbing magnate from Cleveland. He was fat and furious, mostly at his wife for making him late for his tee time. But he was also mad at his club pro who swore his latest lesson would fix his incurable slice.

He'd already shanked six balls so badly off the practice tee the players next to him politely pulled up stakes and left their positions for fear of being hit.

So incensed was this jerk from Ohio, he never saw the white flag. He simply re-teed ball after ball, swinging wildly as his anger increased with every bad shot.

Then, against great odds, he caught one. It left the tee on a clothesline headed straight for the green golf cart, just as Butterbean opened the cage door. From 180 yards away, the Titleist arrived like a bullet, slamming into Butterbean's skull, right where the platelets meet, dropping the boy like a sack of range balls.

When he came to, he heard voices but saw nothing. He was rushed to the Medical University in Charleston where they ran tests. All came out the same: Butterbean Green was blind.

CHAPTER 9

Orrie Adger never knew Butterbean when he could see.

Orrie grew up on Butler Island and played with the black boys down at the caddie shack where Butterbean was a highly sought after looper. Not only was a blind caddie great cocktail party conversation for New York bankers, he was the best of the bunch, barefoot and all.

Occasionally, somebody would scoff at the idea of a blind caddie. But after he toted their bag, gave them yardages, told them how their putts would break, and where the alligator might be sunning himself on the other side of the bunker, they became believers. To them it was a parlor trick well played. But to Butterbean it was a computer game.

During the building of the golf course, he'd mentally absorbed every inch of the layout, understood the hydraulics, the drainage, the feel of the fairways, and the slope of the greens. He knew the pins would be front-left on Thursdays, allowing errant shots and poorly hit putts to funnel down within six inches; or tucked tight back-right on Sundays, into unforgiving corners where the hole might as well be a clown's mouth guarded by a windmill on a Putt-Putt course.

But Butterbean always maintained a certain air of mystery about himself, wearing a hat pulled down low over sunglasses so that when he spoke, it sounded like the word of God coming from somewhere within a mannequin.

And he could talk golf. When a player skulled a shot that ran up on the green, Butterbean would snatch up the bag, start walking away and say, "That was an O.J."

The golfer would turn to his caddie and ask what he meant.

"Means you got away with it, Mistuh," Butterbean would mumble as the clubs rattled on his back.

Or if someone hit a decent shot that wasn't that great, Butterbean would lean back and say, "Dat dere's a son-in-law shot. Not 'zactly whatcha had in mind, but it'll do."

One of his favorites was when a big hitter would blister a drive far past the player he was handling. That's when he'd turn to his man and say, "Dat's a Ronstadt, Mistuh. He just *blew by you.*"

It would take some men a moment to correlate the term into Linda Ronstadt's sultry hit song, "Blue Bayou," but it always made them laugh.

Which was Butterbean's business plan. If rich white men were able to play an expensive golf course badly, but enjoy the experience because a blind caddie kept them laughing at themselves, his tips grew exponentially. At the end of each round, Butterbean would stand next to the golf bags holding his hat in his hand like a tin cup, tapping the ground with a broken putter shaft he used like a cane. After the foursome stuffed wads of money into his hat, he'd stick it all in his jacket pocket, and get ready for the next group coming out of the clubhouse.

Later, the caddie master would fold each bill according to denomination so Butterbean could tell a twenty from a ten.

Orrie watched all this from a child's perspective and thought Butterbean was the smartest caddie on earth.

But there were other stories about Butterbean that weren't so funny.

Jake Sizemore, a retired physicist from the bomb plant, surmised that the golf ball that struck Butterbean's temple had somehow magnetized particles in his brain, causing him to pick up signals from the fourth dimension.

The more pot Jake smoked around the campfire at Healing Springs Baptist Church and Country Club, the more he rambled on about how normal people only see three dimensions, when actually there were a total of nine, separated in time and space by a fraction of a second, and invisible to the human eye.

Other scenarios from the past, he claimed, were happening all around us, but we were unable to see or connect with them. Thus he surmised that Butterbean's blindness somehow enabled him to see these other dimensions, for better or worse.

That was one explanation for what others called Butterbean's "moments of madness;" those times when he would act like he was going under a spell, his eyes would roll back in their sockets, and he would start to channel other people from other times.

Some were legendary, like the first time anybody remembers it happening back on Butler Island. Butterbean was just a teenager when he suddenly went stiff, his body turned cold, and he started singing slave songs.

"I've been in the storm so long, Lawd," the words came slowly but painfully from his mouth, which barely moved.

"You know I done been in the storm so long," and his head would drop, then suddenly jerk upright.

"Gimme mo' time to pray, Oh Lawd," he moaned.

"Just look at the shape I'm in, Oh Lawd. Just gimme more time to pray."

Then tears would burst from his sightless eyes like dew drops forming on a flower petal, ready to run to the river without any say in where they would fall.

"Lawd," Butterbean would scream in a primal voice of a slave hoeing taters and beans in a field so hot and dry no man could live through a day, much less a lifetime.

"Lawd, hear me now," he would groan, barely audible. "I's ain't got no mo'. No mo'. No mo'. Lemme be, oh Lawd, lemme be."

It took several of these incidents before people screwed up enough courage to talk to Butterbean when he entered into one of these fits. But slowly he told them his name was Willie Ware, a slave on Butler Plantation, who lived and died on the barrier island in the early 1800s, or thereabouts.

Sometimes Willie was so sad he couldn't explain his torment. He spoke in Gullah of his children who he barely got to name before they were taken away, and his wife Eulah, who died of the fever on Christmas Eve. It was all in there somewhere, jumbled between praise-house songs and talk of whips across his back.

It seemed Butterbean was able to connect with restless spirits wherever he went, never knowing who would force their way out of the forgotten past and present themselves for all to see and hear.

Like the day he bitched to his fellow caddies, in a curt British accent, about the mosquitoes and lack of rum.

"They treat us like swine," he said, pretending to raise a musket to his shoulder and aim it into thin air. "One day soon I'm going to put a ball in the back of the leftenant's 'ead, I am. And if you doubt me, try me. I'll put one in the back of your 'ead, too."

When Tom Adger, Orrie's father and the owner of Butler Island, heard all of this, he had a doctor from Charleston examine Butterbean to see if he was of sound mind. Turned out, the doctor said, the blind black man was channeling the dead, picking up signals from those who had passed this same way long ago and still had something to say.

While it wasn't a recognized scientific phenomenon, there had been cases of channeling reported since the beginning of time. Most had been challenged and written off as hoaxes. But some are uncannily accurate.

Once, as a tropical storm swept over Butler Island, Butterbean became a lost boy, maybe 9 or 10 years old, running through the pine forest, falling into the mucky marsh, screaming for his mother, not knowing which way to go. As five people tried to hold him down, the boy thrashed about, his voice slowly fading, as he eventually tired, fell limp, and apparently died alone in the storm.

The last anyone heard from the lost child was his distant whimpers, "Momma… Momma…oh, Momma, please…."

Even Orrie had experienced Butterbean's sudden departures from the present.

It happened one day when he was playing a qualifying match at Musgrove Mill near the town of Ninety Six. Orrie asked Butterbean if he should hit a 6- or 7-iron to an elevated green with a front pin placement and a left-to-right cross wind.

"Never make it," Butterbean said, hat low.

"But I can hit a draw with the seven, hold it against the wind, and carry the trap with some to spare," Orrie said, still staring at the flag flapping in the breeze.

"Too many Cherokee," Butterbean said. "Never make it. Stay in the fort."

At 16 years old, Orrie wasn't up on his state history enough to realize Butterbean had morphed into an 18th century scout who led hunting parties into the wilds of western South Carolina where Indians still roamed, ruled and occasionally scalped unsuspecting white travelers.

Unfazed and confused, Orrie hit the 7-iron, and the ball ballooned against a gust of wind and fell short in the trap to the right of the green.

"Damn," Orrie muttered as he slammed the club back into his golf bag. "I should'a hit the six. Now I'm plugged."

Butterbean, eyes still glassy, simply walked past him and muttered, "You shoulda stayed in the fort, like I told you, white boy. Now you's dead."

CHAPTER 10

Holly Holladay was holding a Diet Coke and talking to an administrative aide from Fritz Hollings' office when she saw Brumby McLean come through the door.

Unlike other people she'd met on The Hill, Brumby didn't fit the mold. He wasn't from a prominent family. He wasn't a political junky. He didn't wear a college ring. He wasn't a frat boy. Granted, he was a little overweight, but he had great dimples.

She also knew he was a few years older, but his floppy blond hair and his habit of wearing Weejuns without socks made him look younger.

When he saw her across the room, the East Coast Party Band was returning from its first break, so he walked over and extended his hand, trying to ignore the guy standing next to her.

"I'm Brumby," he said. "We met before in Congressman Spratt's office."

Holly nodded and introduced Bobby Trouche, one of Hollings' constituent service gurus who specialized in military affairs.

"I remember," Holly said, shaking Brumby's hand. "Bobby was just telling me about some proposals for the new budget. Are you interested in the National Guard's pre-mobilization plan?"

Brumby looked at Trouche and smiled, allowing his dimples to do the work, then turned to Holly and said, "I'm much more interested in asking you for the next dance."

Right on cue, the band broke into Marvin Gaye's "Stubborn Kind Of Fellow" and Holly accepted, handing Trouche her empty Coke can as she and Brumby moved through the crowd en route to the dance floor.

People from South Carolina usually don't bother asking each other if they can dance. It's assumed that everybody from the Palmetto State can do the state dance, the Shag, in one form or another.

As Brumby took Holly's right hand and dropped his left shoulder on the down-beat, she followed as if she'd been taught the sensuous dance by Mo Oswald herself, the lady who taught every boy from Bluff County how to Shag.

After showing off a few of his best moves, Brumby proved that for a fat boy, he was light on his feet, and soon felt brave enough to lean in and ask, "So, how'd you get the name Holly?"

She felt comfortable in Brumby's loose embrace, turning when she was supposed to do so, hanging back in a sultry sway when he made a move. The Shag, after all, is a man's dance, designed to show off the male's sensitive side, his musical soul, his rhythmic, restless sensuality.

"My parents were hippies," she said as the music ended and they walked off the floor. "I grew up outside Abbeville, in a commune. My parents still live there. Only now it's an organic food and herb business."

Brumby laughed, saying he'd heard about the mushroom farm near Due West, where a rock concert turned into an orgy back in the early '70s.

"My sister was conceived at that concert," Holly said, blushing slightly. "We're all named for trees in the forest. Her name is Cypress."

They both broke up laughing and turned toward the bar when Brumby noticed Holly wasn't wearing the engagement ring he'd seen earlier.

"Did you lose your ring?" he asked innocently.

"No," Holly said. "I lost…."

The lead singer leaned into the microphone and crooned, *"You never close your eyes, anymore, when I kiss your lips…."*

"…that loving feeling?" Brumby replied, finishing the title to the Righteous Brothers' song and leading her back through the crowd for a slow dance.

"Yeah," Holly said as she put her head against his shoulder. "That."

CHAPTER 11

Headwaters of the Salkehatchie River emanate near Par Pond, a large catch basin inside the gates of the Savannah River Site, a top secret facility created when the federal government confiscated 300 square miles of South Carolina for the production of plutonium during the Cold War.

While it takes only 11 pounds of plutonium to make a nuclear bomb, the United States produced 36 million metric tons of the material between 1953-58 at the facility everybody called "The Bomb Plant."

Older folks, especially the ones in small communities relocated to make way for the facility, called it "The Bum Plant." Yet it was a money machine where people could get good jobs, government health insurance, and a retirement plan.

But what a mess they made. By the mid-80s, all five reactors at SRS were shut down, leaving tons of nuclear waste in shallow graves that had been leaking ever since.

Underneath it all was the Tuscaloosa Aquifer, a giant water supply that feeds the entire Southeast. The only thing between all that toxic waste and the local water supply was a natural clay barrier and the Right Rev. Macon Moses.

When he wasn't preaching the gospel at the Healing Springs Baptist Church and Country Club, Moses worked as a security guard for Nu-Chem.

Preaching, of course, was a calling, and he dearly loved the Lord. But Moses had child support payments from a previous relationship, a gambling habit, a scam he was running on a black girlfriend, a not-so-secret sexual liaison with a white girlfriend, and a few part-time jobs to make ends meet.

But so far, at the age of 46, he'd avoided going to jail, which was his first and foremost objective. He'd seen his father go in and out of prison and wanted none of it. His mother saw to that, telling him God was calling him to the ministry, and he had to follow. But to get there, he had to play football.

At 6-6, 240, Macon Moses' name was on every college recruiter's list, with an asterisk beside it noting grades. While he led Blackville-Hilda to a state title in Division A, his SAT score lacked a comma, and he was relegated to play at S.C. State, the historically black university in nearby Orangeburg.

Despite making first team All-MidEastern Athletic Conference two years running, a knee injury his senior season sidelined his NFL dreams. Still, Macon Moses managed to turn name recognition, natural charisma, and his mastery of Bible verses into a profitable avocation.

The Healing Springs Baptist Church and Country Club was his stage and his congregation was the audience he'd sought all his life. He even got Orrie and Butterbean up early one Sunday morning to hear him preach, which was no small miracle.

While neither one came forward to be saved that day, he considered it a successful effort toward race relations because they stayed awake, put some money in the collection plate, and didn't puke on the pews.

On average, Moses collected about $200 a week when they passed the plate, mostly cash because few in the congregation had checking accounts. The offertory hymn, therefore, was his favorite tune. While Nu-Chem Security paid his bills, his flock funded his lust for sex and gambling. And he had other occasional jobs that helped feather his nest.

"I can see myself retiring and settling down with a nice pension," Moses would tell Orrie when they talked about their lives. "I grew up a sharecropper's son on Boss Cantey's farm, not far from here. So I'm doing pretty damn good for a black man in South Carolina. You know, I got a job. I drive a nice truck. I own a home. I'm supporting my kid. I give blood.

"You, on the other hand," he said, looking down at Orrie, "are a worthless white piece of shit."

Orrie thought about that for a moment but couldn't argue the point. Ever since the accident, he'd been on a downhill slide. The garbage truck completely crushed the left side of his body. What remained could barely lift a beer bottle much less play golf.

And that was all Orrie knew how to do. He'd been pampered his entire life, living in a resort, playing golf, chasing rich girls, going to private schools, totally avoiding reality. Until that big green garbage truck hit his little yellow sports car and the world rolled over on his leg.

For a year, maybe more, he hardly remembered not being in surgery, ICU, or some rehab facility where he became a test case that couldn't be solved. Too much damage. Lucky to walk at all.

But, if all you're gonna do is sit around a one-hole golf course and drink beer and smoke pot all day, he was in pretty good shape. Most days he could get around without a walker, unless he was really wasted. Then he kept one under the pulpit, along with a bottle of Wild Turkey, just in case.

Still, Orrie couldn't decide which one he missed the most, his golf swing or his dick. Not only did the garbage truck smash his legs, a piece of steel from the radiator grill speared his groin, severing nerves he didn't know he had until he lost them.

He remembered hearing the word "impotence" for the first time as he awoke from a drug-induced sleep. Two doctors were standing at the end of his hospital bed, talking about his wounds, and how he might be impotent.

"Nerves," one doctor said, shrugging to the other. "You never know whether they'll grow back or not." Now, in the prime of his manhood, Orrie hadn't had an erection in years, and no place to use one if he did.

As far as Orrie was concerned, the sooner it was all over the better. He had no desire to kill himself; he just had no desire. All those competitive juices that once flowed through him were gone, dried up, in the back locker room with the losers who hear the cheers through the window and wonder what it would be like in the spotlight. They'd never know because they never had it. Unfortunately, Orrie had heard the cheers, and they haunted him.

CHAPTER 12

Brumby and Holly were thinking about leaving the party when they saw Henry Smalls heading for the door.

"Hey, Henry, it's Brumby, how's it going?"

Henry didn't hear Brumby and appeared to be in a huge hurry. It wasn't until Brumby grabbed his coat sleeve that his old acquaintance from high school turned in his direction.

"Oh, hey Brumby. I didn't see you, man. How you doing?"

"Good," Brumby said to Henry, a light-skinned black guy, always popular with women. "So, you still at Energy?"

"Yeah, public affairs, what a dead-end job, huh?" Henry said, noticing Holly as he completed his turn. Suddenly he wasn't in such a big hurry.

"So, who's your friend?

It had been a few months since Brumby had seen Henry Smalls. The son of an African-American bomb plant worker from Barnwell, he'd ridden affirmative action through college and up the political ladder to a job here in Washington where he was a deputy assistant to somebody in charge of something.

On previous occasions, Brumby had been happy to see Henry, or anybody from his home state. But with Holly by his side, he suddenly became defensive. Henry had a reputation with white women, so Brumby was on guard.

Henry, despite being only 5'6, had proven himself a snake when it came to the ladies. He once stole the quarterback's girlfriend a week before the homecoming dance. Nobody could figure out his charm. He was, after all, shorter than most of the girls in high school. His secret, some smirked, was in his pants.

"Um, this is Holly, she works in Spratt's office," Brumby said.

"Nice to meet you, Holly. What a nice name," he said, taking her hand and kissing it lightly. "I'm Henry, moving up over in DOE, been here since Reagan's second term. Is that your real name?"

"Yep," Holly said politely.

That's when Brumby knew he was in trouble. When a guy like Henry Smalls starts sniffing around your woman, you have to hit him upside the head with a 2-by-4 to knock him off the scent.

"She's just passing through," Brumby said, trying to move his body in between Henry and his prey. "She's moving to Charleston to start medical school; leaving town tomorrow."

Holly managed not to flinch when Brumby created her medical career out of thin air, but played along to see where it would go. "Yeah," she said, catching on quickly. "Proctology. Should be fun."

"Absolutely," Henry said, taking a half step back and tightening his butt cheeks. "Sounds like a blast. Where'd you do your undergraduate?"

"Erskine," she said proudly. "Played volleyball for the Flying Fleet!"

"Good school," Henry said, realizing she was a full head taller than he was. "So, Brumby, how about give me a call, I might have a story for you."

And then Henry was gone. That's when Holly looked at Brumby and they both broke out laughing.

"Med school?" she asked.

"Proctology?" Brumby said, snorting a laugh.

"Just following your lead," she said with a smile.

CHAPTER 13

Henry Smalls was in a hurry because he needed to find Luke Thompson, and he needed to find him fast. Thompson worked for the AARP (Alliance Against Radiation Proliferation), an acronym that often got him discount hotel rooms and more than a few confused looks at cocktail parties.

At 56, Thompson was a senior citizen in Washington World, a storybook place where youthful innocence is routinely replaced by more youthful innocence. Thompson, bald and cynical, stuck out in crowds, which he avoided. His favorite entertainment was taking his four-year-old twin grandsons to the National Mall to play Frisbee with his Golden Retriever, Chopper, on the weekends.

Smalls had known Thompson since he came to Washington in '87. They'd met at a public affairs seminar about radioactive waste and what the country could do about it. Over a case of Coors Light, they decided not much. But in due course, they established an adversarial friendship that allowed them to exchange personal cell phone numbers and therefore, private information.

Thompson, a Citadel graduate, was an unlikely advocate for peace and tranquility. He'd served in Vietnam, a decorated soldier who, like most, seldom talked about combat. He grew up in the small town of Batesburg slightly north of the Salkehatchie River, and was home-schooled before going off to college.

Although South Carolina reluctantly integrated its schools in the late 1960s, racial and economic chasms actually widened when most of the white families in small towns fled the public schools for private academies. Others, who thought hastily built schools named for Confederate generals were substandard, tried home schooling.

Guys in Henry's generation fared no better than the blacks who came before. They ended up surrounded by other black students and taught by black teachers, only in different buildings.

Thus Luke and Henry grew up in parallel universes, separated by time and color.

People who knew the Thompson family joked the kids were homeschooled because they were too ugly to leave the house. That applied to Luke, whose hard face and angular features cast him in the Charles Bronson mold.

This was kind compared to what kids said about his younger sister, Gertrude. They said she was uglier than a bowling shoe, but she seemed oblivious to the ridicule en route to a full ride to MIT where she currently taught astrophysics.

While both were odd, Luke, at least, was sociable. He always wore a sly smile, like he knew something amusing you didn't know. But that was not his tone of voice when he left Henry Smalls a voicemail late that Friday afternoon.

Henry had departed work early, hoping to meet somebody like Holly Holladay at the South Carolina party. But when he checked his messages about 8 p.m., it was Thompson's voice that sent him scrambling for the door.

"We've got dead cows, Henry," was all it said.

That's all it took for the blood to rush out of Henry Smalls' face and make him start walking briskly to find a quiet place to return the call. After reluctantly breaking off the conversation with Brumby and his new-found friend, Henry pulled out his flip phone and dialed Luke Thompson's private number.

"Yo," Thompson said, answering on the first ring.

"Luke, it's Henry."

"Uh, yeah, man, I got something your office might need to know about," Luke said, trying to pull pajama tops over the heads of his two rambunctious grandsons. "My guys say your guys found some dead cattle on the Cantey farm outside Elko, down near Snake Creek."

There was an awkward silence on the line before Smalls responded bureaucratically, "Well, you know how cows are, Luke. They're like fish. They die every time the weather changes. Could be anything."

Another awkward interval arrived, filled with the muffled sounds of small boys struggling with nightclothes, before Luke said, "There are 63 of them, Henry. And they've all got high numbers. Real high numbers."

Henry knew what that meant. The University of Georgia lab at the Savannah River Site had been running groundwater tests for years in three areas downstream from the nuclear site. The results were predictable.

In 1995, a toxic soup of various "iums" was dispersed in small parts per million in the water table. That was to be expected. Everything from fertilizer to parking-lot runoff could make the needle move a little bit.

But in 1997, the needle moved again, this time more abruptly. A few farm ponds and shallow wells showed signs of contamination; six public school children, all black, were hospitalized with high fevers and unacceptable levels of cesium, and the wells were summarily closed.

Henry remembered preparing the press release acknowledging the incident, using all his abilities as a propagandist to disguise the alarming reality. He talked a local doctor into saying, and he quoted, "We believe it was mold fungus that made these children ill for a day or two. They were back in school the very next week."

One newspaper in the region ran the story, hacking out the technical mumbo-jumbo and focusing on the children missing school. The next week *The Aiken Standard* ran an editorial, using the event as a hook, to blast the county school board for poor maintenance on the school's air conditioning units.

Sixty-three dead cows, however, was a different story.

"Who knows about this?" Henry asked.

"Oh, you know, the usual suspects, a couple of researchers, a department head or two...." Luke said, waiting for the right amount of tension to build before adding, "And me."

Henry took a deep breath, trying not to sound alarmed, and said, "Look, Luke, it's probably nothing. Give me a little time before you bring in the protesters. I'll get down there Monday and check it out, see if anything serious is going on."

Another long pause was followed by the sound of Luke kissing his grandsons goodnight and whispering into the phone, "And if there is...?"

CHAPTER 14

Orrie was stoned and Butterbean was driving.

"Just keep it aimed straight ahead, Butterbean," Orrie said, holding on to the side of the golf cart as it sped down the dirt road toward the highway. "You're doing great!"

Of all the things Butterbean Green couldn't do because of his blindness, driving wasn't one of them. He remembered driving the golf carts at Butler Bay and knew difference between an EZ-Go and a Club Car by the way they accelerated and handled in the turns. While there were 75 sliver-and-mauve Club Cars in Butler Bay's cart barn, the Healing Springs Baptist Church and Country Club had only one basic green, broken-down, EZ-Go at its disposal.

But it was Butterbean's pride and joy because every day he'd get to drive it down the mile-long dirt road to the highway to get the mail. Sporting a green Penny Branch Golf Club shirt and red-striped Bermuda shorts, Orrie almost fell out of the cart as he reached out to grab some leaves off a mulberry bush sticking out over the sandy, rutted road and said, "We're almost there, Butterbean, slow it down some."

"I know dat," Butterbean said with a sense of disgust. "I kin feel da ruts in da road and da heat from da highway, smell da change in da air when we leaves da pine thicket, hear dem crickets go silent when we pass dat big gum tree. I can even taste dem diesel fumes left behind by da truck that went by last night."

Orrie regained his balance, managing not to fall out of the golf cart after all, and said, "Well, I can tell because I can see the road up ahead and a cop car sitting there with his blue light flashing."

That's when Butterbean hit the brake, locking the golf cart down as it slid to a halt in the soft white sand.

"Whas he want, you reckon?" Butterbean said.

"Prolly nothing," Orrie slurred. "Pull on up and let's see."

As they rolled to a stop at the edge of Highway 300, Butterbean heard the clicking of the cop's flashing lights, leaned over to Orrie and said, "Dat's a state trooper. County cops ain't got dem new halcyon light packages yet."

Orrie, as usual, didn't give a shit. He stepped out of the cart and staggered toward the officer who was leaning against their sign that read, "Welcome to Jesus Saves, S.C., Home of the Healing Springs Baptist Church and Country Club."

In fact, it said the same thing on both sides of the sign.

"Something wrong, man?" Orrie asked, grabbing the mailbox that was supported by a broken 3-wood stuck in the ground.

The trooper squinted at the disheveled drunk, dropped his sunglasses on his nose, looked over the top and said, "You know, you look an awful lot like a guy I used to know, something Adger, the golfer. Yeah, your nickname was Mudpuddle, or something like that."

Orrie winced a little, leaned on the mailbox, sighed and said, "Puddles."

"Yeah, that's it," the cop said, taking off his Smokey the Bear hat. "It's me, man, Parish Chaplin. We played against each other in that junior tournament down in Beaufort. You beat me like a drum, you bastard."

Orrie stared into the pulsating blue light, trying to recognize the man in uniform. Hearing the name "Puddles" always put Orrie on the defensive, like hearing a haunting voice from the past, the kind that signals one to run away.

"Yeah, Chaplin, sure, I remember. You double-bogeyed the last hole at Fripp Island. Got plugged in the greenside bunker, had to take an unplayable. Tough break, man. Bummer."

Parish Chaplin hadn't seen Orrie Adger since that day, but he knew what happened to him and his promising golf career.

"Wouldn't have mattered," he said. "You birdied the last hole and won going away. Like you always did in those days. How's it, uh, going for you now?"

Orrie shuffled his feet, waiting for Butterbean to bail him out, but the blind man was silent in his orange jumpsuit and sunglasses.

"I'm good, I'm okay," Orrie said, uneasily. "Got a little place out here. Getting by."

Chaplin looked over at Butterbean with suspicion and asked, "Is that guy okay?"

Orrie realized his partner looked like he should be picking up litter on the side of the road, and said, "Yeah, yeah, you know, he's like a, um, disabled vet. Blinded in

Baghdad. Roadside bomb. Terrible, just terrible. So, what's with all the lights, man?"

Parish Chaplin put his hat back on, leaned in a little so he could hear the chatter on his police radio, and said, "Oh, you know, routine stuff. We got a shipment coming through tonight. Big flat beds from Oak Ridge. We just make sure there ain't nothing in the way to slow 'em down."

Orrie nodded his head, knowing all about the shipments to Nu-Chem, the ones that were supposed to be top-secret.

"They still dumping all that shit in the ground over there?" Orrie asked, trying to determine which way to point.

"I guess so," the trooper said. "You know, we don't ask questions. It's one of them need-to-know deals, and I guess they think we don't need to know."

Orrie nodded, opened the mail box, saw nothing inside, turned back toward the golf cart, shoved Butterbean out from behind the wheel, mangled a three-point turn, and waved goodbye to the Parish Chaplin, whispering to himself, "Ain't it so, brother, ain't it so."

CHAPTER 15

In his prime, Orrie Adger was a magician with a golf club. But that was a long time ago. These days, when Orrie was really high on weed and Wild Turkey, he'd grab a pitching wedge from the barrel of mismatched clubs by the front door, ease off the porch, and limp to the first tee.

Everybody around Healing Springs Baptist Church and Country Club knew the stories about how good Puddles used to be. But none of the local boys ever saw him play. Mostly they were from somewhere else. Welders and steel workers who wandered the country from one nuke job to another, living in campers along the riverbanks where they loved to hunt and fish and screw and lie about all three.

Winston Sellars was typical. The bearded, barrel-chested man from New Hampshire entered nuke world right out of the Navy when the business was booming. He'd earned his certifieds the hard way, moving 16 times in 28 years to reach Level Three Inspector, of which there were not many.

While he'd made more than $100,000 a year for almost 30 years, he'd spent it all on good times and bad times, but mostly bad. Especially when he mixed whiskey with almost anything. Recently, he announced he was only drinking beer because hard liquor made him break out in handcuffs. But that didn't last. Nothing worth a shit ever did, it seemed. But at least his camper and bass boat were paid off, and he only had six more payments on his Ford Explorer.

All the other boys who hung around there were about the same. Either they were from way off, or too young to understand that history stretched further back than their last erection.

All they knew about Orrie was he drank a lot, smoked a lot of pot, and was in a bad wreck that left him a little off kilter. Only a few of the transient workers knew Orrie when he was a champion, a stallion, a win or two away from the PGA Tour. But the Salkehatchie swamps were full of people who were almost something. That's why they lived here, so they could do their forgetting in peace.

Such grace occasionally came to Orrie on sleepless nights when he stood on the tee box with a full moon shining down on the first hole like a spotlight from heaven.

He'd always thought he would end up on tour, hanging out with Freddie, living on the whims of the golf gods, taking the good with the bad, and moving on down the line. He never dreamed he would end up here, less than 50 miles from Magnolia Lane, living in an unplayable lie.

That's when he'd drop a scuffed-up Titleist from his pocket, touch it with the toe of the wedge, try to find a grassy spot, then take dead aim at the tattered flag that fluttered 135 yards down the hill.

While most golfers would spend time deciphering the elevation drop, which was considerable, and the wind velocity, which could be a factor, Orrie simply stared at the moonlit target, waggling his wedge like a cocker spaniel anticipating dinner. When he was set, he'd drop the club face behind the ball, set his shoulders, take one more look at the flag, and begin his take away.

It was in that short distance between the time the club started back until it returned in full force that Orrie's golf game once lived. It was so graceful and pure that it was poetic. It seemed untouched by natural forces, unfazed by unfavorable conditions, an utterly unbelievable thing to behold.

But it was gone. Probably forever. And Orrie knew it. Deep down, he knew it, but he couldn't accept it. Not until he reached the pinnacle of his swing, started back down, and felt his left side collapse as he wiped across the ball like a hacker, was he reminded of his condition, undeniably.

The only thing that left the tee box with authority that night was the divot, freshly dug, with the ball dribbling halfway down the hill, as Orrie doubled over in pain. The club, in fact, went twice as far when he slung it in anger, watching it helicopter down the fairway, and land in the weed-choked rough.

The next morning Butterbean found Orrie asleep against the wooden bench beside the first tee, snoring, drooling, aware of nothing, and caring even less.

Knowing what happened, Butterbean leaned over, felt the fresh scrape on the tee box, then walked slowly down the hill to collect the golf ball and the club, his bare feet leaving ghostly footprints in the morning dew.

CHAPTER 16

Henry Smalls caught the first flight out of Reagan Monday morning, connected in Atlanta, then touched down in Augusta by 9 a.m.

An intern from the bomb plant picked him up in a government fleet car, and they drove through the gates at the Savannah River Site, a place Smalls never liked to go. His father worked at the Bomb Plant, something to do with the E-Reactor, but never talked about his job.

All Henry knew was Randall Smalls died of colon cancer two years earlier. He was only 57. The doctors said they got it all the year before, but they didn't. So Henry was holding his father's hand in the hospital when he took his final breath. Even more heart-wrenching than witnessing the exact moment when his father's life ended was what happened next.

Also in the room was Henry's white mother, Ruby, who quickly lifted the sheets, plucked two tissues from a bedside box, reached under his father's hospital gown and wiped away a small issue of feces that came forth when his dead muscles finally relaxed, just a moment before the nurses came into the room. It was, Henry thought, the most powerful gesture of love he'd ever witnessed, and one he was sure he would never know.

While some people considered him a mulatto Casanova, it was all part of his little-man complex. Ever since he stopped growing in the seventh grade, he began searching for something that would make him fit in. Being smart and half white didn't exactly endear him to his black classmates who labeled him "beige" because he made good grades and talked without a gangster accent.

That bothered him when he wanted to be accepted in high school, but he soon learned white girls liked him because he was nice to them, unlike the bully brotherhood of Neanderthals that populated the football team. Being short, he discovered, was a non-threatening entrée into the world of women, who actually liked guys who liked what they liked.

So he learned to cook from his mother, wore nice clothes, and joined the cheer-leading squad. That was his ultimate stroke of genius. As the only male cheerleader at his high school, he'd just flash that Cheshire Cat grin when he'd hoist Patti Gatens on his shoulder, palm her crotch, then lift her up for the entire student body to admire, including the football players.

Because of Henry's close proximity to pussy and the way the girls fawned over him, there were only two possible conclusions to be drawn. Either he was gay or a ladies man. And the answer was never as clear-cut as it could be.

Even Henry questioned his sexuality. He liked girls just fine. In fact, he loved the curve of their hips, the sweep of their legs, and their shoes. If he'd been born a girl, he would be the biggest shoe whore in town.

But there were other things that caught Henry's eye. Like the time Brumby McLean walked in on him naked in the showers at band camp. Henry was 16 that summer, showering all alone at the camp near Lake Lure where he perfected snare drum rolls. Brumby, then 15, was a trombonist.

It happened so fast and so long ago that Henry should have forgotten it. But he hadn't. It replayed itself in his head for years to come — Henry was soaping his genitals, stroking slowly because he was alone when Brumby turned the corner.

Brumby was wearing a towel around his waist, and a pair of green flip-flops that echoed in the cavernous shower when they slapped against the wet floor. He also had a bar of soap in his hand. Ivory soap, Brumby thought, wishing he didn't remember every detail.

Turning toward the noise, Henry held himself proudly as Brumby stopped dead in his tracks and stared.

While group showering was common in summer camps and football practice, most boys learned not to look down for fear of being branded queer, or fag, or homo.

But that moment, which lasted only few seconds, seemed like forever in the slipstream of time. Because both boys froze like statues, unwilling, or unable to move, then turned shyly away.

That's when Brumby's towel loosened around his ever-expanding trunk and fell to the floor, exposing his involuntary erection. That neither boy ever mentioned that moment became an unspoken bond that hibernated for years until they stumbled across each other in the nation's capital.

Henry was a fine specimen with a triple-digit IQ, and the girls always liked having him around. But he was unlucky in love. Seemed white Southern girls liked having a smart, black boy around with whom to flirt and flaunt, but that infatuation never led to the bedroom.

Being used as a jealousy toy was frustrating for him, but not as tormenting as the lack of black girls to balance the scales. The ones he knew growing up were nappy-headed baby machines his parents told him to avoid. One example they kept using was his cousin TaShanna Williams, his daddy's brother's daughter, who delivered her first child when she was 16 years old and was pregnant with another from a different boy by the time she was 17.

No sir, his parents had higher hopes for Henry. He would go to college, get a degree, a job, marry a nice girl from a good family, get a government job, have a couple of kids, and make his parents proud. It was a dream he'd been cast in since he could remember, but the sharp sound of a 300-page report landing on the table in front of him brought him back quickly to the small meeting room on the second floor of the Savannah River Site headquarters building.

"I got dead cows," Joe Moskos, an environmental specialist for the Department of Energy, said, walking around the end of the table to take a seat across from Henry. "A bunch of dead cows. Sixty-three to be exact. What's going on, Henry? I thought Washington was going to fix this shit."

Henry knew what this shit was, but he didn't know how to fix it. He was a political science major from the College of Charleston. He didn't know an isotope from a breeder reactor, despite working in the industry for 10 years.

"It's an aberration, Joe," Henry said, apologetically. "The guys in the director's office say it's okay, nothing to worry about. It's happened before. It might happen again. But in the long run, everything's okay."

Joe Moskos wasn't so sure. He'd come to SRS after 24 years in the Marine Corps and didn't need a master's degree in hydrology, which he had, to know that crap runs downhill.

"Our guys, the ones who actually go out into the field to see what's going on, think otherwise," Moskos said, his New Jersey accent coming through loud and clear. "In fact, they say the entire system from Lower Three Runs Creek down into the watershed is starting to glow."

That, Henry knew, was the worst-case scenario. For decades the government had denied that radioactive waste even existed at the Savannah River Site. It wasn't until Luke Thompson and the AARP gained access to classified files through the Freedom of Information Act that the feds officially confirmed nuclear materials on site. Even then, they wouldn't say how much. The Alliance Against Radiation Proliferation, however, knew exactly how much there was, how it was stored, the possibilities of disaster, and that the government was accepting even more low-level waste from other states without a backup plan if something went wrong.

Stories like that appeared in *The Washington Post* from time to time, but barely got legs in South Carolina, where the press was more interested in Gamecock football than other similar unsolvable mysteries.

"I'm serious, Henry," Moskos said, leaning his 6-foot frame across the table to get his attention. "If I have to drive up to Washington and get the director and bring him down here and make him drink a bottle of water taken right out of the Salkehatchie, I'll do it. Sooner or later, somebody's going to have to answer for this shit."

So far, nobody had.

For half a century the area known as the CSRA (Central Savannah River Area) had been sacrificed on the altar of progress without a second thought of eternal outcomes. And for decades the people who lived in this backwater region learned to live in a dysfunctional marriage, the love-hate relationship they endured with the Bomb Plant.

Away from official ears, of course, some bomb plant workers said CSRA stood for Citizens Sacrificed for the Rest of America. Those with scientific degrees and engineering backgrounds, of course, chose to live upstream from the facility in towns like Augusta, North Augusta and Aiken. The poor souls who didn't know any better lived downstream and downwind in a sparsely populated, agricultural area best described as "po-ass South Carolina."

Henry enjoyed telling people he grew up behind the Pine Curtain in the hyphenated athletic conference where all the schools had names like Williston-Elko, Allendale-Fairfax, Bamberg-Ehrhardt, and Denmark-Olar because the towns were so small they had to be scrunched together to come up with enough kids for a football team.

This, however, was ground zero if the dam broke. That's how people who worked at the Bomb Plant spoke when they whispered about doomsday, the worst-case scenario. If, they said, the millions of gallons of contaminated sludge buried inside the fences at SRS and Nu-Chem ever leaked into the water table, the show would be over. The area fed by a thousand nameless streams would quickly become a graveyard, uninhabitable for thousands of years, maybe more.

"Salkehatchie Soup," Moskos said emphatically, staring Henry in the eye. "That's what we'll have on our hands, Henry. Sticky, stinky, radioactive, Salkehatchie Soup. And when it comes gushing out of here, it ain't gonna be a good day for me, for you, for the director, or for anybody else who has to explain how in the world we let this happen."

CHAPTER 17

D r. John Edmunds was in a congressional hearing when an aide whispered in his ear that he had an urgent phone call.

A dentist by trade, Edmunds had been appointed director of the Department of Energy by President George W. Bush, a tip of the hat to the former governor who led the Reagan Republican revival in South Carolina. His job, he said when he accepted the position, was to eliminate the department all together, dismantle its unmanageable machinery, roll it over into a new, more effective agency yet to be named.

But the department had actually grown in size and budget during his time in Washington with no end in sight to its myriad problems. For half a century the agency had been in collusion with contractors like Dupont and Westinghouse, conglomerates that systematically enjoyed free reign within the wire fences of SRS where they could conduct experimental operations without oversight.

Now the cows were coming home. Literally.

"Dr. Edmunds, I hate to bother you, but we've got an issue that needs immediate attention," Cole Campbell, Edmunds' local liaison, said on the phone from his office in North Augusta.

"Yes, Cole, I'm aware of the cows along the Salkehatchie," Edmunds said. "It's containable. No big deal. We'll handle it as we always do."

Cole Campbell had been working for DOE for 20 years. On most days he was proud of his accomplishments, the certificates of commendation that hung on his office wall, pictures of his beautiful wife and three children, his work in the Sertoma Club, and his position as an elder in the Silver Bluff Presbyterian Church.

But none of that, even his steadfast belief in the Almighty, prepared him for what he was facing. A native of Wisconsin and a graduate of N.C. State's vet school, he knew more about cows than the average guy. His father was a dairy farmer. His brothers were still in the family business. But nothing he knew about animal husbandry applied to this situation.

"Um, sir, Dr. Edmunds," he stumbled slightly, "it's not just that the cows are dead. They're, you know, kind of fried."

CHAPTER 18

Hello Darling, nice to see ya, it's been a long time....

Conway Twitty's voice hung like Spanish Moss on the old oak trees around the country club. That's what Orrie and Butterbean were discussing as they listened to the radio and shared a breakfast doob.

"I'm pretty damn sure there's more moss growing in Bluff County than there is any other county in this damn state," Orrie said, using the tail of his "Savannah River Nuclear Solutions" T-shirt to clean the bowl of his bong, which he used only on special occasions.

"Barnwell," Butterbean said. "Maybe Beaufort. Definitely not Bluff. Too much pine. Moss don't like no pine. Simple as dat."

Orrie thought about that for a minute then forgot what they were talking about because the song ended, and he started listening to Carl Gooding, the voice of WDOG, Big Dog Radio, in Groton.

"Ya'll ain't gonna believe a word of this," Carl said in his usual hound-dog voice. "But somebody told me that Judianne Rollins out there in Barton is pregnant with her seventh child and wants to put it up on Swap and Shop if it's another boy. Said she's got six of 'em already, and she don't want no more. You can even have naming rights. She wants to start the bidding at $1,200 because that's how much she needs to get Rufus out of jail."

Everybody within the Big Dog's 50-mile signal knew this was just Carl being Carl; that ain't nobody gonna auction off their unborn child on the radio. But Carl didn't let on to nothing.

While waiting for the phone lines to light up, Carl launched into one of his many downhome commercials about Adam Loadholt's diner known as The Garden of Eat'n.

"If ya ain't got no plans for lunch and you find yourself in the Groton area when your stomach starts growling, just pop into Adam's Garden of Eat'n for some good old fried chicken with rice and gravy, butter beans, sweet potatoes, cabbage, and cornbread," Carl drawled. "Best food within four miles of downtown Groton, so get yourself in there today and tell 'em Carl sent you."

With the commercial out of the way, Carl heard a voice come through his headset and said, "We got us a bid, ladies and gentlemen. Harvey Womack over in Ulmer said he'd give Judianne $1,500 for the child if she'd come along with it. Seems he's got a thing for pregnant white women with multiple tattoos. While she's thinking over that proposition, let's talk about your lying, double-crossing, church-going, cheating heart...."

With that Orrie and Butterbean caught up with Hank Willams.

You'll toss and turn, the whole night through…your cheating heart, will tell on you.

"That's good shit, ain't it? Country music, I mean," Orrie said, hitting the joint and swaying with the music. "I know you like Motown, and who don't, but you gotta admit, they both pretty much tell it like it is. I mean, white country and black blues, it's all the same shit, different day, different color."

Butterbean had no opinion on that particular subject because he was thinking about how much Orrie had changed over the past three years, wearing cut-offs and flip-flops and seldom shaving. While Butterbean couldn't see his good friend clearly, he could smell him and knew what he was wearing and how long he'd been wearing it.

"'Bout time to revisit the Goodwill," Butterbean would say when Orrie got a little on the stale side. "Think yo clothes done seen better days."

Back when he was playing golf, Orrie was a meticulous dresser. He didn't wear anything but the best: Polo shirts and FootJoys. But all that went out the window when the Kuwaitis took over, Orrie got hurt, and he had to re-invent himself. The problem was, the accident took away the only thing he knew how to do.

Fortunately, Butterbean made enough money for both of them. Those marijuana plants scattered throughout the Salkehatchie swamp behind the church produced more than $200,000 last year, and they were running out of places to hide the cash.

They'd solved their housing situation when they met a contractor who built hotels for Embassy Suites. He'd come to the country club one weekend with some buddies who worked at the bomb plant.

Orrie said he'd always envisioned himself staying at Embassy Suites on the PGA Tour, putting golf balls across the carpet from one room into the other, going down every morning for the free buffet breakfast.

The new guy said he could get 'em some rooms if that's what they wanted. Said they were like modules, you just stack 'em anywhere you want 'em, and he had a few damaged ones on his farm in Saluda.

So, for a few thousand dollars cash, some jackleg builders showed up one day with two Embassy Suites units on a flatbed truck. They were the real thing, completely furnished, with king-size beds, two television sets, wet bars, nice bathrooms, and pullout sofas for visitors.

It took the better part of a morning once they hacked down a few trees, but eventually they wedged the two units into a shady spot about a 9-iron from the campfire, and leveled them up with some concrete blocks so they'd be even.

Naturally, the town of Jesus Saves didn't offer sewage, so a couple of Orrie's plumber friends rigged up a disposal system of pipes and elbows that ran down the hill and dumped directly into the Salkehatchie River. The air conditioners and lights ran off a wire that hijacked power from the Healing Springs Baptist Church.

Orrie's room had the number 201 on his door, and Butterbean's was 432.

They also had maid service. Nicety McNeil, a loyal member of the Healing Springs congregation, worked as a maid cleaning rooms at the Augusta Marriott. So she was hired to do the same for Orrie and Butterbean. She even tied the ends of the toilet paper rolls to look like roses, a trick she learned on the job.

Another church lady named IdaSue Middleton worked at the S&S Cafeteria in Aiken and agreed to supply the boys with regular meals. For $100 a week, she would bring home Styrofoam to-go boxes filled with roast beef, mashed potatoes, and green beans; or fried fish, rice pilaf, and steamed squash; or chicken fried steak, macaroni and cheese, and pinto beans.

The menu at the S&S was endless. One night there would be chicken and dumplings with broccoli, the next would be southern fried chicken and okra, followed by veal parmesan and Brussels sprouts. All the meals would be topped off with a dessert like blueberry custard, coconut, apple, key lime, pecan, or pumpkin pie; or chocolate, key lime, or carrot cake.

It was no wonder Orrie gained 30 pounds. Butterbean, on the other hand, ate like a horse, sopped up gravy with buttered biscuits, and never gained a pound.

"It's da genes," Butterbean would say, wiping his mouth with the back of his hand. "It's all in da genes."

All Orrie knew was he now had to look for size 38 pants instead of 32s at the Goodwill store. Either that or he had to quit smoking pot before dinner and go on a diet, neither of which was likely to happen.

So Miss IdaSue kept them fat and happy, and they paid in cash, something that was even more plentiful after they added three video poker machines to the clubhouse. These electronic bandits were mainline heroin for problem gamblers who came across the Georgia line to play and drink and leave their money behind.

Butterbean didn't approve of gambling or the people it attracted. But profits from those three poker machines tripled every month for the first year, so they got six more shipped in and turned the place into a haven for slot machine junkies.

There came a point, in fact, when the two pronounced themselves millionaires, decided God had blessed them with such riches they were going to start tithing to the church. Of course they were stoned, so it actually turned out to be a one-time donation of an organ for the Healing Springs Baptist Church and Country Club, which served two purposes. One, they weren't about to give cash to the church because it would go straight into the Macon Moses' pocket. Second, it made Wednesday nights a lot more interesting.

Wednesday night was choir practice for members of the "Healing Springs Choral

Choir of Angels," eight big black women who dressed in flowing white gowns on Sunday morning and let loose with some serious gospel. Orrie's favorite was "Peace in the Valley" because he liked the solo part when Hattie McCall would sing,

There will be peace in the valley someday, there will be peace in the valley for me; I pray no more sorrow or sadness or trouble, there will be peace in the valley for me.

Orrie told everybody Hattie was talking about the Horse Creek Valley, this god-forsaken stretch of rolling hills between Augusta and Columbia where the red clay of the Appalachians mixed with the silted sand of a long-gone shoreline.

He and Butterbean would get stoned and sit out on the porch on Wednesday nights, slapping mosquitoes, listening to the organ music, and singing along with the choir the best way they could under the circumstances. Butterbean liked "Amazing Grace," and would tear up when they got to the part that said, *"I was blind, but now I see...."*

They'd end up crying on each other's shoulders and promising to do something better with their lives. Then Orrie and Butterbean would pass out and forget to follow up on the promises made under the influence of Negro spirituals.

Orrie was thinking about the pleasant words to "Peace in the Valley" when he saw Nicety leaving his room and decided it was safe to go back in and take his morning dump. But he stopped short when he heard Carl come back on the radio.

"Hope none of y'all were hanging around the Bomb Plant last week," Carl said. "Heard them big trucks were rolling in so fast that Highway 300 was lit up like a Christmas tree. They said the boys in orbit could see the glow from the space shuttle."

Carl Gooding had been on the air on the Big Dog for 25 years, owned the radio station, and knew darn well he wasn't supposed to be chatting about secret shipments of nuclear waste on the air, but figured what the hell. He already had a hundred warnings from the FCC tacked on the studio wall. What's a couple more?

"Yessir," Carl said, leaning back in an easy chair down at the station, "Jazzbo McMillan from Snelling, the laziest man in three counties, said that stuff done caused his tomatoes to rot. That's right. Jazzbo said his 'maters were doing just fine until he decided to irrigate by running a hose from that branch down by his chicken house. Said he filled up the troughs real good, then watched every one of them 'maters wrinkle up and die."

About that time you could hear the phone ringing in the background, and Carl picked it up and put the caller on the air.

"I had the same thing happen to my okry plants earlier this summer, Carl," the caller said. "I think there's something in the water down here in Sycamore, too."

Carl let out a big hound-dog howl, allowed it to echo over the airwaves for a few seconds then leaned into the microphone ,and said, "I think the Big Dog done uncovered us something suspicious, something downright worrisome, perhaps even something...*evil.*

"We'll keep on eye on them 'maters down in Snelling and them okry plants over in Sikkimo, and let Jim Ed Brown take us to the national news with one of our favorite Southern hymns...."

There was an ever-so-slight pause before you heard Jim Ed's slow country voice.

Pop a top a—gain, I've got time for just one round; set 'em up my friend; then I'll be gone, and you can let some other fool sit down.

Orrie got up, took a PBR from the cooler where it had been bobbing in lukewarm water, shook it, then handed it to Butterbean. "It's not just for breakfast anymore," Orrie said, laughing as he unsnapped the top button on his Army fatigue pants and limped toward his hotel room door.

Butterbean popped the top of the beer and it spewed all over his pants leg, causing him to throw the can down the hill. It clanked against some others that didn't quite make it to the campfire over the weekend. But that was all right. Willy and Billy, the two boys from the congregation, would pick them all up for the few quarters Orrie and Butterbean paid them to police the area every day.

All in all, Butterbean figured he'd done all right for a blind man. He had a one-hole golf course, a swamp full of reefer, all the beer he could drink, and a choir practice lady who liked to visit his hotel room on occasion.

Her name was LeeBelle Simmons. She sang soprano in the choir and said she wanted to marry Butterbean, but he'd have none of it.

"Never own nothing that flies, floats, or fucks," he would counsel young Orrie when he was coming of age. "Just rent it. Cheaper in the long run."

CHAPTER 19

Brumby woke up in his small, efficiency apartment on 4th Street Southeast, on the corner of South Carolina Avenue, rolled out of his Murphy bed, and pushed it back into the wall.

His place had once been somebody's third-floor bedroom when the old house was a single-family dwelling. But the house had been converted into a six apartments sometime during the Kennedy administration. When he rented the place, he thought the climb up three flights of stairs would help him maintain his weight, but it only made him hungrier and more disappointed when he'd open his fridge and find some leftover pizza and a jar of pickles.

His entire dwelling was almost as sparse, consisting of the disappearing bed, a writing desk, a small kitchen and an even smaller bathroom that was an afterthought.

While the rent was a little high, Brumby took it the first day he saw it because it was four blocks from the Capitol. There was a small grocery store on the corner, a park across the street, and he could walk to work, even if it did mean stepping over homeless people on the way.

One block away was Advent Methodist Church. It ran a soup kitchen in the basement, attracting a variety of vagrants, which was bothersome. One block in the other direction was Little Beirut, a lawless section of the District where you could turn the wrong corner and end up dead.

Brumby quickly accepted the fact that sometimes, late at night, he could hear gunfire. One morning he saw a trail of blood on the sidewalk that disappeared into the park. Being that close to violence, however, was nothing new to residents of our nation's capital. Unless you lived in Georgetown or DuPont Circle, you were never far away from a knife fight or a drive-by shooting.

"It's life in the big city," Brumby told Charlotte McKennon, his high school flame, when she visited the first year he was there.

Charlotte was a nurse in Blackville and had seen what gunshots look like on the receiving end. Together they thought they were a pretty well-matched couple. They spent a long weekend looking at monuments by day and rolling around in his Murphy bed at night.

But nothing came of it. She never came back to visit. Said she'd rotated to weekends at the hospital and couldn't work it out. Soon after, Brumby heard Charlotte married their former gym teacher, Glenn Holcombe, and was pregnant with twins, which he knew were not his.

But it didn't matter much to Brumby. He'd moved on in a way few back home could imagine. Living in Washington had become a way of life for Brumby, and he liked it.

He liked the feel of political tension in the autumn air when Congress came back into session, the smell of perfume when the cherry blossoms lined the Potomac River Basin in spring, and the sense of importance he felt when he showed visitors from back home where he worked and the people he worked around.

They were always impressed when they saw somebody like Andy Rooney or James J. Kilpatrick saunter through the press gallery. Once, when he was showing his former high school principal around, Bob Woodward of Watergate fame came whisking through, stopped when he came to a hallway blocked by construction, looked around in bewilderment, and asked Brumby about a shortcut to the Senate Cloak Room where reporters could buttonhole legislators on their way on and off the floor.

Without thinking, Brumby answered, "Just follow the money."

That made Woodward laugh, and became a legendary story back home after the principal told it at his next Rotary Club meeting. Brumby also wrote about it in his weekly column, making the story part of the historical record.

Up until then, his "Washington World" column had been a sprinkling of news about the South Carolina delegation and various projects they were promoting. But when he wrote the one about Bob Woodward, he actually got fan mail. People loved reading about what went on behind the scenes in Washington. And they wanted more.

That made Brumby a must-read in the editions of 11 weekly newspapers and a popular speaker at the Sertoma and Kiwanis Clubs when he came back home.

"Washington is like a wishing well," he told the Barnwell Kiwanis Club a few months later. "People throw money in and hope to get something in return. But more often than not, it's like a video poker machine. You throw money in and get nothing back."

That caused some of the local bar owners to squirm because there had been strong anti-poker sentiment stirred up in the state and things were about to come to a head. Already on the front burner in Columbia was a referendum that would allow the citizens of South Carolina to vote on whether to keep the evil machines or get rid of them for good.

They had become such cash cows that tacky, temporary buildings filled with electronic video poker machines had sprung up all along the state line, from North Carolina to Georgia. The parking lots and bar stools were always full of fools who thought they could outwit a computer.

It had been going on for about eight years without much fuss. But now the papers were filled with stories about mothers leaving their babies outside in hot cars while they went inside to play video poker; about families breaking up because daddy sold everything he could find to keep playing the electronic bandits.

The Conference of Southern Baptist Churches led the charge against this courier for the devil, even though local politicians were willing to accept cash bribes to turn a blind eye.

The issue had become a pimple on the face of the Palmetto State that was about to burst when the South Carolina Supreme Court suddenly ruled, a month before the public vote, that the referendum was unconstitutional and all video poker machines had to be removed from the state within 30 days.

That, along with some fried hamburger meat on Jack Cantey's farm, would have been front page news when Granville Trinity was in charge of the newspapers. But he'd just moved to Florida.

CHAPTER 20

Brumby actually heard the news from Holly Holladay, which made him feel pretty stupid. He had talked her into a picnic lunch on the east lawn of the Capitol building when the crape myrtles were blooming and the air was heavy with the weight of summer.

"I heard your papers were sold yesterday," she said, not realizing the importance of her words. "Congressman Spratt said something about it last night. Said it was a sad day for local journalism. Do you know what he's talking about?"

Brumby had no idea, but politely excused himself, and ran back to his cubicle in the press gallery where he found a pink message slip that read, "Call Your Office."

"Alice Ann," he said when she finally answered the phone. "What's going on?"

There was a pause before Alice Ann could bring the words from her heart to her lips, then she said, "Mr. Trinity sold the newspapers, Brumby. Some group out of Utah. I'm supposed to tell you to come home immediately."

Brumby couldn't believe it. After three years of getting to know his way around the wacky world of Washington, was he done? Just like that? No thank you, kiss my ass, nothing?

"Is Mr. Trinity there?" he asked Alice Ann. "Can I talk to him?"

"He's gone," she said, starting to cry. "He cleaned out his office over the weekend and left a note. Said he was moving to Miami. He wished us luck."

"What does that mean, Alice Ann?"

"I don't know, Brumby," she said, snuffling her tears. "The new owners will be here next week. They want to talk to us Wednesday afternoon."

Brumby found himself looking out the window of the press gallery, onto the east lawn where moments earlier he'd been sitting on a blanket with Holly Holladay, fantasizing about them being together, maybe here in Washington, a power couple hobnobbing with important people.

"Are you coming home?" Alice Ann asked, making him drop the imaginary drumstick he was holding for Holly, just waiting for her to take a bite.

"Sure, um, Alice Ann," he said. "I've got to think about this. This is terrible. It's actually worse than terrible. It's unbelievable."

Granville Trinity clicked his drink in a toast at a bar in Miami with Chris Gardner, a man he didn't like and would never see again. It was Gardner, a Californian, who brokered the deal for Community Press Inc., a newspaper consortium that now owned 53 other media properties from Nevada to Florida.

At a time when the Internet was threatening major dailies around the world, Community Press seized the opportunity to expand, knowing that the smaller the newspaper, the more likely its survival.

"All News Is Local" ran under the masthead of every paper they owned, and would soon grace the front page of *The Barnwell Bugle,* once the paperwork was finalized.

Trinity hadn't really wanted to sell his little empire, but he couldn't afford not to do so. He was over 70, had a heart condition, an irritable ulcer, smoked too much, drank way too much, and wanted to retire in style.

The $3 million Community Press offered him would make that possible, so he took it without even saying goodbye, except to his son on the wall in Washington, where he wept and promised to use the money to find out what really happened that July day in Vietnam.

Whether or not Granville Trinity knew exactly what Community Press was or who was behind it, Brumby wasn't sure. He only knew things would probably never be the same for him or the people of po-ass South Carolina again.

CHAPTER 21

Henry Smalls's first priority was finding out what really happened to the cows.

After he left Joe Moskos' office, he adjusted the seat forward on a motor-pool Plymouth and drove out Highway 316 to a place just outside Elko, where Jack Cantey raised Black Angus beef. The entrance to "Cantey Ranch" was graced with an iron sculpture that resembled the golden arches of McDonald's. Beneath the arches sat a brown Crown Vic, the kind of Ford every cop in the country drove. This one belonged to the SBI, State Bureau of Investigation.

"Henry Smalls, DOE," he told the man in the black suit when he pulled up and flashed his ID badge. "I'm here to see Mr. Cantey."

The SBI agent looked twice at Henry, wondering how a black midget got such a job, then opened the swinging metal gate that guarded Jack Cantey's 3,000-acre agricultural enterprise. As Henry drove down the dirt road that led to Jack Cantey's house, he saw a picture of Southern farming's slow, generational decline.

To the right, the dirt road turned into an avenue of oaks that led to Jack Cantey's big white colonial with four columns out front and an incongruous carport on the side protecting his wife's new Cadillac.

Next to that, down a paved asphalt driveway, was a three-bedroom, brick ranch belonging to his son, Jack Jr. It was in a pecan orchard, with an above-ground swimming pool out back, covered and unused.

Just down from there, amidst some sawed-off pine stumps, was a doublewide trailer with a well-worn awning cocked crooked by the last storm that blew through. This is where Trey Cantey, his ex-wife Tracey, and their three unruly kids once lived, alongside a broken-down dirt bike and a wrecked racecar up on cinder blocks.

Jack Cantey, 76, was sitting on his veranda, whittling on a stick, when Henry pulled up and waved. He'd known Mr. Cantey all his life, and like everyone else, was scared to death of him.

"Now you're gonna act like you give a shit," said Cantey, who still looked like he could rope a steer, brand it, and cook it for dinner before one could decide which side of bed to roll off in the morning. "Come on, Henry, are you the best thing they could come up with?"

Henry didn't take the comment personally, knowing the old man was rightly pissed off at the government and needed to take it out on somebody, and it probably made old Jack feel better to take it out on him.

This was not the first time Jack Cantey had tangled with the government. He'd been dueling with DOE and DuPont for years, filling out forms and filing claims, trying to get some answers about the water in the area.

"It's like trying to get answers out of S.C. State," he'd bark, noting his ill-fated endeavor as a board member trying to get reliable financial statements from the black school's administrators. "It's a black hole," he'd been quoted in the paper.

Things like that didn't endear Jack Cantey to the local black populace, but he didn't care. Like most older white folks in the area, Cantey was of two minds when it came to blacks. On the whole, he thought they were lazy, shiftless people who did just enough to get by. But individually, there were certain ones he loved. Like Zeke, his ranch foreman, and Bubba, who graded his cattle. Half breeds, like Henry Smalls, fell somewhere in the middle.

Which is why Cantey didn't put much faith in Henry or any bureaucrats for that matter. So, Cantey commissioned an independent study, brought in some scientists from Florida. They took water samples back to Tallahassee, tested them for every bad thing they could imagine, and reported it contained them all.

When Cantey's findings gained no traction with DOE, he sent them to Strom Thurmond's office and got a form letter thanking him for his concern and offering him a $10,000 seat at the next Republican fund-raiser.

Sen. Hollings wasn't much help either. He sent an aide from his Columbia office out to talk about it, but that guy didn't know one end of a cow from the other, so Cantey threw him off the farm.

Indeed, Jack Cantey was known for two things in addition to his prize-winning cattle. His uncontrollable temper and his devotion to the way things used to be. That included women barefoot and pregnant in the kitchen and black folks poor and uneducated in the fields.

So far, he'd managed to keep his black workers under control, which meant living in substandard housing and earning substandard wages on the farm. But he was losing his grip on this latest generation, and he knew it. His daughter Autry, the youngest, had a taste for chocolate that drove her old man nuts.

"Hey, Mr. Cantey," Henry said, feeling even smaller than the time he came here to take Autry to the local drive-in. He was 16 then, she was 15, but he had his driver's license and heard Autry Cantey would make out with you if you took her to a movie. So he asked, and she accepted. But Henry distinctly remembered Jack Cantey threatening his life when he drove the family car to the big house to pick Autry up for the date.

"She's sick," Jack Cantey told him abruptly, nestling a rifle in his arms.

"Oh," Henry had answered shyly. "Is she going to be all right?"

"No time soon," the old man said.

Henry concluded it was the kind of virus that struck every time a black boy asked a white girl out to a movie and the white girl was backhanded by her father for saying yes.

Indeed, the next week, heavy makeup barely disguised a bruise on Autry Cantey's left eye.

That was the last time Henry officially dealt with Jack Cantey, known to everyone in these parts as Boss. Until today.

"How's it going, Boss? How's Autry doing these days?" Henry asked shyly.

"Not worth a flying fuck, on both accounts," Cantey roared, rising from his seat, still holding on to the stick he was sharpening with a buck knife. "My daughter's living in Blackville, mothering a half-breed baby, shacked up with God knows who, and I've got dead cows. Fried cows. Sixty-fucking-three of 'em. I had to move my entire herd to the north end of the ranch so they wouldn't drink from that same filthy stream. Y'all better have some answers, some Goddamned good answers."

Henry, of course, knew nothing and could do nothing. He was the agency's first sacrifice, sent in to take the heat, see how bad things really were, and report back to the brass.

"I'm sure this is a containable issue, Mr. Cantey," Henry said, uneasily, trying to get a better position by going a step higher, then stepping back down again. "You know we'll do everything possible to reimburse you for your loss. About how much is one of those cows worth, approximately, you know, ballpark?"

Cantey stepped to the edge of his front porch, looked down at Henry, and snarled, "It ain't about the money, son. It's about the fucking future. Y'all been telling us for years that there was nothing to worry about. That everything was under control. Well, as you can see, it ain't!"

With that Cantey stomped down the steps, opened the door to his 1963 Chevy pick-up truck and told Henry to get in. After a bumpy ride across a pasture, they came to a sliding halt near a stand of river birch trees where Henry saw the problem first hand.

As Henry stepped out of the truck, the smell of decaying flesh hit him full force. He turned as if he were going to puke, but didn't, saving it at the last second. Twenty yards away, two black men used backhoes to push the cow carcasses into a pile away from the trees, then soaked them down with kerosene, and were about to strike the match.

"Shouldn't somebody look at those before we, um, light the barbecue?" Henry asked cautiously.

"We saved two, put 'em on ice down at the peach shed," Cantey said, motioning for Zeke and Bubba to go ahead. "Figured y'all might want to test 'em, figure out what happened. My guess is it ain't hoof and mouth."

Henry was trying to think of something official to say when he heard the fire swoosh behind him. He turned around and saw the pile of cows go up in a flash, their hides and hair curling in the flames, sending dark smoke high into the South Carolina sky where an eastbound breeze whisked it away as if it never happened.

CHAPTER 22

Over the years, the Rev. Macon Moses had been to six sessions at Quantico Marine Corps Base in Virginia where he was trained on the latest technology and brought up to speed on the best intelligence regarding the safety of nuclear material.

In his Nu-Chem Security truck, he now carried night vision goggles, an electronic radiation detector, a high frequency radio, a laser-guided sniper rifle, three clips of hollow-point ammunition, and an empty bucket of Kentucky Fried Chicken.

The chicken was gone before midnight, so he was happy to see his relief coming down the perimeter road in a government-gray Chevy truck.

Twelve on, twelve off, for two days, then a two-day break, then twelve on and twelve off. That had been Macon's circadian rhythm for the past three months, but it was about to change from nights to days, which would cause his bowels to seize up, but it was worth it.

In between shift changes he often had four-day weekends when he would disappear to meet his girlfriend in Savannah, telling his congregation he was on special assignment for the government and couldn't say where he was going.

That was the beauty of working at a top-secret government facility. You could tell civilians anything, and then tell them you couldn't talk about it.

As he watched Neal Bradberry's truck coming fast in his direction, he thought about how much of his life he'd spent staring at these long, ugly trenches where the nuclear waste was stored.

When he started, back in the '80s, Nu-Chem's footprint was about the size of a football field where carefully constructed pits with rubberized linings were supposed to contain a spill, should anything happen. Over the years, however, the plutonium plantation had grown exponentially, with rows and rows of imperfectly packaged poison.

And Moses knew exactly what to do if terrorists came over the fence, or parachuted into the compound, setting in motion a "Broken Arrow," a Cold War security condition that meant nuclear material was at risk.

During his weeks at Quantico, he and other security contractors from around the world had been put through the ringer, attacked by ground troops, swarmed by fanatic infidels, and bombed by mortars. Regardless of reality, they always pencil-whipped the outcome to make it look good on paper.

His personnel file, in fact, was filled with meaningless commendation letters designed to keep him on track for pay grade increases that came with or without meritorious service.

The only problem was nothing ever happened. Absolutely nothing. Which gave a man time to think.

For a black man in South Carolina, Moses considered himself upper middle class. He'd been raised on Jack Cantey's "plantation" where his parents lived in a three-room, shotgun house on the edge of the property. His daddy was a black cowboy, although Jack Cantey never liked that term, figuring it put black folk on par with western stars like Roy Rogers and Gene Autry. Especially Gene Autry.

Jack Cantey loved Gene Autry and had seen all his old movies and TV shows a thousand times. He named his daughter for the stylish cowboy of yesteryear, which is where the trouble started.

When Moses was home from S.C. State one summer, he seduced the 16-year-old Autry, who had a habit of driving her Mustang convertible around the farm where the field hands were working. She liked their muscles, the songs they sang, and the way their skin glistened with sweat in the mid-morning sun.

That, and the fact Moses never saw a white woman he didn't want to bed, led to big trouble with Jack Cantey, who caught the two of them buck naked in a barn and threatened to kill the young football player on the spot.

Though cooler heads prevailed that particular morning, Cantey swore there wasn't a jury in the Horse Creek Valley that would convict him of murdering the black bastard who deflowered his little girl.

Truth is, Moses always had a way with the ladies, which was why he wasn't higher on the sociological food chain. Wives and babies proved to be expensive, a problem he later solved with a confirmed bachelor status.

Not, however, before he'd knocked up Autry Cantey, who was now 24 years old, living in a trailer with their 6-year-old daughter, Maisey, and claiming to be pregnant with Moses' second child.

His once-simple life had become complicated. But during those lonely hours sitting in his truck watching those trenches, Moses had dreams of something better for himself. Something that involved palm trees.

Moses bought Bubba's Used Cars after Trinity inherited the local newspaper and moved up a notch on the chain. If everything went as planned, Moses could retire from the government in his mid-50s, always have a nice ride, and still have plenty of time to enjoy life. And while his pension was fine and the church kept him in spending money, Moses always wondered if there might be more.

He often let his mind drift off to various possibilities. The last two hours of every shift were the worst, or best, for daydreaming. It was during those fitful, restless hours when he thought he hadn't fulfilled his potential. Perhaps he was missing out on something.

As Neal Bradberry's truck drew closer, he rubbed his eyes and tried to shake off the cobwebs of three months of night shift. He was eager to hand his log book over to Bradberry, clear his weapons back at the security shack, hop in his Dodge Ram, and head for Savannah.

Only this time, when Moses pulled out of the parking lot, a black Plymouth pulled slowly out from a side road and followed him out of town. Unfazed, Moses popped a CD in his dashboard player and let Michael Jackson plead his case.

Billy Jean is not my lover,
She's just a girl who
Says that I am the one,
But the kid is not my son,
She says I am the one,
But the kid is not my son.

CHAPTER 23

O n the first of every month Orrie took the golf cart into Barnwell to get his meds.

Actually, the pain was a better calculator of time than the calendar. It always came back at least a week before the pills ran out, like somebody stabbed him in the leg and left him to die on the side of the road.

It started in his left hip and shot down to his knee where it spread out like a spider web, regrouped, then ran down his calf and made camp in his ankle. When that happened, twice a day, steady as a tide chart, Orrie couldn't get out of bed until it passed. Maybe an hour. Sometimes two. But always the same intensity.

Over three years of living this way, he learned a few things about his new room-mate, pain. It never knocked, never slept, didn't care, and wouldn't leave. Once it started, Orrie knew what the next few days would be like, so he'd ask Butterbean for the good stuff.

The 50 marijuana plants Butterbean had growing in the swamp came in four varieties that dated back to slavery times. In order of potency, Butterbean called them Rope, Paper, Sack, and Shine, names that came from the early days of the country when hemp was a staple of colonial society. Even during the days of our Founding Fathers, wearing homespun cloth made from locally grown hemp was a sign of a revolutionary spirit. But the land owners didn't grow it; the slaves did.

"We got real good at it," Butterbean would say, inhaling a bowl of Shine and passing it over to Orrie. "Maybe 'cuz we needed it mo'."

Orrie had heard Butterbean's stories about how the seeds were heirlooms, passed down through generations of slaves, kept secret from the masters, and shared only amongst themselves.

"Dey talk about dem happy slaves down on da plantations," Butterbean said, the smoke poring from his nose. "Dat's 'cuz dey was high as buzzards."

All Orrie knew was a few hits of Shine pushed the pain away until he could replace it with legal narcotics, so he inhaled deeply.

Shirtless, he drove the golf cart down the dirt road, his dirty blond ponytail, which now hung halfway down his back, stirred in the breeze, as did the tiny Confederate flag on a stick that flew from the rooftop.

In this part of South Carolina, the Civil War never really ended. Some still talked about the "truce" and clung to the Confederate flag as a symbol of resistance and the illusion of state's rights. What Orrie learned after moving to Jesus Saves, S.C., was that it had nothing to do with any of that.

The main reason country boys flew the Confederate flag was because it pissed off the niggers, plain and simple. They didn't know A.P. Hill from Appomattox or Chickamauga from Chancellorsville, and they never would because they didn't really care. All they needed to know was there was somebody on this earth more worthless than themselves. And this was all they could come up with to elevate their sad status.

Having grown up on Butler Island, Orrie never understood race relations because he was raised in an all-white community supported by an all-black infrastructure. From the family home to the golf course to the dining rooms to the guest cottages, Butler Island was a controlled environment, catering to Yankee visitors, with just enough Negroes running around doing the dirty work to give them a modern taste of what plantation life was like, even though it wasn't.

Life behind the Pine Curtain, however, was different. Whites and blacks lived in parallel universes, seemingly together, but always apart, except when they rubbed up against each other, and sparked like flint.

Orrie and Butterbean never talked about the racial divide. It never really came up because there wasn't much they could do about it. Orrie never bothered to tell Butterbean about the Confederate flag flying above the country club, and his black friend never asked.

Mostly, they stayed stoned and talked about esoteric issues brought forth by cannabis and beer. They considered, for instance, the dog-dick gnats that constantly plagued the area during the long, hot South Carolina summers.

"Why dey call 'em dog-dick gnats?" Butterbean asked one day as he brushed the pesky insects away from his face.

"'Cause they go after moisture," Orrie explained. "When a dog gets a hard-on, that pink, wet thing attracts them gnats like bees to honey. They also like to flock onto little children's eyeballs and scabs."

Butterbean thought about that for a minute or two then said, "I believe dey's a finite amount of water on da earth. That it's used and re-used over and over again in many forms."

Orrie didn't blink at the abrupt change the conversation took. He was used to it.

"I bet dat beer you're drinking, two hundred years ago, was Napolean's piss," Butterbean pontificted.

"Probly," Orrie answered, pouring the rest of his PBR on the ground. "Tastes like it."

In town, Orrie had become a familiar figure, pulling his golf cart up in front of People's Drug Store, parking sideways in a parking space. On his way in, he saw the sign, "No Shirt, No Shoes, No Service," so he kicked off his shoes in defiance.

"Remember, young man," the aging pharmacist repeated when Orrie collected his refill. "These are Level Five narcotics, very potent stuff. Make sure you take them properly, twice a day, and with food."

As usual, Orrie ignored the old man, letting his eyes wander to the young pharmacy technician who stood behind the counter, her smock barely disguising her breasts.

After paying in cash, Orrie took the bottle of pills back out to the golf cart, popped open a Blue Ribbon, shook four pills into the palm of his hand, threw them into the back of his mouth, swigged the beer, saw the pharmacist watching him through the window, and shot him the bird as he pulled out into traffic.

Within minutes the drugs were in his system, seeking out the pain like marauders systematically searching a house. Only a few more minutes until they found it, attacked it head on, and knocked it down, one milligram at a time, until it was almost bearable.

After hitting the drug store, he always stopped by McDonald's drive-through for a Big Mac without pickles, large fries, and a vanilla milk shake. Since he couldn't understand anything they said over that tin-can ordering machine, he always pulled straight up to the window where he heard Shanniqua talking to Antoine, who was making the fries.

"Ain't nobody gone tell me when I can and when I can't go to Mr. Dusty's," she said loud enough for everybody inside and outside the restaurant to hear. "If I want to spend my entire paycheck on my hair-do, I will, and ain't nobody gone tell me I can't, so dere."

Antoine looked at Orrie, then at the black and purple hair wrapped high on Shanniqua's head and said, "You paid money for dat?"

"You shut the fuck up, Antoine," she said, no doubt breaking several rules in the McDonald's employee handbook in one short sentence. "You just shut the fuck up."

Orrie listened to this conversation with the same rapt attention an alligator gives a fly. All he wanted was his Big Mac without pickles, some fries, and a milk shake. The last thing he wanted was trouble.

"Whachu think of dat hair?" Antoine asked out loud, directing the question toward Orrie.

Orrie looked around, saw no other customers in line, then said, "Who, me?"

"Yeah, man," Antoine said, leaning out the to-go window, enlisting his help. "Would you put up wid a woman who spent nine hours and a hundred dollars at a beauty shop and came out looking like dat?"

Orrie was drunk, stoned, and high on prescription meds, but still knew better than to answer that question.

"I just want my Big Mac, man," he said. "And hold the pickles."

When his order finally came up, he looked inside the bag because they always got it wrong.

"Uh, ma'am," Orrie said, looking down into his McDonald's bag. "I don't think this is a large order of fries. And I see pickles on my Big Mac."

Shanniqua slammed the cash drawer shut, turned to Orrie and said, "What the fuck do you think this is? You want it your way, go to Burger-fucking-King! "

Orrie thought about that for a moment, considered the hassle it would be to get his order changed, shot Shanniqua the bird, and pulled the golf cart over under a shade tree where he removed the pickles from his Big Mac and ate it in four bites.

As he pulled away, he could still hear Shanniqua barking at Antoine, "So, who died and made you mayor of my hair…?"

From there Orrie drove the golf cart two more blocks down past the Dollar General store and the Check Cashing/Title Loan shop to the town's Goodwill store. While Orrie wasn't much of a shopper, he'd found a friend in the store's manager, Laura Trellis, a skinny, gapped-toothed woman who once worked as a bartender at the Confederate Club until she was fired for no good reason, according to her.

During better times for both, Laura had known Orrie as the fair-haired boy who came there to play golf, always amidst talk of the future and how he was going to be a pro someday.

The next time they met was in the Goodwill store when Orrie stumbled in looking for a shirt to wear. After he knocked over several racks, Laura came to Orrie's rescue, offering to pick out a shirt for him.

With the skill of a haberdasher, her gnarled hands flipped through the hangers and pulled out a golf shirt with a "Patriot's Point" logo on the front.

"I slot six-under there one time," Orrie said, slurring his words.

"Then wear it with pride," Laura said, hustling him out the door.

Since that day, Laura Trellis would grab all the golf logo shirts that came in on donation and squirrel them away for Orrie.

"Got three good ones for ya, champ," Laura said as she escorted him out to his golf cart in the parking lot, "Got one from Paw Paw, one from Fairdale, and another one from Augusta National."

Orrie loved the shirts with the identifiable logo on the front, a map of the United States with a golf flag stuck in Augusta, Ga. He and his buddies used to joke about how to play that hole.

"If the tee box was in Cuba, it'd be an easy 9-iron," Orrie would say, then burst out laughing. Butterbean said he should play it from the back tees, in Ecuador, which would bring the Gulf of Mexico into play.

Both agreed, after much consideration, that you could hit the ball behind the pin, up into North Georgia, and let it spin back toward Augusta. But, they said, if you hit into northern Florida, you'd have an uphill putt.

Slackjawed, Orrie handed Laura a $50 bill for the effort, thanked her, tried to kiss her, missed her face, stuffed the shirts behind the golf cart seat, then pulled out into traffic, barely avoiding an on-coming car.

On his way home, Orrie felt the veil of agony beginning to lift as the road dipped into a shady glade, overhung with oak trees, where a branch of the Salkehatchie slipped through the landscape and an old concrete bridge let cars pass over without notice.

Coming down the hill, Orrie rode the brake so he could see who was fishing for what. There were three black men standing on the east side, two on the west side, and three women down under the bridge sitting on paint buckets.

As he pulled up, a black man named Eli snatched a pretty red breast from the dark waters, swung it high over the bridge railing, laying it down on the sandy roadbed where the poor fish flipped and flopped and breaded itself before it got off the hook.

"Nice catch," Orrie said, watching Eli slip the barb from the fish's lip in the fading light.

Not one for talking much to white people, Eli dropped the pan fish into a paper bag, listened to him scraping around inside with the other prisoners, looked up at the flag flying on Orrie's golf cart, and sarcastically said, "Not bad, for a colored boy."

Orrie nodded, accepting the chasm between them, flipped the switch that lit up the search lights mounted across the top of the golf cart, and drove away into the oncoming night.

CHAPTER 24

Headlights can only do so much in the Dixie darkness, which is why Brumby was being extra careful driving the Ford Taurus home through the tiny South Carolina railstop kingdoms of Norway and Sweden.

Pretty soon he would turn left at Denmark and follow the narrow farm-to-market roads to Kline, where his parents lived in the parsonage next to the First Baptist Church of the Redeemer.

Brumby grew up listening to his father preach of hell and damnation, places that sounded pretty good to him, considering the alternatives. Now he was at another crossroads in life. He was about to lose his dream job because a new company bought his newspapers. Seems you're on top of the world one minute, run over by it the next.

But luck comes and goes, Brumby realized, when Holly Holladay announced she needed a ride to South Carolina. He considered it a wild shot in the dark when he mentioned her riding with him. He was, after all, a little older, a lot less educated, kind of shy, somewhat inexperienced, possibly out of work, slightly overweight, and drove a Ford Taurus, perhaps the worst car ever made.

But she said yes immediately. Her internship had ended, and she was going to visit an old college roommate in Barnwell. How quickly she accepted his offer made Brumby wonder how often she rode off with men she hardly knew. That bothered him only slightly because he was absolutely gobsmacked by the young girl's natural beauty and wistful attitude toward life.

In conversation along I-95 between D.C. and Fayetteville, she told him how her parents weren't really hippies in the Woodstock mold, just a couple of kids who liked sex, drugs, and matriculation, pretty much in that order. Her father taught philosophy at Erskine College, where she earned her undergraduate degree. Her mother taught chemistry at Belton-Honea Path High School.

"They're great," Holly said as they drove into the Southern darkness. "There are five of us kids all together. Cypress, the oldest, lives in Asheville, married to a gynecologist. Twig is a senior at BHP headed for Davidson College in the fall. Berry is 13 going on 30. And Woody, the youngest, is 10. He's convinced he's adopted."

"Cypress? Twig? Berry? Woody?" Brumby said. "I thought I had an unusual name. But at least it's a family name. Where do these names come from?"

Holly slipped off her sandals, folded her long, beautiful legs underneath her on the car seat, and said, "Well, I told you about Cypress. Twig is named for, well, twigs on the trees. Berry's named for the Burberry Bush. And Woody is named for the Dogwood trees."

And, Holly added casually, she grew up in a tree house.

"What?" Brumby said. "A real tree house?"

"Yeah," she said. "Daddy had this thing when he was growing up about the book *Swiss Family Robinson*, and always wanted to live in a tree house. When he married my mom, Rebecca, his childhood sweetheart, they started this commune with some of their college friends and built their dream home.

"It took a couple of years. Mainly because my dad wasn't much of a carpenter, and because he refused to pound any nails into the tree."

Their home, she said, had many levels, carefully laid into the limbs of a sprawling oak, with rope-twined bridges between each section, and a sliding board for exiting easily to the ground.

She said her family never owned a television, the children weren't allowed to listen to the radio, and she didn't even see a movie in a theater until she was 16 years old.

Her father's only vice, she admitted, was golf. He'd learned the game early from his father, who caddied for the DuPont family when he was a boy growing up in Camden.

The DuPonts were wealthy Yankees who wintered in the small South Carolina town along the Wateree River and the Seaboard Coast Line Railroad. They liked the river because it provided a water supply for the plant where they produced Orlon and Rayon.

They also liked the railroad because it delivered them to the front door of the Camden Country Club, a family treasure built by the famous Scottish course designer, Donald Ross.

"Daddy learned the game from my granddaddy and from caddying for the rich and famous himself. So when he grew up, he would shoulder his golf bag and walk five miles to the Erskine College Golf Club and play 18 holes on Sunday mornings," she said. "I loved to walk with him and talk about things. He said golf was as close to understanding the meaning of life as man would ever come."

Randy Holladay taught his daughter how to swing the club, strike the ball, and play the game correctly, without malice.

"He said the beauty was in the balance," Holly recalled. "We never kept score. We just walked the course, talking between shots, playing the ball as we found it, accepting the good with the bad.

"That's the way Daddy sees life," Holly said. "You take the good with the bad and move on to the next hole."

Brumby thought about that for a moment as they peeled off the Interstate onto a dark, lonely highway.

"What about your mother?" he said, curious about this strange world she grew up in. "What's her irresistible vice?"

Holly didn't have to think about it long, but answered the question carefully.

"Medicinal herbs," she said matter-of-factly. "She's an expert."

Brumby laughed at the answer, comparing it to his parents' relationship, and said, "Your world sounds like a Disney movie. I'd love to see it sometime. I'm afraid my parents' house isn't anything like that. In fact, it's a little scary."

Dr. Phillip McLean, pastor of the First Baptist Church of the Redeemer, had never read *Swiss Family Robinson*, or any other literature other than the Holy Bible. He was convinced beyond any doubt that everything man needed to know was in the Good Book, you only had to understand the word of God. It was his job, as a servant of the Lord, to deliver that message with a savage and relentless verve designed to scare the absolute shit out of everybody in the church.

So he did that every Sunday morning, with great pleasure.

Brumby was about to explain his mother when Holly punched a penlight, stared at the road map in her lap, and said, "This reminds me of Abbeville County. Man, when it gets dark out here in the country, it gets really dark."

Brumby looked away from the road long enough to admire Holly's blonde hair as it hung down and touched the edges of the road map. If there was a prettier girl in South Carolina he hadn't seen her. And for some unknown reason, she seemed to like him.

Holly thought Brumby was a nice guy with cute dimples, but a little on the plump side and, therefore, not necessarily do-able. Despite having led a sheltered life growing up, she was not as innocent as everyone thought. There was this boy, Darrell, from Hodges, who came to the commune each month when his father delivered hog manure for fertilizer.

To get away from the awful aroma, she and Darrell would sneak off into a field of wild flowers and make love. Granted, they didn't know that's what they were doing when they were 14, but they knew better than to tell anybody about it.

Darrell dropped out of school when they were in the tenth grade, and she lost touch. Later, she heard he got his GED, went to Piedmont Tech, learned welding, and worked at SCE&G's Sumner Nuclear Plant near Jenkinsville.

Holly could find it on the state map, but she'd never been there. She figured Darrell had married somebody by now anyway. She was about to tell Brumby about Darrell when he asked, "So, what happened with your last boyfriend? You were engaged, weren't you?"

Fumbling the penlight slightly, Holly said, "It just wasn't, um, meant to be."

Glancing over at her, then back to the road, Brumby heard Holly click out the penlight and zip it back into her purse.

"Of course, it's none of my business," Brumby said.

"No, it's no big deal," Holly said, thinking it through. "It just took me a while to realize he was a jerk. I should have seen it coming sooner."

"Well," Brumby added awkwardly, "at least you found out before you married him."

"Yeah," Holly sighed. "It was a lot of wasted energy. So I threw away the checklist."

"What checklist?" Brumby asked.

"The one I developed in college, mostly because of my sorority sisters. We made up lists of what we wanted our future husbands to be like."

Brumby knew right away that pleasantly plump probably wasn't high on her list, but he plowed ahead anyway.

"Like what?" he said, feigning a smile.

"You know, rich, good looking, Ivy League, funny, family man, wants 2.3 children, did I mention good looking?"

"Yeah," Brumby said. "Several times."

"Well," Holly allowed, "I thought I'd hit a grand slam with Ted. He was gorgeous, a graduate of UNC-Chapel Hill, which likes to think it's Ivy League. And, he was rich. Very rich. Too damn rich, actually."

"Culture clash?" Brumby offered.

"Yeah," she said, rolling her eyes. "I was a human being and he wasn't. The rich are different, you know."

"So I've heard," Brumby said.

Another mile of rural South Carolina passed beneath the headlights before Brumby asked, "So, did you keep the ring?"

Holly giggled and was about to answer when Brumby's eyes widened in fear.

"Son of a bitch!" he shouted, slamming the brakes. Instinctively he threw his right arm across Holly's chest so she wouldn't fly into the windshield. Her seatbelt, of course, was fastened and would have saved her. But she didn't mind that Brumby wanted to protect her.

"What's this stupid bastard doing in the middle of the road?" he screamed breathlessly, pointing to the green golf cart parked sideways in the highway with a shirtless man slumped over the steering wheel.

As Brumby hit his emergency flashers, he told Holly to sit tight as he got out of the car and walked slowly to the golf cart, thinking the man might be dead. Orrie Adger, lifting his head slightly, was disoriented by the flashing yellow lights from Brumby's car and misinterpreted their meaning.

"I'm sorry, ossifer," he said. "I think I zigged, you know, when I shoulda zagged."

When Brumby realized it was Orrie, he wasn't surprised. Everybody in the area knew about the golf prodigy who lived in the woods with a black man named Butterbean and the odd arrangement they had with a church.

Brumby tried to write about them once when he first started working for *The Bugle,* but the story made no sense. Every fact Orrie gave him checked out wrong, and Butterbean wouldn't talk to him at all, saying he might be blind, but he wasn't stupid.

Holly stayed in the car until she realized there was no danger, then stepped out to see what was going on.

"Is he your run-of-the-mill drunk or just a burned-out hippie?" she whispered to Brumby, noticing Orrie's long ponytail and scraggly beard.

"Hard to categorize," Brumby said, trying to push the golf cart off the road. "Just one of the many crazy people who live out here behind the Pine Curtain."

About that time, the beer and the meds in Orrie's stomach decided it was time to leave.

"Damn," Brumby said, skipping backwards to keep Orrie's vomit from splattering on his shoes.

That's when Orrie raised his head, wiped his mouth with the back of his hand, then slowly dragged his hand through his tangled hair so he could see where he was puking.

It's also when Holly, looking closer at the man in the golf cart, squinted quizzically and said, "Puddles? Is that you, Puddles?"

CHAPTER 25

O rrie woke up in his Embassy Suites hotel room with a foot in his face. The most beautiful foot he'd ever seen, in fact. It was sleek and sultry, with perfect toes, painted pink, the kind of toes you'd like to kiss, maybe even lick a little.

And tattooed across the bottom of the foot was the word *"left"* in italic script, which made him laugh, which he shouldn't have done.

As he moved, it felt like somebody planted a hatchet in his head. The deep, splitting pain caused Orrie to close his eyes and lay perfectly still. It was, unfortunately, a familiar feeling. The kind that came when he mixed drugs and alcohol. The kind he'd experienced for years upon waking up.

That's when he felt a hand moving up his left leg, slowly, back and forth at first, then up again, past his knee, carefully avoiding the worst scars, floating across his pubic hair, his rounded belly, onto his chest, then stopping with a gentle brush against his cheek.

Orrie opened his left eye enough to see blonde hair draped across his arm. Then he felt the warmth of a woman's curvaceous body pull up against him, like a ship berthing in a familiar port.

"Are you alive?" the gentle voice asked.

Orrie wasn't sure, but moaned and tried to cover his head with a pillow.

"Maybe I better check your vital signs," the voice said.

With that, Orrie felt the hand rubbing a slippery substance on his stomach, then farther down, inching, rubbing, touching, massaging, and finally grasping, which caused him to jump.

He opened his eyes and frantically looked about the room, searching for the usual disorder — clothes on the floor, bottles against the wall — just to make sure he wasn't dreaming.

Everything seemed the same. Except the smell.

Orrie couldn't quite place it at first. It came from far away, somewhere in the past, somewhere he'd been before. Unable to focus in the dimly lit room, he let his nose seek out the solution, like a sommelier snuffling a merlot, allowing the sweet odors of human essence to invade his nostrils, swirl around his olfactory nodes, wipe their pollen on his memory banks, and skip away like a young girl running in the rain.

It had been so long since Orrie focused on the flesh that he'd forgotten how to handle the sensory surge that came with arousal. So many times, in this same bed, on dark and endless nights, Orrie had let his mind drift to places he could no longer go.

Like the cleavage of the young pharmacy tech behind the counter at the drug store. The way her breasts swelled beneath her smock, pressing against the top button, casting a shadow in the crevice that plunged into places he would like to explore.

Because of his youthful celebrity, Orrie felt he'd skipped a step in sex education. His first experience came when he was 15, in the cart barn of the Sea Island Club at Jekyll Island. He was putting his clubs away when Miss Pluff Mud, a 17-year-old socialite, said she wanted to crown his achievement.

He didn't know what that meant until she undid his belt, unzipped his pants, carefully ran her hands down the sides of his hips, and slipped him into her warm, wet mouth.

Orrie felt his knees buckle, grabbed the top of a golf cart, and watched Miss Pluff Mud work her special magic.

In a matter of seconds, with perfect timing, she rolled back on the seat, spread her legs, and pulled Orrie in, where like a jackhammer he almost shoved her out the other side of the cart.

But this was not her first golf tournament. Miss Pluff Mud grabbed the straps securing the golf bags and pushed back, causing Orrie to explode before he was ready. As he rolled off, panting, she laughed, saying he needed to clean himself up before going upstairs to accept his trophy.

Before Orrie could catch his breath, she was gone. Walking out of the cart shed and tucking in his shirt, he saw her hop playfully into another boy's Range Rover and pull away, laughing. He never knew her name, but made mental love to her a thousand nights since, always awakening just before the finale, a frustration he was learning to accept.

He was supposed to receive counseling, but never did. After the accident, his doctors recommended sex therapy once a week, but his limpness was a low priority compared to his other injuries. There hadn't been much demand for it anyway.

So when Orrie tried to pull himself up in bed, he felt a long forgotten feeling. Instead of the usual, agonizing aches and paralyzing pains, he felt spent all over, like he'd run a marathon and somehow survived.

"You're amazing, Puddles," the voice said softly in his ear. "It was everything I always hoped it would be."

Orrie was confused. He thought he was dreaming about the pharmacy tech, but she never talked. This was something new. Rolling right, he shifted carefully on his elbows to keep weight off his left leg, then came face to face with an angel. She had a small, golden cross hanging around her neck.

Holly Holladay was born with the kind of beauty that looked as good at midnight as it did at daybreak. Without makeup, without sleep, without anything, beautiful.

The first thing Orrie saw were her blue eyes, friendly beacons bedded down in the pillow next to him, surrounded by tousled blonde hair.

Did he know this girl? Surely this was a hallucination brought on by good drugs and bad booze. He'd been on this trip before. But it never ended like this.

"Hi," he said, trying to get that simple word off his tongue and past chapped lips.

"Hi," she said, brushing his tangled hair away from his face. "I know you don't know me, but I'm the girl you're going to marry."

Orrie closed his eyes tight, thought about it for a moment, then opened his eyes again to make sure she was real. "I'm Orrie," he said, suddenly realizing how painful it was to say two words instead of one.

"I'm Holly," she said, smiling. "Holly Holladay."

"Nice to meet you," he said, trying not to moan. "Who…I mean, how…?"

Without blinking, Holly dipped her fingers into a glass jar beside the bed, slid her hand under the sheets, grabbed Orrie and began stroking gently as he slowly rose to meet her touch.

"When I was a little girl," she said, looking him in the eyes and watching him squirm, "my father took me to a junior golf tournament at Musgrove Mill. I think

I was 14. No, wait, it was in June, just before my 14th birthday."

Orrie looked at her, letting his eyes roll slightly back in his head, then refocused and said, "I played there. I won there."

"I know," she said softly in his ear. "I followed you the entire last round. You were the most beautiful boy I'd ever seen. The sun lit your hair and you moved like a young lion on the prowl. Every step you took, every swing you made, I watched, and I marveled at the way your body folded and unfolded itself when you swung the club.

"You were magnificent. When you lifted that trophy over your head on the last hole, I turned to my father and told him I was going to marry you. That you were the love of my life."

Orrie stared at the beauty lying beside him, stroking him, and started to cry. "What is...that stuff?" he said between soft sobs, pulling up the sheets and staring at his immaculate erection.

"Something my mom gave me for graduation," Holly said, continuing to stroke him gently. "She makes it herself. You know, eye of newt, wing of bat. Except this is herbal-based with root juices and some other special ingredients. She calls it Love Potion Number Nine. Said every girl should keep a jar handy, you know, in case of an emergency."

As painful as it was to speak, Orrie asked, "Your mom gave this to you when you graduated from high school?"

"No, silly," Holly said with a giggle. "Junior high."

Then, without warning, Orrie climaxed.

Feeling the surge and sudden thrust, Holly guided her lover to a grunting conclusion, slowly releasing her grip as his body geared down in spasms.

"This isn't real," Orrie spluttered, trying to catch his breath. "It can't be real. It's been...I mean, I'm...."

"No you're not," Holly said, slowly licking her fingers. "Not anymore."

CHAPTER 26

That same morning, Brumby awakened in his old room, the one with the picture of the Jesus praying hanging on the wall. Outside his door, he heard his father flush the toilet and exit the only bathroom in the parsonage where he grew up.

His boyhood home had always been the property of the Great Redeemer Baptist Church, a fact the board never let his father forget. It was all part of the plot, Brumby thought, to keep preachers in their place.

And it worked. Any time his father started to gain a grip on the congregation, started feeling his oats, thinking he was more than a mere messenger, that he had some kind of power over the people, the Men's Club would take notice and raise the rent.

"Evil doers," the Baptist fire-breather brayed when he was away from the tender ears of the church. "Little do they know their despicable, evil ways will go unrewarded when the Judgment comes."

Unfortunately, if God were actually keeping score like the Good Book said, Brumby's father was in a world of shit. Beneath his black robe and holier-than-thou attitude beat the heart of a sinner. The worst kind of sinner. The kind even a forgiving god would never forgive.

Brumby's mother should have known. She was his only hope. As the only son of the devil, he was sacrificed early. He was only 12.

It happened the first time on his birthday, after his friends left the party and his mother went to the church to set up communion trays for services the next morning. Brumby was in his room, playing with his Etch-A-Sketch, when his father came in and locked the door behind him.

Brumby didn't know what was wrong, only that a bad whipping usually came when the old man pulled his belt from his pants. But this time the pain was different.

Brumby remembered crying when his mother came to tuck him in. She had no idea. She couldn't have known. Then again, how could she not? He had since grown irritable. Cut his hair. Started smoking cigarettes in the dark behind the house.

It lasted four years until finally one day, at age 16, Brumby took a butcher knife to bed. That's when he slayed the dragon, sticking the blade into the old man's crotch, swearing to slice and hack at will if he ever entered his room again.

The preacher, scolding his son with arcane indecipherable scripture, skulked out and never returned, except in Brumby's nightmares. Even now, with the old man in a wheelchair and his door securely locked, Brumby never felt safe in this house.

In his on-going fantasy world, he'd hoped to spend the night somewhere with Holly Holladay. But somehow she ended up with Orrie Adger, the drunk, the pot head, the has-been, dirty, rotten-smelling, bum that lived somewhere deep in the woods with a blind black man.

Brumby still didn't know exactly how that happened. One minute he was looking at Holly's legs and the next they were taking "Puddles" home. And Holly chose to stay with him. Why? What went wrong?

Brumby always blamed his father for his failure with women and his weight gain. Every time he got close to being close, something inside him seized up, like an engine without oil, with all parts working against each other, metal against metal, grinding, halting, devastating.

Most times, a piece of his mother's cheesecake or some other desserts brought home from the covered-dish supper at the church would tamp down the self-loathing. He thought by now the law of averages or the mercy of God would bring a woman to his bed, but it never happened. Something always broke down. He would say the wrong thing, or they would say something that turned him away.

In Washington, where he thought he'd escaped the reach of his humiliation, he slept alone in his Murphy bed. Even the stories he told himself about Charlotte McKennon were not true. He simply told the lies so often he started to believe them.

Now, as he lay awake in his childhood bed, he heard his father's wheelchair creak down the hallway and stop in front of his door. He froze like a frightened little boy.

CHAPTER 27

M acon Moses saw the black Plymouth tailing him out of town. It wasn't the first time, and it wouldn't be the last.

Random background checks on employees with top secret clearances were no secret among the guards at Nu-Chem. All his buddies had been followed, harassed, had their records pulled, their girlfriends interrogated, and their homes invaded.

It's how DOE kept up the image of security. Why look for bad guys when the good guys are so much easier to find?

This happened so often that Moses recognized the different FBI agents assigned to follow them. This one was Bud DeWitt, a former Marine who joined the agency when the standards were low. After an undistinguished tour of duty as a mess officer at Fort Gordon, Bud was assigned to a desk job in Augusta where his claim to fame was working undercover at the Masters Golf Tournament every year, looking for troublemakers.

Bud asked the members one time who exactly he should be looking for in the crowds jamming Augusta National every April. Protesters, he was told. Just be on the lookout for protesters.

Nothing ever happened at the golf tournament, and Bud never saw anybody he considered suspicious. So he spent his time munching on pimento cheese sandwiches and getting autographs from the players when they came through the scoring tent just off the 18th green.

His requests, of course, were against the rules. But few golfers refused when he flashed his badge and made a big deal out of himself. Eventually, after hearing enough complaints, the green jackets had Bud reassigned to the parking lots.

To the 40 men who worked with Macon Moses, Bud had come to be known as Dumb-ass DeWitt. They all played games with the hapless agent, knowing he would only make up his reports anyway.

Usually he just wanted to be seen giving chase, a ruse he played until he came across a cinderblock beer joint. Bud, it turned out, was a sucker for cinderblock roadhouses and the women who served beer and shot pool inside.

So losing Bud DeWitt had become a game to Macon Moses. He simply pushed his Dodge Ram up to 80 miles an hour as he tore out of town on Highway 3, a single-lane road that stretched down the South Carolina side of the Savannah River.

Once he got to U.S. Highway 301, he checked his rearview mirror to make sure the black car was topping the hill behind him, then Moses executed a U-turn and headed right back at the G-man, doing 90 miles an hour.

He blew past Bud DeWitt so fast the agent fumbled the pack of Cheetos he was eating and almost ran off the road. By the time he turned around to give chase, here came Moses again, headed back in the opposite direction, doing 100 miles an hour. DeWitt became agitated, tried to make a three-point turn, but his car slid backwards into a ditch.

Moses saw it all in his mirror, slowed down to the speed limit, grabbed a cold beer from a cooler on the floorboard, and cackled as he topped the next rise and disappeared into the fading light.

CHAPTER 28

Make no mistake. Macon Moses was not a man without a plan.

From an early age, sometime after his first marriage failed, Moses realized the key to complete freedom was the triangle. He'd seen it work for his Uncle Horris when he was growing up in Edgefield.

Horris worked the triangle to perfection. He lived in a trailer in Edgefield, worked in Williston, and partied on weekends in Augusta. That way, nobody ever really knew where he was or where he was supposed to be.

Moses admired that in a man, so he worked the triangle theory to suit his particular plan. That meant he worked at Nu-Chem in the tiny town of Snelling, lived in a double-wide near Healing Springs, and did most of his serious carousing in Savannah.

While he occasionally entertained local women in his trailer during the week, his main squeeze was Nicole Davis, a part-time hairdresser/masseuse/stripper from Brunswick, Georgia, who had a non-vocational triangle theory of her own.

Nicole, who was at least 10 years younger, had Moses convinced they were going to retire with proceeds from a condo they bought together on Skidaway Island near Savannah. That's where they would rendezvous on weekends and holidays, drinking, fucking, and watching the property value of their mutual investment rise on the high tide of beach-front real estate.

An enterprising entrepreneur, Nicole also operated a lucrative phone sex business, the proceeds from which she conservatively invested in tax-free municipal bonds. The third leg of her triangle was MSgt. Dock Drayton, her Army husband, who was stationed in Germany. Nicole had him convinced they were going to retire together on his pension.

What neither man knew was she never intended to see old age with either of them.

It seemed the Rev. Macon Moses and MSgt. Dock Drayton had the same problem. They were men. That was the simple weakness Nicole Davis exploited from the days she met each of them. Both were so sure they had her wrapped around their little fingers, they never considered the alternative.

The male ego, she would tell her stripper friends, is a terrible thing to waste.

CHAPTER 29

After making love to Orrie that morning, Holly Holladay left him sleeping and slipped out the door of his modular Embassy Suites room. She did not get a good look at the compound the night before, but wasn't surprised to find a pile of beer cans smoldering in the campfire with Coca-Cola crates, liquor bottles and pieces of a busted guitar scattered on the ground.

As she exited the room, she tripped over a truck driver who'd passed out on the steps the night before.

"Damn," he said, looking up at Holly. "Where the hell'd you come from?"

"In there," she said politely, stepping over him gracefully, her long legs peeking out from underneath one of Orrie's old golf shirts that had a Persimmon Hill logo on the front.

"Yeah, well, I see that, ma'am," he said, rubbing his eyes and trying to find his hair. "But I didn't think…I mean…he ain't never…I mean…you know…I don't know what the hell I mean, ma'am."

About that time Holly looked up on the nearby "No" tree and saw the sign announcing "No Women." She laughed. Without hesitation, she walked over to the tree, wiggled the sign until the nail came out of the bark with a screech, threw it into the bushes, turned toward the truck driver and announced, "New rules."

"Oh shit," the trucker said, gathering his shoes and socks. "I think it's time for me to go before Butterbean gets up."

From inside his room next door, where he'd been groping the choir lady named LeeBelle, Butterbean heard Holly's voice, cocked his ear to the sound and smiled, knowing things were about to change for the better around Healing Springs Baptist Church and Country Club.

CHAPTER 30

At high noon, Brumby pulled up in front of the small brick building on Main Street, parked his car, wiped the sweat from his brow and headed into *The Barnwell Bugle*.

This was one of many times he wished he'd lost the 20 pounds he swore he was going to lose last year, and the year before that. He'd always been pudgy.

His mother said it came from her side of the family, that all her brothers were husky, which he considered a nice word for fat. But he knew what caused it. And he despised and cursed his father for it every time he tore open a pack of wedding cookies.

That was an ongoing problem for Brumby since he was young. This, he convinced himself, was an immediate problem, one that had a beginning and an end, unlike his unspoken abuse.

Granville Trinity had obviously sold them down the river. With a new group taking over the newspapers, things were sure to change. Nobody else in their right mind had a Washington correspondent writing for weekly papers. He knew it was unusual, but after a while he'd convinced himself he was special.

But all good things must come to an end, he told himself. Maybe he would go back to school. He heard chiropractors made a good living, and there was a two-year school in Spartanburg.

With a deep sigh, he climbed three steps, opened the door, and stepped inside. As always, Alice Ann was sitting at her desk behind the counter where customers paid for classified ads and extra copies of the paper, which typically contained an article about their grandson's Dixie Youth baseball game or some such from the week before.

Next to her was a man in a tan suit, but no tie. He was 40-something, Brumby guessed. He was thin, with large hands and feet. He smiled and extended his right hand when Brumby came in the door, something he didn't expect.

"I'm Dexter Young, with Community Communications," he said, shaking Brumby's hand and holding the smile. "You must be Brumby."

"Yes, sir," Brumby said, his hand feeling small in Dexter Young's firm grip. He'd assumed since he talked to Alice Ann that this meeting was an execution, and that hand would soon be wielding an axe.

"I was just telling Alice Ann how much I admire your work," Dexter said, pulling another chair up for Brumby to sit in. "I think *The Barnwell Bugle,* indeed all our papers, are lucky to have a guy like you in Washington, keeping an eye on local issues, telling it like it is."

Brumby cut a glance over to Alice Ann ,who met his eye with an innocent shrug. Apparently, they weren't getting fired. Maybe.

"Well," Brumby said, trying to regain his composure. "I've really enjoyed covering Washington, and I think people like reading my stuff. I'm just not sure what y'all, the new owners, are going to, um, do, you know, with the position."

Dexter Young had no intention of making Brumby suffer. He was a Midwesterner, innately incapable of bullshit, so he cut to the chase.

"Brumby, I was just telling Alice Ann that the only changes you're going to see around here are changes for the better," he said. "My grandfather and father published *The Lynndyl Ledger* in southern Utah. My brother and I inherited the paper 15 years ago. Since then we've added about 50 other weeklies across the country and couldn't be happier with the way things are going.

"Our little company is known as Community Communications, which just added 11 more papers here in South Carolina when we were fortunate enough to strike a deal with Mr. Granville Trinity. The addition of these fine papers to our family business makes us as happy as apple jack."

Brumby cut another glance at Alice Ann hoping she might know how happy apple jack might be, but he figured it was a Midwestern thing so he'd leave it alone for now.

"So, we're not getting fired?" Brumby asked, cautiously.

"On the contrary," Dexter said. "You're all getting a raise. We're meeting with all the employees at the other papers this week and making sure everybody feels comfortable with this change. We figured a pay raise might help morale."

Brumby still wasn't sure this guy was for real, but he liked what he was hearing so far.

"So, you want to keep the Washington bureau?" he asked.

"Absolutely," Dexter said. "In fact, my brother and I want to expand it."

Dexter's identical twin, Donald, was the business mind behind the Mormon family enterprise.

"Once we saw what your writings bring to these papers, we decided we could use your brand of homespun journalism in our other papers as well. We want you to be the Mark Twain of weekly newspapers. You know, tell it like it really is. People love that stuff.

"My brother, Donald, who handles the marketing, says we can make you a star. We want you to ride in local Christmas parades, come to Illinois and attend the county fairs. "We'll discuss it further when we have more time, but we want you to file for all our current papers, and we'll probably be buying up even more in the future. You're going to be syndicated, Brumby. What do you think about that?"

Brumby tried re-crossing his legs from right to left, but his thick thighs rejected that move. So he just stared at Dexter Young with a look of amazement, cut another glance at Alice Ann, who was smiling ear to ear, and simply said, "Wow, I didn't see that one coming."

CHAPTER 31

As usual, spring in the South Carolina Lowcountry lasted eight days. As soon as the azaleas fell off the bushes, the heat rolled in and nasty, aggravating black gnats invaded, causing doors to slam and air conditioners to hum.

After a morning with Jack Cantey's dead cows, Henry Smalls took the afternoon off to visit his mother in Denmark, one of many small towns struggling to reinvent itself in the South's post-agricultural economy. As he rode down Main Street, all he saw were shuttered storefronts of family-owned businesses where children went off to college and never returned.

He recognized the smell of small-town decay because he was one of those kids. After graduation from the College of Charleston, he took the first job that got him out of South Carolina.

At Oak Street, he turned right and down a shady lane that led to Happy Days Rest Home where Ruby, his mother, waited out her final days on his late father's bomb-plant pension and disability benefits.

She had lost both legs to diabetes, and the former nurse almost didn't notice when her only son came through the door. An aide standing next to her wheelchair pointed when he arrived.

"Miss, Ruby," the black woman named Annelle said. "It's yo' son, Henry. He done come to see you."

As a white woman who was married to a black man, Ruby Smalls got indifferent treatment from the all-black staff at the nursing home. Some resented her taking a good black man from their pool of possibilities. Others just resented her on general principles.

"Did you get the Mother's Day package I sent?" Henry asked, kissing his mother on the cheek. "I hope you liked the flowers, Mom. Can't send you chocolates like I used to."

He was about to joke with her about going for a walk when he realized she hadn't said hello or kissed him back.

"She ain't quite right, Mr. Henry," said the aide, Annelle, who was short, black, and as round as she was tall. "Miss Ruby done stroked. A week ago last Thursday. We thought she'd just had a spell, but it left her this way. Tried to find your sister, but she ain't around much, you know, less she needs something."

Henry was not surprised. His younger sister, Hannah Jane, had married a guy from Leesville who sold mobile homes for a living. And even though South Carolina was the manufactured housing capital of the world, he couldn't seem to make more money selling trailers than he lost playing poker. Indeed, Bobby Jenkins was a self-destructing man. Everything he touched turned to shit, including Henry's sister.

While Henry was the color of caramel, Hannah Jane was somewhere between dirty dishwater and a charcoal briquette, depending on the day. Her complexion actually changed, like a chameleon, depending on her mood.

Sometimes, when she had her black hair pulled up tight away from her face and she hadn't been drunk for a month, she looked like an African princess, albeit with an acne problem. But when she was riding the bottle and sucking down pills, her hair would kink up, and she looked like somebody's "high yellow" sex slave.

"She been here lately?" Henry asked of Hannah Jane.

"A week or so ago," Annelle said.

"Has Momma been getting the money I send her?" Henry asked, cautiously.

"Yessur, but I think Miss Hannah Jane talked it right out of her pocket," Annelle said, lowering her eyes. "You knows how she is."

Henry knew all too well how she was. Hannah Jane had never met an alcoholic, a junky, a con man, or a wife beater with whom she couldn't fall in love.

"She still living in Olar?" Henry asked.

"I heard dey moved again," Annelle said. "But I ain't know for sure. I just heard."

Henry held his helpless mother's hand and let out a sigh. Tracking down his sister could be tougher, and perhaps more dangerous, than tracking down what was killing those cows on Cantey's farm.

CHAPTER 32

Neal Bradberry leaned back in the swivel chair inside the guard shack, lit a cigarette, blew three consecutive smoke rings, and watched as a summer thunderstorm swept across his field of vision. That was pretty much his job, watching the rain slap into the tilled soil stretching out a half mile in front of him, trying to decide if it was washing dangerous radiation into the watershed.

Actually, that last part was the job of the scientists who worked in the main administration building down at the Savannah River Site. They were the ones tasked with filling out the federal forms and guaranteeing the world that the 30 tons of radioactive waste buried eight feet deep in the South Carolina soil were nothing of concern. That, after all, was all anybody wanted to hear.

So, like 40 other Nu-Chem guards, he penciled in when it rained, how much it rained, and whether or not any of the nuclear waste was washed away from its underground clubhouse. The paperwork, of course, always said no. But Bradberry and all his buddies knew the real answer.

While he wasn't the valedictorian of his high school class, Bradberry understood the basics of gravity, and how water always seeks its lowest point. His science teacher, George Warren Chavous, used to demonstrate that fact by pouring a glass of water on the floor of his classroom so his students could follow the liquid as it seeped toward the outside wall and disappeared beneath a window casing.

"Where does it go from there?" Mr. Chavous asked the class at New Ellenton High School, just outside the Bomb Plant.

"The Salkehatchie River," the class would respond in unison.

They'd been trained by their teacher to say that because it was true. Everything in the Horse Creek Valley eventually ran into the town's storm drainage system, through some open ditches, past the town dump, into Barnyard Creek, and eventually ended up in the Salkehatchie. There it joined water droplets from other industrial and agricultural runoff to form a filmy flow that slipped silently downstream, through the swamp, under the fishing bridges, where it settled in the tidal creeks, waiting to be swept out on a salty tide.

Even Neal Bradberry was clear on that point. He often chuckled to himself when he recalled Mr. Chavous saying to the class, "It's part of the plumber's handbook, ladies and gentlemen. Remember, there are only three rules in the plumber's handbook."

Bradberry poured some coffee out of his Thermos and repeated the three rules: "Shit runs downhill, payday is Friday, and don't bite your fingernails," he mumbled.

Then he looked out over the field he was guarding, put his feet up on the windowsill, and began filling out the form.

"I should have been a plumber," he said to himself. "More money, less paperwork."

The truth was, Bradberry and his fellow trench watchers made damn good money for showing up and punching a clock. While security was mandated by the federal government as part of the nuclear waste pact, it was hardly necessary. Who would want to steal low-level nuclear waste? And what would they do with it?

Even the state of South Carolina, whose legislators thought it was doing the world a favor by agreeing to store the stuff, was having second thoughts about its role in this ruse.

Just last week Bradberry read an update in *The State Sentinel* about the flimsy agreement Palmetto State legislators had with North Carolina to take on some of this burden. A committee was formed. A study group assigned. A year passed. Then two. And all they had to say was they were working on it.

But they weren't. North Carolina politicians were inherently smarter than South Carolina politicians and wanted nothing to do with nuclear waste. They'd already screwed up by allowing so many hog farms in the Tar Heel state that excrement was polluting rivers from Raleigh to Wilmington. The problem was hyper-exposed when a tropical storm tore through the holding ponds and spilled crap into the water supply.

No way North Carolina representatives were going to sign anything having to do with nuclear waste when they were already up to their armpits in hog shit. Everybody seemed to understand that except the legislators in Columbia who kept allowing their sister state to sidestep responsibility. Meanwhile, radioactive junk from New Jersey hospitals and worn out rods from Connecticut reactors kept arriving in the dark of night and disappearing beneath the sandy loam of the Palmetto State.

Bradberry figured there was nothing he could do but show up for work, collect his paycheck, and keep his log book up to date.

And so he entered, *Rained all day Monday. Trenches filled with water. High winds knocked over the monitoring equipment. No data available. Chug Newton, my relief, was 15 minutes late…again. Neal Bradberry, Badge 31.*

CHAPTER 33

Nu-Chem guards liked their badges. Macon Moses kept his shiny bright shield pinned inside his wallet so state troopers and other law enforcement officials were sure to see it when he reached for his driver's license. Which was often because Moses also liked to drive fast. His black Dodge Ram had a 456-cubic-inch engine that sucked gas like a battle tank and flew like a fighter jet.

When he showered down on the accelerator there was a tug-of-war on his dashboard with the needle on the speedometer going one way and the needle on the gas gauge going the other. But he didn't care. He loved to fly down Highway 3, a ribbon of a road laid down through the swamp like a dock in the marsh. Once known as plantation row, it was a serpentine stretch of two-lane blacktop following the curvature of the river.

Both sides of this lonely road were lined with paper-mill pine trees, perfectly planted in straight lines. And on days like this, late in the afternoon after a summer rain, it was as spooky as a graveyard, with steam rising off the hot pavement and apparitions appearing in the mist.

On one occasion, Moses swore he saw a woman in a white nightgown, clothes aflame, running through the swamp holding a silver candelabra. He tried to rub his eyes, hoping the vision would disappear. But then he saw the puff of a rifle discharge in the distance and watched as the woman fell face first into the mud.

In the distance, he smelled wood smoke and saw the dull glow of a house in flames. He even thought he heard muffled screams, and hoof beats thundering off to the north.

This was, after all, where Old Dixie died, where desperate Confederate conscripts tried to slow Sherman troops tromping up from Savannah en route to burn Columbia. The cause, however, was lost long before the battle.

Sherman's troops split off into marauding bands of war-weary men a long way from home. En route, they felt it was their duty to extract a pound of flesh from South Carolina, the incestuous home of slavery, and make it pay for starting the war.

That price would be doubled and tripled by individuals with little military discipline and even fewer scruples. What they didn't burn, they ate. What they didn't eat, they destroyed. And what they couldn't carry away, they left broken and bleeding.

Seldom did the Yankee soldiers encounter experienced troops. Gen. Robert E. Lee's army was up north in Pennsylvania where he thought the war could still be won. But Sherman had brought it home, down through Georgia in a gashing maneuver that split the South like a melon and left it in the sun to rot. Then, pushing back to the north, the Union general burned a path through the Carolinas that would bring the Confederacy to its knees.

Even these days when the Civil War should be a distant memory, Moses witnessed the remnants of its effect on those whose families suffered the worst of it.

Once, when he was waiting for some paperwork in the headquarters building at Savannah River Site, he heard an engineer arguing with his supervisor about a business trip up North.

"It says here I'm to check into the Sherman House Hotel," the man said in his South Carolina drawl.

"So," his supervisor said, "what's wrong with that? It's a pretty good hotel from what I hear."

"But, sir," the young engineer said. "There's no way I can tell my mother I'm staying in the Sherman House. She'll disown me."

Moses thought it funny at the time and shared the story with his fellow black guards back at the nuclear dump where they worked. While his generation knew nothing of slavery, they found the white man's guilt about the peculiar institution an easy pot to stir when they wanted to shame them into trivial concessions.

He took it to extremes when he filled out a form requesting government disability payments for Post-Traumatic Stress Disorder. He knew some Army guys who'd been deployed to Iraq who got checks every month because of what they witnessed in combat. On the line where it asked Moses to fill in the nature of his trauma, he wrote, "Grew up black in South Carolina."

He was still waiting to hear back on that one. But what the hell, it was worth a try.

Moses was thinking about his white supervisors and their naiveté when a flashing blue light suddenly filled his truck cab. Glancing at the speedometer, Moses saw he was cruising at 93 miles an hour with a beer bottle between his legs and a roach clip in the ash tray.

At the same time, his cell phone lit up with a call from "Autry," which he definitely didn't need at the moment. The problem was, she always called back, over and over until he answered.

"What?" he screamed into his phone as he lowered the windows to remove the smoke from the cab. "What the fuck do you want now, bitch?"

Autry Cantey was standing in the middle of a doublewide, watching their 6-year-old daughter dance around to a rap song about prostitutes and pimps. "I need money, you motherfucker!" Autry said, trying to be heard over the wind whipping around in his truck. "You owe me seven hundred dollars! You said you'd pay me this week! Your daughter is hungry! Your son is kicking like he's the next Pele! You need to...."

"Shit, Autry, I gotta call you back," Macon said as he turned his cell phone off and gave his full attention to the cop car behind him. "I hope I know this sumbitch," he muttered.

Real cops, in Moses' opinion, were a major pain in the ass. Especially for black people.

Didn't matter if you worked for the government or preached at the church or played golf at the local country club. If you were black and lived in South Carolina, you were a nigger until proven otherwise. That much hadn't changed in 200 years.

Moses, of course, was known to most law enforcement officers as a good nigger. Didn't cause no trouble. Didn't smart mouth. Kept his cool. Which is why the good reverend was surprised when the police vehicle behind him suddenly flipped on four big swamp lights mounted on the hood. The candle power of those babies lit the world up like the Rapture.

Hopefully, Moses thought, this guy would see his "dealer" plates on the truck and recognize the bumper sticker that said, "Bubba's Used Cars: The Walking Man's Friend."

A lot of his customers were cops, which was good and bad. If this guy bought a lemon, he was screwed.

Moses blinked twice and reached for his sunglasses. Who the hell was this, anyway? It wasn't a state trooper because it wasn't a Ford. It wasn't County because they drove Chevys. And it wasn't the Estill town cop because he happened to know Chief Chuck Brewer's daddy just died, and he was out of town for the funeral.

Pulling over, he squinted into the glare as the driver appeared in his side mirror walking toward the truck, backlit against the bright lights, wearing a drill instructor's flat-brimmed hat, epaulets on the shoulders, bloused riding pants, and calf-high boots.

Then the dark figure was next to him, tapping on the truck window with a riding crop. All Moses could see was a shadowy face behind a pair of wrap-around Dale Earnhardt sunglasses, the kind that could make Mother Theresa look evil.

"Yes, yes, officer," Macon allowed, lowering his window, playing it cool. "Did I do something wrong?"

Snapping to attention, the ominous figure turned a flashlight into Macon's eyes, blinding him further, then swept the beam through the truck cab, back in the driver's eyes, and said, "License and wegistration."

"Oh, sure, just a minute," Moses said, fumbling with his wallet, trying to make sure his DOE security badge was in plain sight. Then, it hit him.

"Wait a minute. Did you say 'wegistration'?"

The officer fell silent. The flashlight swept back across Moses' face.

"License and wegistration," the officer repeated.

"Come on, Charlie," Macon said, squinting, recognizing the voice. "Why do you always have to be so damn dramatic? You scared the hell out of me. Last time you showed up at my house as a census taker. The time before that as a school crossing guard near my kid's school. Are you getting your rocks off on this shit, or what?"

The flashlight clicked off and the officer snuffled a laugh.

"Wocks off?" he repeated, haltingly.

"Oh, shit," Macon sighed. "Rocks off, Charlie! Like getting your wocks off! Shit! Nevermind!"

Charlie looked left and right down long stretches of empty highway, slipped his Smokey-the-Bear hat off his head, held it under his right arm and whispered, "Weren't you getting tired of dwopping stuff off at the town dump? I need some excitement in my life, man. The old lady's dwiving me nuts. I got a teenage daughter who thinks she's Madonna. Another Chinese joint opened up a few months ago across town using weal chicken. It's a jungle out there, man. This spy stuff is the only thing in my life that makes sense anymore."

Moses let out a sigh, closed his eyes slowly and said, "Ok, Charlie, if that's what it takes to make you happy. The bag is right behind me in the truck bed. We got some interesting parts this time. I don't know what any of it is. That's for your guys to figure out."

As Charlie illuminated the duffle bag with the flashlight, Macon thought about how he got himself into this business deal.

It was, of course, about the money. Moses was always looking for another source of income, something to pad his much-anticipated retirement years. So when Charlie Wong said he wanted to buy garbage, he saw no real problem with it.

For a grand a month, he'd be happy to supply the Chinese government with as much low-level radiation material as they wanted. After all, we couldn't give the shit away. Nobody else wanted it.

To Beijing, however, Charlie Wong was a valuable and gifted field agent. His ability to infiltrate the United States, worm his way into a small-town society, and supply his superiors with important information about the United States' nuclear program was vital.

Because, the wizened Chinese reasoned, it's not about what you know, it's what you don't know that wins the day.

Moses had been doing business with Charlie Wong for three years, ever since he and his wife moved to Barnwell and opened a Chinese take-out place called Hung Chow. Not realizing it was an ethnic joke about constipation, Charlie figured it was the perfect cover for a Chinese spy. And he was right.

It didn't take Charlie long to get a list of all the guards who worked for Nu-Chem, cultivate a relationship with a local man of the cloth, and fulfill his mission.

So for three years now, like clockwork, Macon Moses had surreptitiously supplied Charlie Wong with plastic garbage bags crammed with bits and pieces of stuff uncovered from the ground at work: Bolts. Medical tubing. Lab coats. Pants. Boots. Air conditioning parts. A heavy-duty crank. Some screwdrivers. It varied from month to month. But Charlie always seemed interested. And he paid in cash.

"Can I go now?" Moses asked, sticking the cash-filled envelope into the truck's glove compartment as Charlie Wong lifted the bag from the truck bed. "Where'd you get all this police stuff anyway? You've been going to those pawn shops in Augusta, haven't you? I knew it. You're hooked on law enforcement. Happens to about four percent of the population. Even illegal Chinese immigrant spies. Can't resist the uniforms, the power, the guns. You gotta gun, Charlie?

Suddenly the flashlight clicked on again

"Not yet," he mumbled. "Can I went yours?"

"No, you can't went mine, Charlie. Now get the hell out of here before some other lost soul comes down this road and sees us together."

Macon Moses dropped the Dodge Ram into gear, jerked it back onto the pavement and laid rubber for 20 yards, blue smoke pouring out the tail end of his southbound truck.

He assumed Nicole had already arrived at the Skidaway condo and was most likely knee deep into the Crown Royal. God, he loved that woman. He liked it when the sultry hairdresser with the husky, smoker's voice talked dirty to him and made him feel like a stud. She was good at that. Turned out she'd learned that trick working phone sex when she was only 16 years old.

"Men love being teased," she told Moses one Sunday afternoon as they lay naked on the bed at Skidaway. "Sometimes it's better than sex."

These days she only worked the phones when she needed a little extra cash. She'd just let Morine know she was available, and her cell phone would start ringing. Thirty minutes, 50 bucks. Then it doubled every 15 minutes as she turned up the heat, taking these poor souls down a trail of temptation that always ended with them jacking off in their sweat pants. Once the climax arrived, Nicole talked them down, cooled them off, and invited them back another time. They always came back for more.

Reaching for his cell phone, Moses punched in a number, waited for the ring, got Nicole's recorded message and said, "Hey, baby, it's me. I'm running a little late. Got hassled by the man. Threw me a little behind schedule. You just wait for me there, honey. And please, don't start without me."

Nicole Davis saw the light flashing on one of her three cell phones, looked at her watch, and assumed it was a message from Macon Moses.

"Excuse me, sweetheart," she said to an older man sitting next to her at the bar. "Duty calls."

CHAPTER 34

Orrie awoke with a jerk that immediately sent a painful jab through his head, and he sank back into the pillow moaning.

Opening one eye, he tried to decide if he'd been dreaming. It seemed so real. The feel of her skin. The softness of her lips. The heave of her breasts. Her legs wrapped around him. Him on top of her. Feeling the power. Using the power.

How many nights did he have the same dream? Always a blonde. Could never make out her face. But her body, oh God, her body. Like the young groupies who hung around after golf tournaments. Having cut his sexual teeth on Miss Pluff Mud, he got to know other women at tournaments all across the South. More than once he knocked off a piece on the putting green after hours, in the pro shop during an awards banquet, on the hood of his Porsche before he left town.

One sweet thing told him she was practicing to be a PGA Tour wife. She had the hair, the look, the poise, the visor, the fake smile, the polite patience, and the ultimate plan. They would live in Ponte Vedra with all the other touring pros, travel in style, have a few kids.

She showed him how she practiced running out onto the 18th green, little children in tow, planting a big kiss on the champion, then stepping aside as her man hoisted the trophy and spoke in clichés to a breathless sportscaster about the winning putt.

But all the characters in that play were fading memories. Whereas Orrie had once seen himself holding the trophy and toasting his competitors, now the player in his dreams was faceless, as was the blonde tour wife, the children, the sportscaster, and the officials who were holding the oversized check.

Even when he dreamed of sex, he never got any. His impotence ran deeper than his nerve endings. It infiltrated his brain, the place where all things sexual begin. While blood makes a man hard, it's his mind that allows him to score the ace.

But ever since the accident he'd been mentally mute. If his sleeping, alcohol-soaked brain did stray into the parlors of pleasure by mistake, it was like an old man staggering from memory to memory, reaching out for familiar fragrances and feelings that seemed to belong to him but never did.

His dead zone, Orrie thought, must be similar to the feeling amputees experience when they talk about ghost limbs. It's there, but it's not. It's gone, but it isn't.

For a while, in the early days after the accident, he tried to convince himself the feeling would come back. But when months of nothingness turned into years of frustration, he moved those thoughts to the back of his mind, into a dark closet to share space with his broken golf dreams.

Yet sex still teased him in his dreams. The touch of a tit. The soft brush of pubic hair. The scent of a woman giving herself, on the verge of consummation, the precipice of pleasure. But at the height of arousal, he would awaken, wrapped in bed sheets, sometimes sweating, often crying.

That's when the door suddenly opened, a streak of sunlight slashed his bloodshot eyes, and the angel of mercy reappeared.

CHAPTER 35

The 22nd Annual Bluff County Cooter Festival Parade was delayed by an early-morning rain but kicked off only an hour late when Punkin Parsells' 1938 Farmall tractor cranked on the first try and spit smoke all over the Shriners' Hillbilly Clan No. 31 from Horry County.

During the 1970s, almost any town of any size could fill out a form and get state accommodations tax money for almost any kind of festival that would promote tourism.

Radio personality Carl Gooding had raised the rallying cry that Bluff County should celebrate the cooter, a colloquial name for the turtles than were in abundance in the Salkehatchie Swamp.

"Our cooters are the best cooters in the country," Carl would croon on his morning radio show, stifling a laugh, knowing how close he was to the line of decency, which he had no qualms about crossing. "Ain't nobody got no cooters that look as pretty or smell as good as ours. I was telling the missus just last night how sweet her cooter smelled when she scrubbed it with a little Dutch Boy cleanser. Yessir, I told her she oughta enter that thing in the cooter contest, and we'd have the prettiest little cooter in the county."

People who listened to Carl Gooding's morning show were accustomed to his brand of blatant buffoonism that bordered on blasphemy, and they loved it. A guilty pleasure, the ladies would admit. There was just something about Carl that allowed him to be a little bad boy, despite his gray goatee and gimpy leg.

Indeed, he carried the joke all the way to the state capital where he actually obtained a $5,000 annual grant from the state to start the Cooter Festival, most of which went to his radio station for advertising.

Nobody seemed to mind much because Carl was always the Grand Marshal, riding in his Corvette convertible, throwing stuffed turtles to the children and condoms to the adults.

Then he'd preside over the main event, the Cooter Race, where locals would bring snapping turtles out of the swamp, line them up, then turn them loose, to see which one would waddle toward the strips of smelly squid that had been lying out in the sun all morning.

"Oh, my, something smells fishy to me," Carl would say over the loudspeaker as a hundred people gathered for the Cooter Race in front of the Bluff County Courthouse. "It couldn't be these cooters, 'cause our cooters don't smell, right boys?

"Well, maybe now that the race is co-ed, I suppose it could be Carolee Atkins's cooter I'm smelling. Is that your cooter, Carolee, the one bringing up the rear?"

Carolee Atkins weighed 335 pounds, worked at the Waffle Hut in Hampton, and didn't take any shit off anybody. Especially Carl Gooding, her second cousin by marriage.

"I don't smell nothing but your breath, Carl Gooding," she said, poking her cooter with a stick to get it going faster. "That's why you're on the damn radio. You too damn ugly for people to look at."

Carl hooted at Carolee's comment, urged the other contestants on to victory, declared a winner by default because none of the cooters were interested in eating half-baked squid, then closed the ceremonies with his usual flair.

"I wanta thank all y'all for coming to the 22nd Annual Cooter Festival," he said, holding the microphone with one hand and stretching out the cord with the other. "As usual, it's been a big success. We've crowned another Cooter Queen, Miss Rosalie Rushing, and she'll be representing us in the Miss South Carolina Festival Contest this fall.

"Furthermore, I'd like to say that our womenfolk are obviously to blame for the fact our cooters were not exactly up to par this year. I was hoping we'd have better cooters than last year, but it seems y'all ain't been taking care of your cooters the way you should.

"Now, if any of you ladies need private consultation on the care, feeding and grooming of your cooters, I'll be holding a clinic next Saturday night at my house because that's the weekend my wife will be in Beaufort counting her daddy's money."

The crowd laughed as they dispersed, stepping over a few runaway cooters. A few folks looked around to see if Carl's wife was in the crowd, but she wasn't. Never was.

Lisa Gooding was the secret to Carl's success. Her daddy owned six radio stations from Beaufort to Barnwell, including Groton's WDOG (93.5 FM), which had been turned over to his son-in-law right after the wedding.

A gifted performer and natural entrepreneur, Carl turned the sleepy country music station into his own private empire from which he broadcast the news of the world as he saw it, which was perverse.

For years he'd made fun of, embarrassed, humiliated, cajoled, and harassed every living soul within ear shot of the 5,000-watt radio station, and became a folk hero for it.

People tuned in just to see how irrepressible, sacrilegious, unrepentant, irresponsible, and irascible Carl would be on that particular morning. And they loved it when he assigned nicknames to somebody they knew, because they knew everybody.

"You know, it's a good thing Earl 'Short Bus' Walker has such big ears," Carl would say, in relation to nothing. "If he didn't, when he and the lovely missus Walker were experimenting with oral sex, he'd fall in and never be heard from again."

Or, "I ain't saying Bill 'Dookiebird' Kearse is behind on his personal hygiene or nothing, but I saw a buzzard sitting on top of his house the other day with a sandwich board sign around his neck that said, "All You Can Eat."

Without stopping to take a breath, Carl launched into another commercial spot for the Garden of Eat'n restaurant in Groton where chicken-fried steak was the special of the day.

"Tell you what goes good with that chicken-fried steak," Carl swooned. "Sweet Tea, y'all. And ain't nobody got sweeter tea than them waitresses over at the Garden of Eat'n. Just tell 'em Carl sentcha."

Sometimes Carl would ring a cow bell in the control room while he laughed at his own jokes, then lean into the microphone and say, "How 'bout somebody go over to brother Ephraim Polite's house and tell him the Civil War is over, that we won, and he needs to report back to the plantation immediately."

While people listening in their cars and kitchens moaned and groaned when he said things like this, Carl would punch a button on the control panel that would automatically release a pre-recording of one of his listeners trying to imitate his patented "Big Dog" howl.

After a few seconds of unrecognizable sounds coming across the airwaves, Carl would say, "I think that was Bert Kerwin's rendition of the Big Dog. Good God, y'all, sounds like he got something caught in his zipper, don't it?"

This would go on for four hours every weekday morning until Carl took off his headset, hitched up his pants, pulled a Titleist cap down tight on his head, and hopped in his red Corvette waiting outside to carry him to Sweetwater Country Club, 15 miles away in Barnwell.

There he would play golf with local cronies, bet on long drives and short putts, swill liquor drinks until sundown, then go home to Miss Lisa, his high school sweetheart.

He was, by local standards, a genuine celebrity, and he loved every minute of it.

"If life was any better," Carl would tell his golfing buddies, "I'd be me with a bigger dick."

CHAPTER 36

Hannah Jane Smalls Bartow Sullivan Jenkins was face down on the bar at the VFW Club with a string of spittle dangling from her mouth. Normally, they didn't serve black people, but nobody could exactly figure out into which category Hannah Jane fell. Only that she fell, and often.

In fact, she hadn't moved since she passed out the night before and Hall Boylston, the bartender, wasn't about to wake her up. Hannah Jane was a mean drunk and even meaner when hungover.

As a few local boys drifted into the low-slung, dimly-lit, cinderblock building just outside Blackville, they saw Hannah Jane's body slumped over and chose to sit on the other side of the room.

On the jukebox the Lonesome River Band sang a bluegrass whiner called, "I Ain't Broke, But I'm Badly Bent."

Well I'm going back to the country,
I can't pay the rent,
I ain't completely broke,
But brother I'm badly bent.

"Gimme a Budweiser and buy one for Hannah Jane there when she wakes up," Buddy Gillam told Hall when he was ordering. "Maybe she'll pass back out and we won't have to deal with her."

That's because nobody could deal with Hannah Jane. The only thing worse than an alcoholic, brass-ankle, drug-abusing, trash-talking, knife-throwing, man-hating, ugly-ass bitch like her was one just like her who knew karate, which she did.

That skinny skank of a woman with her left boob hanging out of a wife-beater T-shirt ran away from home and joined the Marines when she was 17, survived boot camp at Parris Island and six months in Kosovo before being discharged for getting impregnated by an inferior officer.

Despite a medical discharge and military training as a truck driver, Hannah Jane never obtained suitable employment, finding it easier to marry white men with worse addictions and financial problems than her own.

Two of them, Oliver Bartow, a motorcycle mechanic, and Phillip Sullivan, a land surveyor, turned up dead, which was fine because Hannah Jane was sick of them anyway. But neither one had any life insurance, which is why she hooked up with Bobby Jenkins, who was on parole for burglary and buggery, having pled to the latter charge in order to get the former charge reduced, though he denied ever meeting the horse in question.

During a break in the conversation, the jukebox clicked and whirred and spewed forth some of Tony Joe White's "Polk Salad Annie."

Everybody said it was a shame,
'Cause her momma was working on the chain gang,
…a wretched, spiteful, straight razor-toting woman.

"I heard Henry was back in town," Buddy said to Hall, casting a cautious glance over at Hannah Jane, who was snoring. "How 'bout calling him and asking him to come get her."

"I would," Hall said, "but we ain't got no phone. They cut it off last week. It was that or the beer chiller, and you know, we got priorities."

Buddy sipped his beer, thought a minute, then said, "I got a cell phone."

Hall thought about that for another minute, weighing the consequences of waking Hannah Jane up against letting a sleeping dog lie.

"I don't know, man," he said. "I'm thinking…."

About that time the battered metal door to the VFW club creaked open, sunlight rushed into the darkened bar, and Henry Smalls, dressed in a three-piece suit, walked in.

"Howdy, boys," Henry said, ignoring the "No Civilians" sign and letting the door slam behind him. "Hope my baby sister hasn't been too much trouble. I know how she can be. Tell you what, I'll buy a round if you'll help me load her up."

A couple of veterans looked over at Hannah Jane, glanced down at their empty mugs of beer, and went back to playing gin rummy.

"Come on, guys," Henry said, whipping out his wallet. "I've got to take her back to the VA in Augusta, and I don't want to get my suit all messed up. I've got meetings to go to today."

The men said nothing.

"Okay, how about 20 bucks?" Henry said, holding up a Jackson.

The old men stirred a little, knowing $20 would get them well on their way to happy hour, but they balked.

"She bites," one of them said.

"And she might have AIDS," another grumbled.

·Henry walked over to Hannah Jane, asked Hall for a towel and draped it over his sister's exposed parts.

"Tell you what," Henry said calmly. "If you boys'll put her in the back seat of my car, I won't tell the SBI about those illegal poker machines y'all are hiding in the back room. *Capiche*?"

That's when the bartender motioned for the veterans to pitch in and haul Hannah Jane's sorry ass out of the bar and dump her in the back seat of Henry's government car.

Fortunately, she never woke up.

When she was buckled in, Henry gave the vets the $20 bill, thanked them, and said, "Remember, boys, you can choose your friends, but you can't pick your family. Y'all let me know if there's ever anything I can do for you up in Washington."

Nodding in agreement, the veterans took the folding money back into the bar to finish what they'd started as Willie Nelson's "Pancho and Lefty" spilled out of the jukebox.

Living on the road, my friend,
Is gonna keep you free and clean,
Now you wear your skin like iron,
Your breath as hard as kerosene.

As Henry pulled out of the parking lot headed for the VA Hospital in Augusta, Hannah Jane threw up in the back seat.

CHAPTER 37

Tuesday night was Nigger Night at the Healing Springs Baptist Church and Country Club. Orrie supplied the marijuana, and guys from three counties would show up with various contraptions for smoking the stuff. Everything from expensive Oriental Hookah pipes with multiple hoses coming out the top, to something as simple as a cardboard toilet paper roll with a scrap of aluminum foil stuck in a hole on top.

Fancy or functional, the object of the game was to get as screwed up as humanly possible and still tell racist jokes. The crowd usually consisted of shade-tree mechanics, used car salesmen, farm hands, welfare recipients, and anybody who didn't have to be drug tested to keep a job.

The winner got a bag of free pot.

The loser had to drink the bong water.

They chose Tuesday nights because that's when Butterbean went bowling with Miss LeeBelle and the church ladies from the choir. When asked if he could bowl, Butterbean just smiled and said, "Da ladies lines me up and tells me where to put it. You knows, just like every other night." Nigger Night, of course, was not much different from Fart and Burp Night, which was an unannounced event that occurred when the group around the campfire was too drunk to remember any jokes.

The loudest and smelliest fart as judged by the panel of experts on hand was usually awarded some pickled eggs, which led to more of the same. Burping was a talent everybody thought they had until one night a man passing through from Alabama pronounced the entire alphabet in a single burp barrage that left the encampment stunned. Then he recited the Pledge of Allegiance in a single belch and the group was unable to think of a prize befitting such expertise.

But the only title to be retired because it was deemed unbeatable was that of the Caddyshack Champ. That belonged exclusively to Orrie, who as a 13-year-old watched the Bill Murray-Chevy Chase movie 175 times in one year.

The game started as a bet between two truckers about who could remember more funny lines from the 1980 golf classic.

While they were stumbling through a few scenes, Orrie stood up with a bottle of Wild Turkey in his hand, took a hit from a joint, turned to the gentlemen participating in the quote-off and declared he could recite the Top 20 lines from the 1980 golf comedy, in order.

Challenged to do so, he began with Judge Smails saying to Ty Webb, "You know, you should play with Dr. Beeper and myself. I mean, he's been club champion for three years running, and I'm no slouch myself."

To which the drunken crowd responded in chorus, "Don't sell yourself short, judge. You're a tremendous slouch."

The crowd loved it, so Orrie continued with Sandy the Scottish groundskeeper saying to Bill Murray's character, Carl Spackler, "I want you to kill all the gophers on the golf course."

To which Spackler replied, "Correct me if I'm wrong, Sandy. But if I kill all the golfers, they're gonna lock me up and throw away the key."

"Not golfers, you great fool!" Sandy shouted. "Gophers! The little, brown, furry rodents!"

"We can do that," Orrie would say, imitating Murray's imbecilic, pot head character. "We don't even have to have a reason."

By then the boys were on the ground laughing, but Orrie was on a roll and threw in Rodney Dangerfield's great line, "Oh, this is your wife, huh? Hey, baby, you must've been something before electricity!"

But the soliloquy that brought the house down was Orrie's re-creation of the scene where Spackler told Chevy Chase about the new strain of grass he was developing, saying, "This is a hybrid. This is a cross, ah, of Bluegrass, Kentucky Bluegrass, Featherbed Bent, and Northern California Sensemilia. The amazing stuff about this is, that you can play 36 holes on it in the afternoon, take it home and just get stoned to the bejeezus-belt that night on this stuff."

Orrie could go on forever because he was in love with the low-budget film about golf. But, seeing his audience was inattentive and more than a little stoned, he simply closed his performance by quoting Ty Webb, bowing and saying, "Thank you very little."

That was random entertainment around the campsite, but Nigger Night always drew the biggest crowds.

What do you call a black abortion clinic?" Eddie France, a plumber, asked before the contest officially started.

"Crime stoppers!" he blurted out, not waiting for the answer.

There was some grumbling and a few snorts of laughter before Little Boy Baxter, all 300 pounds of him, announced that he had a new one.

"So this nigger walks into the bar with a parrot on his shoulder and the bartender says, 'My God, where'd you get him? He's a perfect specimen."

Little Boy waited an appropriate spell before screwing up his mouth so he would sound like a strangled parrot and replied, "Rhodesia, man, they got millions of them over there."

The campfire boys cackled another laugh, not wanting to give anyone a big lead before all the jokes were in. But it looked like it was going to be a slow night for jokes that hadn't been told a hundred times before.

Then they heard an unfamiliar voice step out of the darkness into the campfire light.

"I got one for you," Holly Holladay said, wearing cutoff jeans and a T-shirt with Pabst Blue Ribbon written across the front. "A black man walked into a Saturday night Ku Klux Klan meeting with a shotgun, forced the white men to strip naked, threw their clothes in the fire, then marched them through town while their families were driving to church on Sunday morning."

There was an unsettled silence among the group until Scott Michaux, owner of the only liquor store in Elko, said innocently, "Hell, honey, that ain't funny worth a shit."

Holly turned on one heal, ripped the No Niggers sign off the tree, looked back at the scraggily bunch of bigots and said, "It was to the black man."

As Holly disappeared back into Orrie's room, Eddie France crossed his legs, took a swig of moonshine and said, "Sooner or later, Puddles is going to have to make a choice between us and her."

To which the group muttered and Jim Clark, a retired welder, spit out his tobacco chew and said, "Eddie, you ain't much up on your natural laws of physics is you?"

The plumber scratched his ass, burped, and said, "Huh?"

"You ever heard the Frank Howard story?"

"Which 'un."

"Well," Jim said, balancing his butt on a Coke crate. "It was back when Frank Howard, the legendary Clemson football coach, was recruiting this running back from Elloree. Can't remember his name right now. Don't matter no how.

"Anyway, Howard talked this country boy into coming to Clemson because he could get his shoulder pads down low and run like a deer during hunting season. Problem was, this young stud had a girlfriend and was homesick. So he took off for home after the first week up at Clemson and didn't come back.

"Coach Howard, naturally, got in his car, rode down state and tried to convince the young man to return to campus, which he failed to accomplish. At the next alumni meeting, the heavy-hitting donors in Greenville peppered the old coach about letting this magnificent catch get away.

"Howard, a man of few words, stared back at the group of disappointed football fans and said, 'Gentlemen, this young man had a very important decision to make. He had to choose between playing football for dear old Clemson College and pussy.'

"There was a pause as the men chewed that cud for a moment before Howard finally said, 'And as we all know, gentlemen…pussy is undefeated.'"

Everybody raised a beer can to that one, nodding in total agreement, as the moon began to disappear on the far horizon.

It was three days before Orrie and Holly came out of the Embassy Suites room, and when they did, on a Monday morning, she looked around the campground, cluttered with beer cans and discarded clothing, and declared, "This is going to be our home, Puddles. It just needs a woman's touch."

To which Orrie moaned and softly replied, "Oh, shit…I mean, yep, yep…you're probably right."

CHAPTER 38

Despite Luke Thompson's promise of not leaking news of the dead cows to the militant environmental extremists, 50 of them were standing outside the gates of the Savannah River Site as Henry drove up in his motor pool car.

"Damn," Henry muttered, as he saw the handmade signs attacking the government facility.

"Dead Cows = Dead People" one read.

"Brush Your Teeth With Plutonium To Really Make Them Shine (In The Dark)," another said.

Henry pulled over to the side of the road, parked the car, got out and strolled up to the ring leader, Brett Bursey, an unrepentant hippie whose gray hair was now pulled back into a long ponytail.

"Having fun?" Henry asked Bursey as he looked around at the protesters.

"Not much," Bursey said, rocking his neck back and forth, trying to get the bones to crack. "I'm getting too old for this shit, Henry. You know, I used to protest for your people back in the old days."

"My people?" Henry said.

"You know, civil rights and all that," Bursey said. "You're too damn young to remember what things were like back then. We were your best friends. Actually, your only friends."

Henry removed his coat to fight off the summer heat and fanned away a few gnats that kept buzzing in his left ear.

"Well," he said, "we certainly appreciate all you did for us, Mr. Bursey. But could you hurry up with this? Security's going to be here pretty soon, and I don't want to see 'em bring out the fire hoses and turn the dogs loose on you."

Bursey got the sarcasm and looked around at his disinterested dissenters.

"At least we don't have to camp out anymore," he said. "Nowadays, we just show up, shoot some quick video, upload it to the Internet, and it goes viral. Wish we'd had this technology during the riots at USC. Would've saved a lot of busted heads and broken bones."

Henry knew Bursey's reputation as a troublemaker better than he knew Bursey himself. Somehow, whenever there was a civil rights dust-up, a pro-marijuana rally, or an anti-government protest, Bursey was there, right in front of the television cameras.

Now in his late-50s, the brash young kid who led the riots on the University of South Carolina campus after the Kent State shootings in 1970 still believed he was right and everybody else was wrong. But Bursey knew this new generation wasn't willing to take a nightstick to the head to make a point. Or to go to jail for a cause. Or to do much of anything that kept them away from their video games.

But here was a guy who'd been doing those things for 30 years and didn't care if people thought he was a kook. Because, as he liked to mock the old Barry Goldwater campaign slogan, "In your heart, you know I'm right."

It was people like Henry and his bureaucratic bosses who were wrong and wouldn't admit it. Couldn't admit it, actually. This crime against humanity had been covered up so many times by so many layers of lies it was hard to keep up with the truth, something they seldom talked about.

"All right," Bursey yelled over his shoulder to the rest of the group. "We got the good stuff. Mackey, make sure you got the bomb plant sign in the shot, then upload it and we're outa here. It's getting hot. I need a nap."

Henry saw the Nu-Chem security trucks headed their way and pointed them out to Bursey, who just shrugged.

"What a field day for the heat," he began to sing. *"Thousands of people in the street. Singing songs and carrying signs, mostly say hooray for our side."*

Henry recognized the old Buffalo Springfield anthem from the '68 Democratic Convention when Chicago Mayor Richard Daley's political police busted hippie heads with batons and dragged long-haired kids off to jail.

"This ain't the '60s," Henry said, helping Bursey step up into a van. "People don't give a damn like they used to."

"I know," the old hippie said with a sigh. "I had to pay these guys to be here."

But what the protest lacked in passion it made up for in distribution. The cow story, complete with fingers pointing at the federal government's callous care of disposed nuclear waste, was already winging its way around the world wide web.

CHAPTER 39

B y the time Brumby drove back to Washington, he was of two minds.

One was giddy over the news he still had his job. The other was wondering what his new job was going to be. Flack? Flunky? The new owners planned on making him a star, albeit in weekly papers across the country.

That euphoria, however, was counterbalanced by the dreadful sense of inferiority that returned when he thought about losing Holly Holladay. He had been so close. He'd already seen her in a wedding dress, walking down the aisle, heading straight for him and a lifetime of eternal bliss, and sex, oh God, the sex.

Those heady thoughts, however, were shattered quickly when he reached his cubicle in the Senate Press Gallery, and there was a note to call Strom Thurmond's press secretary.

"Mark," Brumby said from the telephone booth in the press gallery. "Brumby. What's up?"

There was some rustling of papers on the other end of the line before Mark said, "Everybody knows about the cows."

Brumby loosened his tie, pulled out a ballpoint pen and asked innocently, "What cows, Mark?"

Again, six seconds of silence before Mark answered, "Well, then, let me put it another way. Everybody knows about the cows except you."

Brumby flipped hastily through some paperwork on his desk, trying to buy time, when he suddenly saw a printout of a story mentioning dead cows in South Carolina. It was an email from Luke Thompson to every reporter on the Hill about possible radiation leaks into streams outside the Savannah River Site being responsible for the death of a local farmer's cows.

"Quite a barbecue," Brumby said, trying to buy more time to understand what he didn't know. "For some reason, they prefer mustard base in Barnwell County."

Again, sustained silence.

"Thank God Lee Bandy is on vacation," Mark said. "And I don't know if anybody else will pick up on this story. But the Senator wants it squashed."

That was a red flag for any reporter, including the bumbling Brumby, who was scribbling notes as he talked.

"So, has the Senator made a statement yet?" he asked.

"I'm putting one together now," Mark said of *The State Sentinel*'s star political reporter. "It's the usual bramble bush of bullshit, but here's what we need you to do, Brumby. We need you to write a column saying everything is cool. Nothing to worry about. You know, much ado about nothing."

Brumby rubbed his chin, thinking that would help him think faster, but it didn't.

"So, why exactly would I do that?" he asked.

"Because, it's the truth as we want it told," Mark said, suddenly lowering his voice, "and because your new boss says so."

Brumby's mind immediately flashed up a mental picture of Dexter Young, the mild-mannered co-owner of Community Communications.

"How would you know that?" Brumby asked, dumbfounded.

"Because he's sitting right here," Mark said. "Would you like to speak to him?"

CHAPTER 40

It took Brumby 20 minutes to take the elevator down from the Senate Press Gallery to the basement of the Capitol where the trams run underground between the House and Senate office buildings.

As he hopped into an open car for the short ride to the Russell Building and Strom Thurmond's office on the third floor, Brumby scanned the email from Luke Thompson about the cow kill in South Carolina.

While dead farm animals are not front-page news in most newspapers, it was beginning to be a trend around the Savannah River Plant, which meant it was a good story for his newspapers. At least it was when Granville Trinity was running the show.

Trinity's anger at the government for sending his son to die in Vietnam was unrelenting. He had often run front-page editorials denouncing the Department of Defense and whatever party was in charge of sending Americans into battle for political reasons.

Most recently, his ire had been aimed at the boondoggles in Panama, Granada, and the Gulf War.

"Our war on terrorism is going about as well as our war on poverty, our war on cancer, and our war on drugs," Trinity wrote. "The truth is this country has not won a war since World War II, and we were damn lucky to win that one."

On more than one occasion Trinity used Brumby as a stick to poke some politician in the eye. He would assign the young reporter to harass the brass at the Pentagon over some illogical expenditures, or have him wait outside the Metro Station in Crystal City to catch a civilian employee who Trinity thought knew something about his son, whose death had been shrouded in a mysterious bureaucratic cover-up that always seemed to be shuffled off to some other department.

Brumby had learned a few tricks of the trade despite his lack of formal journalism training. Just by watching and listening to the other reporters, he quickly came to understand that the real power of the press was its ability to ask anybody anything, anytime, just because you could.

The First Amendment, he came to realize, gave him the same rights as Jonathon Fuerbringer of *The New York Times*. He could ask any elected or unelected official about anything from how the war was going to how much the government spent on toilet paper in the White House.

Thus he'd taken on an air of arrogance that comes when a journalist enters a joust, knowing he wields the sword of truth in the public's long fight for the right to know. He also enjoyed his minor victories over the bureaucracy and began to feel he could actually write wrongs, a term he read in a novel somewhere and began to believe.

Now, however, he felt a seismic shift. In the time it took to drive back from Washington, his journalistic compass had been hijacked, and he wasn't sure which way it pointed. The answer to that question would come shortly after he was escorted into the inner sanctum of Strom Thurmond's office.

Mark Vandenheuvel met him at the elevator. Without knocking, they walked into Thurmond's long, narrow office and saw the senator, in his late-90s, sitting at his desk, silhouetted in the afternoon sun against the window behind him.

To Strom's right sat Brumby's new boss, wearing a dark suit with a power-red tie and highly shined shoes.

As Brumby moved toward the Senator, he passed through what everybody called the "Tunnel of Time," a tight walk through a gallery of American history, both walls completely covered with framed photographs of Thurmond with popes, astronauts, presidents, governors, movie stars, captains of industry, foreign leaders, scientists, and war heroes. All personally autographed.

This was not Brumby's first visit to Thurmond's office, but he was always impressed with the history within these chambers. The last time he was here, he interviewed the venerable senator about his longevity, both personal and political.

He knew the answer to the latter, of course. Thurmond was a brilliant politician who morphed from a fire-breathing segregationist to a moderate Democrat to a modern-day Republican as easily as a Confederate flag flaps in the wind.

On the subject of his personal longevity, Thurmond went into great detail with

Brumby one day about his eating habits and how important it was to keep things flowing through the body.

"You have to keep the alimentary canal moving," Thurmond emphasized, making sweeping motions with his arms and hands as he illustrated the path food takes from your stomach through the small and large intestines. "It's all about keeping a clean colon, my boy. You should remember that, and you'll live a long time."

Brumby wondered at the time if he really wanted to live as long as Thurmond, who still presented an active lifestyle, but looked like a corpse up close.

That's when Brumby reached out his hand to Dexter, saying it was nice to see him again so soon.

"Actually," said the man in the black suit, rising from his chair, "you've met my brother, Dexter. I'm Donald Young, Chief Executive Officer of Community Communications."

The two men, in their mid-40s, were identical twins, except for the handshake.

Brumby recalled Dexter Young's handshake as strong and friendly, while Donald's was soft and aloof.

"I'm sorry we haven't had a chance to meet until now," Donald Young said. "We've been quite busy with acquisitions, and it's hard to get around and meet everyone working for all our papers.

"But, I especially wanted to make your acquaintance while I was here in town. As you may know, Dexter is Chief Operations Officer of the company and handles the day-to-day production of our newspapers, which is no small task.

"I, on the other hand, deal with the big picture. You know, direction, positioning, forecasting, bottom lines, and, of course, good journalism."

Brumby took notice of where journalism fell in that list of priorities, but simply said it was nice to meet Mr. Young and how happy he was to be working for Community Communications, or anybody for that matter, which he didn't say out loud.

"I gather you've seen the report about the cows," Thurmond said, leaning down to pick up a two-pound dumbbell, which he started curling with his right hand. "We, of course, are vitally interested in the health and well-being of our citizens and this kind of story, if not handled correctly, could cause unnecessary concern, if you know what I mean."

Brumby nodded, pulling the printout from his coat pocket and scanning it once more for details. "So," Brumby said haltingly, "I gather you want me to write something to that effect. Is that why I'm here?"

At that point Donald Young rose from his chair, walked to the window and said, "Actually, Brumby, we want to give you an even bigger scoop. One that might put all this in perspective."

"What's bigger than 63 head of livestock dropping dead from toxic, radioactive materials in our drinking water?" Brumby asked innocently.

Young turned from the window, put his hand on Brumby's shoulder, and said, "What if it's not true?"

CHAPTER 41

Henry Smalls was not an idiot, but he worked for one, which broke his heart. While he'd spent his young life trying to portray an educated black man on the rise in American politics, there were Uncle Toms around every corner in Washington.

One of those was actually an Aunt Thomasina. Her real name was Thomasina Lee Johnson, a black woman from Orangeburg who happened to be the widow of the only black Republican in South Carolina. Thanks to her late husband, Dr. Joseph Johnson, assistant provost at South Carolina State College, Mrs. Johnson was awarded a $130,000-a-year job as DOE's Director of Community Relations and Minority Affairs, a position that previously didn't exist and currently had no directives. Unfortunately, Henry's department fell under the auspices of her federal umbrella, which had many holes.

As far as Henry could determine, of the three years she'd been in office, Thomasina Lee Johnson spent the majority of her time flying to seminars and conventions that happened to be in Las Vegas, Reno and Atlantic City, where she liked to play blackjack.

Indeed, she once assigned Henry to put out a news release stating Donald Trump was under congressional investigation for racketeering and tax evasion, which he was not.

Turned out she had recently lost a month's salary in one of Trump's casinos and the management had to have her forcibly removed from the premises when she loudly proclaimed she'd been cheated and demanded her money back.

Feeling this fiasco was an injustice to the American people and an embarrassment for black people everywhere, Henry did what any good government employee in Washington would do, he leaked this information to the press.

Lee Bandy, of *The State Sentinel,* was his first choice because Mrs. Johnson was a resident of Orangeburg, only 40 miles from the state capital. But the messages he left for Bandy went unanswered, for whatever reason. The same went for correspondents from Greenville and Charleston, who called to get a few facts, but never followed up.

General knowledge said the mainstream media in South Carolina was uninterested and unable to report on black abuse in the system for fear of racial retribution.

Lee Bandy told Henry his newspaper attempted several times to audit the books at S.C. State University, only to back off when accused of racism. So Henry went to Brumby, his only hope, who ran the story under Granville Trinity's nose. It got legs because the Republicans were in power when Trinity's son was killed in Vietnam.

Regardless of the motives, it only took a few columns in 11 small-town weekly papers to raise the awareness of Thomasina Lee Johnson's boondoggle, and the ire of Mrs. Johnson herself.

Once, when Brumby followed her to a cocktail party to ask her about a four-day trip to Vegas to give a 10-minute speech about minority mobility in federal government, she began hitting him with her handbag.

That story caused Dr. Edmunds, her protector, to quietly suggest her retirement, which she took, reluctantly. But not before filing a lawsuit against the federal government for back troubles she suffered while taking all those long flights. She refused to leave office until the case was settled in her favor.

Just before rushing to an appointment to talk to a nuclear physicist about particulate matter in public waterways, Henry received an email that Mrs. Johnson had received a $1.3 million settlement and an enhanced pension plan, which caused him to slam the door on his way out.

"It's a wonder this country has survived as long as it has," he mumbled to himself. "Like white people ain't bad enough."

CHAPTER 42

The sky was clear and an August moon lit the highway like a searchlight as it stretched through the swampy bottoms of the South Carolina Lowcountry.

This was a time Macon Moses cherished, when he could sit back in his Dodge Ram truck, let the big dog eat up the miles between him and the long, luscious legs of Nicole Davis. Between Estill and Savannah, there was not a stoplight or a speed zone, just a zillion pine trees and two lanes of asphalt ribbon custom made for Macon Moses.

As he set the cruise control on 80, Moses slipped open the ash tray, grabbed a roach clip, fired it up, cracked both windows about 2 inches, and let the wind whip through the cab. He sucked hard on the doob, held the smoke tight in his lungs for as long as he could, then blew it out through the open window like a locomotive letting out steam.

Three hits and he was right where he wanted to be, somewhere between reality and nirvana, a place where music and sex and dancing and singing and preaching all became one in his body and soul. Holding the wheel with his left hand, he popped a CD in the player, took one more toke for good measure, dropped the clip in the tray, and settled back as the words of Dr. Jerry Black boomed through his custom-made, surround-sound speakers, spilled out the windows and landed along the roadside like stardust.

But most of it went right into the receptive mind of Macon Moses. Loud and clear. Because this was homework for Moses, the preacher, the man of the cloth who donned his robes on Sunday mornings and performed for his flock at the Healing Springs Baptist Church and Country Club.

While Moses didn't finish S.C. State and never quite got around to actually enrolling in the Southeastern Seminary, that didn't mean he couldn't be a preacher in a black church. Because all you really need to be a preacher in a black church is an expensive suit and a lot of style. Sure, you have to know the scriptures and quote them and note them and use them in parables and shake the roof with them when necessary. But the only actual credential Moses had was the "Clergy" sign above the visor of his truck that gave him free parking almost anywhere.

So he studied other black preachers, stealing things from their sermons, practicing their gestures, their moves, their pregnant pauses. The ones he liked most were the whoopers. They didn't just speak the gospel, they sang and danced and delivered the Word of God in a way that made people dance and sing and raise their hands toward heaven. Which is why, when he had time, Moses listened and learned from the masters.

"I don't know 'bout you," Brother Jerry Black said on the CD, half singing and half talking. "I don't know 'bout you. But I came to Jesus. I found Him a resting place. I found Him a home in my heart."

That's when the organ music kicked in, and Brother Jerry's voice rose and fell with the music, causing some women in the congregation of the Greater Travelers Rest Baptist Church in Atlanta to squirm and answer with repetition and reinforcement.

Which is when Brother Jerry kicked it up a notch.

"Can I get a witness here?" he crooned, as he slowed it down, stepping out from behind the pulpit, taking long, deliberate steps. "'Cause he walks with me. He guides my footsteps. He tells me where to step, which way to turn. He tells me what to do. Where to put my trust. For even here in gator country, everything will turn out all right. Can I get an amen?"

In the background Moses heard the deacons, choir members, and ladies in the congregation shouting out "amens" to the preacher.

"Is there anybody here who has experience in gator country? Is there anybody here who been snapped at? Anybody here who been growled at? Anybody here who been bit sometime? Anybody here who been persecuted some time? Anybody here who been wounded sometime?"

In the background Moses could hear the cacophony of "amens."

"Have mercy, Lord," preacher Black continued. "Well is there anybody here who can testify that the Lord will take care of you? The Lord will take care of you. If you feel the power of the Lord, come forward, don't be afraid, come willingly to the cross, speak of your sin, and be saved."

That's when Moses hit the button on the CD player and replayed the last part. He loved to ask people to testify. There's a certain soul-searching reality to testifying that folks can't resist. Brother Jerry Black knew it, and so did Macon Moses. After memorizing and rehearsing that part twice, he let Brother Jerry finish.

"So as I leave you here, I leave you with the words of an old hymn: Be not dismayed. Whatever the times. God will take care of you. Beneath His wings of love abide. God will take care of you. Won't He do it? Won't He do it? Do you know He will? Do you know He will? Bring you through, Lord, bring you through."

Repetition, Macon learned, was one of the simple secrets of preaching, especially for whoopers, where you turn the words into a song without a melody, but a song none the less, the kind that runs up and down the scale, skipping a few octaves for effect.

Then, when the crowd was worked up and in the palm of his hand, Brother Jerry put them together, holding each other's hands.

"Now turn to somebody beside you and hold their hand," the preacher sang. "Don't turn it aloose. But hold their hand. Look 'em in the face. Look 'em in the eye. And tell 'em these words: I been in gator country. And I had my share of trouble. And I had my share of distress. I been rebuked, and I been scorned. I been through so many ups and downs. But the Lord pulled me through it. The Lord heard my prayer.

"So excuse me, excuse me, but I'm happy, and I don't care who knows it. Excuse me, but you don't know like I know what the Lord has done for me. He been with you in the gator country. If He heard your prayer and brought you out. Then turn to somebody else, turn to somebody else, and shake their hand, and hold their hand with authority, and tell 'em these words — Excuse me if I get excited. Excuse me if I get emotional. But I been thinking about so many times the Lord rescued me, and I been thinking about so many times He answered my prayers. Thank you, Jesus. Thank you, Jesus. Thank you, Jesus. Thank you, Jesus. Thank you, Jesus!"

Five seemed to be Brother Jerry's magic number when it came to thanking Jesus. So Moses replayed the finish of that sermon, where the whooper was thanking Jesus, letting his voice drop, feigning weariness, dropping to a rhetorical knee, and taking the congregation with him, one "thank you, Jesus" at a time.

Not only did Moses enjoy the art of preaching, which he'd been perfecting since he was a child, but he also came to know through the church what benefits are bestowed upon preachers. If he is good enough to hypnotize the congregation every Sunday morning and make them feel as if the Lord himself is speaking through him, then he can have anything he wants.

In some cases, that means fried chicken at somebody's house on Sunday night, or delivered to his trailer on Monday morning. Or it means having free run of the hens in the flock, spreading the Word through personal relationships, even with teenaged girls, entranced by men of the cloth.

But nothing Macon Moses learned in Sunday School, church services, or five semesters at S.C. State quite prepared him for the role he assumed as a black preacher. Because what they don't tell you is everything is free, and all is forgiven.

While he'd only been in business at Healing Springs for seven years, he was considered to be a man of God upon whom people could trust, place faith, support, and who could forgive them when they fell from grace.

And there's another old saying in the black community. "Ain't nothing harder than a preacher's dick." That was certainly true of Macon Moses.

Early in his tenure, he'd been caught drinking and driving with the 16-year-old daughter of a deacon. When *The Barnwell Bugle* published the police report, it caused a stir in the congregation. But when Granville Trinity, writing a gossip column under the pen name Algonquin J. Calhoun, insinuated there was sexual misconduct, the good folks of Healing Springs stood behind Moses, protested in front of the newspaper, the courthouse, and city hall, carried signs about persecution, and swore up and down it was all a big misunderstanding, even though they knew he did it.

Eventually, the paper ran a reluctant, racist, and recalcitrant clarification that read, "The aforementioned allegation will hereby go undiscussed because the party of the first part can't prove that the party of the second part, actually partied with the party of the first part since the party is still going on."

Algonquin J. Calhoun, the lawyer on the old "Amos and Andy" TV series, couldn't have said it better. Soon the protesters melted back into the countryside to handle things their way. Which meant giving the preacher every benefit of the doubt.

Why? Because that's the way it's done in the black church, their only sanctuary from the white world where they have to bend and bow to the white ways; talking white, walking white, and pretending to be white.

But in the church, once those doors are closed, they are African again, hallelujah! Come to Jesus. Closer my God to Thee. Held in the arms of the Lord. Swinging low in the chariot. Among their own kind. Doing their own thing. Their own way.

And even if the preacher is a sinner, he's their sinner, and God will sort it all out in the end when the judgment comes some fine day, sweet Jesus.

That, Macon Moses knew, was every prophet's prophylactic protection, his shield, his sword, his way around the wrongs in life and a narrow path of righteousness that allows him to slip in the side door of heaven, no matter what. Amen.

Jerry Black's sermon ended just as Moses pulled up in the parking lot of the Ocean Breeze condominiums just a block from the beach on Skidaway Island. As he gathered his things in the cab of the truck, he looked up to the third floor where he could see Nicole Davis standing on the deck, a cigarette in one hand, the other on her hip, waiting for her man to come home.

Adjusting himself as he felt a rise in his pants, he climbed the stairway to heaven, two steps at a time.

CHAPTER 43

Orrie, much to his own surprise, hadn't had a beer in three days.

In a matter of weeks, Holly Holladay had taken over the entire camp, cleaned up the trash, told several troublemakers never to come back, organized the harvest, made friends with the black choir ladies, and figured out a way to double their take on the marijuana crop.

"You just have to maximize your yield," she told Orrie and Butterbean as they sat like children in school desks brought in by some lost soul in exchange for pot. "This is primo weed Butterbean's growing. Heirloom stuff. It's mild, smooth, strong, has depth, history, and comes in four grades. It's a gold mine."

Orrie looked over at Butterbean who was mesmerized by Holly's voice and fragrance. There was something about white women that fascinated him. They didn't smell like black women, who could never quite cover up the scent of wood smoke and bacon grease beneath the perfume and powder.

White women, he thought, were dipped in some kind of lavender cream when they were born, a scent that permeated their skin and their soul and made you want to lick them like an ice cream cone.

"So, you wants us to grow mo'?" Butterbean asked.

"Actually, no," Holly said. "I learned from my mother that less is more. Less creates demand, which creates value, especially in something this organic, this historic, this, you know, erotic."

Holly had traveled back to her parents' herb farm, consulted with her mother, established a business plan, and a distribution system. She was ready to bring Slave Weed to market. When she returned to Jesus Saves, she was driving a new Ford Explorer with a false gas tank and extra storage space hollowed out below the back seats, enough room to carry 400 pounds of pot.

By Christmas, she had the women of the church drying the weed in their smokehouses, sprinkling it with a smattering of Healing Springs water for good measure, and bringing in $10,000 a week, which was a problem.

"What are we going to do with all this money?" Orrie asked Holly one night as he walked without a limp across the room to their king-sized bed. "I mean, we've already got it stashed in the ceiling and under the floor and buried out back in pickle jars. Now we've got twice that much and nowhere to put it."

Holly was sitting up in the bed, a pair of reading glasses on her cute little nose, her long legs crossed so that her nightgown barely covered her thighs.

"Daddy's working on that," she said without looking up. "He's been laundering mom's money for years. There are a few hometown banks that will handle some of it. And, of course, we can always go offshore. Ever been to the Cayman Islands?"

"No," Orrie said, sliding under the sheet beside her.

"Then we should go," she said. "I've got this darling little sun suit with a matching muumuu that can easily hide a hundred grand. We used to dress the whole family up in funny outfits and smuggle a half million or so. It was a bonding experience."

Outside, near the campfire, where once there was mud and squalor and vomit and chicken bones and dirty underwear, there was a flower garden surrounded by hand-cut stones that led to the front door of the clubhouse and out to the first tee.

"I'm thinking exclusivity," Holly said, tapping a pencil against her nose. "This little one-hole golf course is a novelty. There's nothing like it this side of the Par Three Course at Augusta National. With the right kind of marketing, we could make a killing during Masters Week. We've got thousands of half-drunk, rich-ass golfers with nothing to do because Augusta is, well, you know, Augusta.

"If we get word out there's a million-dollar par-three hole within 50 miles, I bet they'll come running. We'll charge them a thousand dollars a shot. A hole-in-one wins the money, paid out, of course, over 20 years from an insurance policy. You know how hard it is to make a hole-in-one?"

Orrie thought about that for a moment and said, "Real hard. I've only got two, and I played the game all my life. Well, half my life."

That was all it took for Orrie to start slipping backwards into a place he didn't want to go. Ever since Holly entered his life, he suddenly had a life. Sure, he still smoked a pile of weed every day to ward off the pain, but it wasn't like before when he was soaking his soul in alcohol and hoping to drown.

Holly's magic potion, in addition to her undying and unexplainable love for the man she knew as Puddles, had turned him completely around. He actually took a shower every day. They bought a red VW convertible in Augusta, just for the fun of it. He let Holly cut his scraggly hair to look more like Jesus with a ponytail.

The Son of God, it seemed, was Holly's only other love. One that stirred Orrie's jealousy at first, until he realized the relationship was spiritual, and of course, platonic. The more Holly talked of Jesus walking with them through life, the more Orrie began to believe He could save his forsaken soul. After weeks of reading him scripture at night and praying on bended knees by their bed, Holly took him down to the river one morning, poured a pitcher of Healing Springs water over his head and declared him baptized in the name of the Father, the Son, and the Holy Ghost.

While Orrie had never been exposed to Christianity in his previous life, it looked as though Jesus was his new best friend. Besides Butterbean, of course. And because he couldn't imagine life without Holly Holladay at his side, he waded into her spiritual belief, arms outstretched, head held high, accepting the Lord as his Savior, because it filled an empty place in his soul where his life used to be.

But all it took was a real conversation about golf, and he would fall back into that abyss where the pain reminded him of what he couldn't do anymore. He'd trained his addled brain not to go there, but it did anyway. Back to the open fairways of Butler Bay, where he could hear the ocean rolling in and sea birds screaming overhead as he strolled to the green, lined up a putt, and stroked it in to the applause of many.

He had so much so easily so early, he never knew he should bottle it and save it for days like this. He was young. He didn't know it wouldn't last forever. Nobody cared enough to tell it him it could end. And if they had, he wouldn't have believed them anyway.

Rainy days were the worst. The tall pines and river oaks were dripping wet, the boys had dispersed, and smoke from a smoldering campfire hung low and smelled like death. That's when Orrie slipped comfortably into a place where Jack Daniels served as the doorman to his soul, which was empty.

Nobody had seen him cry since the crash. He'd hidden that emotion so well he couldn't remember where he put it. So sometimes, like a drunk searching for a bottle that didn't exist, he would rampage, ripping up sheets, throwing beer bottles, breaking mirrors.

It was on one of those rainy afternoons that Orrie came face-to-face with his loneliness. Despite Butterbean's steadfast friendship and the constant antics of the boys around the campsite, Orrie's heart ached in places other people don't even know about. Unless they grew up in a five-star orphanage.

That's how Orrie saw his childhood, perfect on the outside, hollow on the inside. Mostly because his parents, Tom and Jeannie, lived in a bottle, like those model ships you see floating on a sea of molded clay, not knowing how they got in there, or how to get out without breaking the bottle itself. Which was inevitable in their case.

Growing up the way he did, inside the bottle known as Butler Bay Golf Resort, Orrie never got a goodnight kiss. His parents were somewhat sociable in the mornings, often visiting the clubhouse where guests dined on omelets and poached eggs, stopping at their tables to chit-chat about the day ahead.

Most of the visitors were eager to tackle the wind-swept golf course that humbled the game's best players when the ocean breeze quartered in from the east.

"Let me know if you break a hundred...." Orrie's father would say as moved between the tables, back-slapping the guests. "...on the front nine," he would say as he walked away.

That would always draw a few chuckles from the happy hackers who paid hundreds of dollars a round to humiliate themselves on the links at Butler Bay. But before they could retort, Orrie's father had moved to another table where he was glad-handing some fat old fart from Philadelphia, mainly because he didn't play golf himself and only knew a few clichés.

"Hey, Angus, I hope you brought your A-game," Tom Adger would say. Or, "I heard Vernon here shot his age yesterday. He looks good for a guy who's 153 years old, doesn't he?"

That was the father Orrie wished he'd had. The real Tom Adger would disappear behind a curtain of bourbon by noon and never had a good word to say about anything his son did or said.

His mother was even worse. Fragile as the crystal wine glass she kept at her bedside, Jeannie Adger seldom left her bedroom, pulling the curtains that blocked the view of the ocean, chain-smoking unfiltered Chesterfields, sometimes spilling pills on the floor.

When Orrie was little, he'd sneak into her bedroom and carefully lift her eyelid to see if she was still alive. Sometimes he wasn't sure. Truth be told, didn't care.

He was raised by Eartha, the house maid, and Butterbean, down at the caddie shack, adrift between the islands of playschool and puberty, tossed in the turbulent ocean of indifference.

And so it was that golf became his world, his only solace. Until tragedy struck and stripped away the only love he had ever known.

Holly recognized that look on his face, the one where he was transported back in time to a place of freshly cut grass and clubs rattling softly on the hip of a caddie. She knew this by now and reached over to touch his face as he dropped his chin.

"You're the best golfer in the whole wide world," she whispered in his ear, kissing his cheek. "The best I've ever seen. The best there ever will be. And right after we turn this hell hole into an efficient enterprise, Jesus will help us get started on your comeback."

Although Orrie had read nothing in the Bible about how to fix a slice or cure a hook, he raised his head, looked Holly in the eye, kissed her sweet, sweet lips, and said, "Amen, my love, amen."

CHAPTER 44

Donald Young and his brother Dexter were identical twins on the outside, but exact opposites on the inside.

While Dexter effused friendliness and made everyone around him comfortable with a casual smile and a hearty handshake, Donald could bore a hole in the front of someone's forehead with a laser-like stare.

Which made them perfect business partners.

During the decade-long build-up to their small-town newspaper empire, Dexter charmed the villagers with his soft smile and dimples, then Donald came in and closed the deal. Much like their doubles partnership in tennis. Dexter was the one who dropped back, looping long, lazy lobs to lull opponents to sleep. Then it was Donald, the emotionless assassin, who rushed the net and slammed it down their throats.

That technique served the boys well throughout junior tennis days in the Midwest all the way to the U.S. Olympic team where they just missed a bronze medal in Barcelona.

At 6-2, 195 pounds, they were impossible to tell apart from a distance of 10 feet. Both had wavy brown hair, big shoulders, tapered waists, and huge hands that made tennis rackets look like ping pong paddles.

The only difference besides temperament was Dexter was right handed and Donald was ambidextrous, with the ability to shift the tennis racket from side to side to further confuse their opponents.

It was his big right hand that grabbed Brumby's shoulder when he uttered the words, "What if it's not true?" in reference to Cantey's dead cow story.

"What do you mean?" Brumby asked, trying to make sense of it all.

Donald Young sat back down in the leather chair next to Strom Thurmond's desk, crossed his legs and motioned for Brumby to take a seat in a similar, but smaller chair, in front.

"Jack Cantey killed those cows," Donald said, nodding toward Strom, who appeared to be asleep. "Fact is, he's the reason for all those radiation scares around the Savannah River Site. He's done this before, and each time he points to the plant and blames the government."

Brumby took that information in slowly, spun it around in his head and said, "But why?"

"Because he's a land grabber," Donald said, rising and walking over to a map of the United States on Strom's wall. "He already owns more than 10,000 acres he's bought up in South Carolina and across the river in Georgia. Everybody knows he has a lot of land, but they don't realize how much.

"In fact," Donald said, running his left hand westward on the map, "he also owns another 10,000 acres in Nevada, where he operates huge cattle enterprises that are ruining the environment."

Brumby screwed up enough nerve to stand and walk over to the map next to Donald Young, then felt the height/weight comparison and moved a few steps away.

"So, what's wrong with that?" he said. "Is he doing anything illegal?"

"Good question, Brumby," Donald said, using his nice voice to make the young reporter feel important. "The fact is, what he's doing is not illegal, it's just dangerous."

"How?" Brumby asked.

"Methane," Donald answered.

"Like gas, methane gas?" Brumby asked.

"You ever spent much time around cows, Brumby?" Donald asked, not waiting for an answer. "Cows produce more methane gas in an hour than humans do in a year. You put a bunch of cows together in one place, and you've got a real problem."

Brumby ran his fingers through his hair, thought about that for a moment and said, "So, we're talking about farts? Cow farts?"

"Flatulence," Donald said, stepping back as if he had just released some. "One of the biggest threats to our environment. Did you know that one cow emits up to 400 quarts of methane gas per day, or 50 million metric tons per year?"

"That's a lot," Brumby said, sitting back down.

"It's too much," Donald said. "All this methane is a threat to the biota. Do you know what the biota is, Brumby?"

Brumby twisted slightly in his seat and said, "Not really."

"The biota is the total collection of organisms that live in a geographic region. The flora, the fauna, the fungi, the wildlife, everything that lives in a biosphere. When you put too many methane-producing cows in one place, well, you've got an endangered biota."

About that time Strom jerked awake and started shuffling through some papers on his desk, forgetting he had guests in his office, then slowly slumped back into a near-death slumber.

"It's all about global warming, Brumby," Donald continued, ignoring the snoring senator. "This gas is clogging the system with carbon dioxide, like we don't produce enough of that already with all the cars and trucks and coal plants around the country.

"This is what I want you to write about, Brumby. I want you to go after Jack Cantey. He's not what he seems. He's killing a few worthless cows to make it look like the government's contaminating the water table around the Horse Creek Valley. He wants land prices to drop so he can buy up more at a cheaper price. He's obsessed with land and doesn't care what he has to do to get more."

Brumby was stunned and didn't know exactly what to say. Nor did he know that Donald Young's real concern had nothing to do with cow farts. What really mattered to the Young brothers was a huge herd of cattle grazing in a feed lot just north of their real estate investments outside Las Vegas. Runoff from Cantey's cows, it seems, was fouling precious water supplies from the White River, and threatened the twins' long-term investments.

"I tell you what," Donald said, motioning for Brumby to rise and walk with him toward the door at the end of the long room. "Let me buy you lunch in the Senate Dining Room, and we'll talk about specifics."

"Okay," Brumby said, somewhat confused. "They have really good cheeseburgers."

"Wouldn't know," Donald said, closing the door quietly behind them so as not to wake the senator. "I'm a vegetarian."

CHAPTER 45

Despite his spiritual progress, there were nights when even Orrie's drugs didn't work, and he'd wander around the campsite like a zombie in search of a grave in which to hide. A few months earlier, when a waxing moon hung high in the Carolina sky, he heard noises and turned toward the usually silent Salkehatchie.

As he moved slowly down the fairway, he squinted to make out two people in the river, naked, bobbing slowly up and down in the gleaming water, gently pouring water on each other. To his surprise, it was Butterbean and LeeBelle, a big woman who looked even larger with her clothes off. With bosoms the size of watermelons, she had an ample belly that became a natural inner tube holding her afloat.

Next to her was Butterbean, his blackness shining beneath the lunar reflection, his hands over his eyes as the choir lady slowly and methodically ladled the water from Healing Springs over his head with her hands.

Moving back into the shadows, Orrie watched but couldn't quite make out the words they were saying. He was too far away to make sense of the mumblings he heard emanating from the woman's mouth. She was speaking, it seemed, in a foreign tongue, one he assumed was rooted in the mysterious world of Gullah.

The white trash around the campsite didn't believe in the powers of Healing Springs. It was black magic, they thought, something left over from the old days, like voodoo and haints.

Then the wind rustled the treetops, swirled and disappeared like static on a radio, and it was dead silent. Sitting on an empty beer keg, Orrie started picking up parts of the conversation as it drifted through the still night air.

"From de depths," he heard LeeBelle say as her cupped hands let water seep through her fingers onto Butterbean's bald head. "Mudder earth she bring de depth and devilment and de light and de glory if she want. She be de healer, de doctor, de root, de decider, and de magic."

Butterbean and the choir lady were onyx and shiny as the river water swirled around their waists, trying to pull them downstream. But they were steadfast in their baptismal stance, leaning against the current like boats at anchor.

As the choir lady ladled more water on Butterbean, Orrie strained to hear the old black caddie moan in a voice he'd not heard before, a voice that sounded both spiritual and primal.

"De water be in me," Orrie thought he heard. "He come down from de hill to de valley to de head to de soul to de heart."

And then, without warning, the couple held hands and lowered themselves beneath the black water surface, disappearing like hippos, leaving only a ripple where they had been.

Orrie watched breathlessly, knowing he had to move soon or his leg would stiffen. That's when the two black figures burst forth from beneath the dark water, exhaling like whales breaching the surface.

Squirming to raise himself, he staggered and tipped over the beer keg which went rolling down the fairway, clanged against a river birch, then slid into the water downstream from the skinny dippers.

By the time the choir lady realized she and Butterbean had an audience for their midnight madness, Orrie managed to crawl up next to the building, out of sight, leaving them standing in the river, naked to the world, glistening in the moonlight.

CHAPTER 46

Nicole Davis, also known as Michelle Rivers, Rachel Rio, Starr Shine, and a few other aliases she couldn't remember, was born in Valdosta, Ga., the third of six daughters by four fathers to a welfare mother who ran a whore house and collected government disability for a work-related back injury.

Whoever her father was, he must have been one good looking son of a bitch because Nicole was drop-dead gorgeous with tits galore and a body that could stop a Mack Truck on a downhill grade.

Her early years were relatively normal as she attended a private school for girls, paid for by her mother's boyfriends. But when the boyfriends left and the money ran out, she was tossed into public schools where she learned the real meaning of life.

At 14, she left home, having been raped by an assistant principal, and took up with a drug dealer in Savannah who pimped her out for three years before she married a soldier and escaped one tragic situation for another. Sgt. Daniel Tanger was an oft-deployed paratrooper who grew up in foster homes and joined the Army to kill as many people as he possibly could, including every woman he ever met.

Nicole nearly bled to death on her 20th birthday after Tanger slit her throat in an alcoholic rage, saved only by a passerby who found her in a gutter behind a convenience store. It was during this downward spiral that Nicole vowed to become a survivor.

When discharged with a neck full of stitches and a plastic bag filled with toothpaste, antiseptic cream and aspirin, she pledged that day would be the end of her struggle or the end of her life, whichever came first.

Her first step up this long ladder of self-sufficiency was marrying a policeman, a vice cop, the kind who fall for hookers, thinking they can save them from the street. His name was Clayton. He gave her shelter and clothes, took her out to nice places, was unashamed of her past, and willing to suffer the cat calls from occasional johns who recognized her.

Except for one, whose head Clayton bashed against a concrete wall after the man licked his chops and said he could still taste the sweetness of Nicole's pussy on his upper lip. She actually married Clayton one night when they were drunk in the small South Carolina town of Groton. It was just across the Savannah River where all you needed was a driver's license to say I do.

The marriage lasted six months before Nicole was bored and took up with a bail bondsman who had more money and better access to drugs. That union, however, was also short-lived. Too many demons living in one house.

She picked up her current husband, MSgt. Dock Drayton, in some bar around Fort Stewart. She played the part of the innocent, lonesome wife, suffering while her husband was overseas, extremely well. Perfectly, in fact. Her plan was to hang on to him long enough to suck him dry. And it was working.

Now, at age 37, she still had her looks and exactly $321,645.66 in a Tallahassee bank account that only she knew existed. And she wasn't done paying herself back for all the hurt men had inflicted on her along the way.

CHAPTER 47

Macon Moses rolled off Nicole Davis with a heaving sigh that expressed his utter satisfaction.

"Lord, woman, you sure know how to make a man feel like a man," he said, falling back into the pillow, trying to catch his breath after 20 minutes of intense sex. "I think I'm in love."

Nicole, leaning over to kiss his forehead, had heard that line before. To her, love was a fruitcake passed around among acquaintances until somebody figured out it was stale.

"You're the best," she lied, as she always did to men whose egos needed stroking. "When I was lying here, waiting for you, it was all I could do not to think of you, touch myself, and shiver like a small animal in heat."

Macon Moses loved it when she talked like that. Nicole had a way of making him feel like he was the biggest, baddest stud who ever walked the earth. Of course, he didn't want to believe her lines had been practiced on phone sex and were guaranteed to please.

"I bet you were the first guy among your friends to have sex," Nicole said, rubbing her hand across Macon's chest. "How old were you, big boy?"

Macon smiled and said it was with a substitute teacher in tenth grade. She cornered him in the gym after school, took him into the showers where he screwed her standing up, then she asked for more.

Nicole laughed like a growling seductress, playing with his left nipple, saying she was a virgin until her junior year in college. That both were lying about their sexual past made little difference in a relationship built on deceit.

Moses didn't have sex until he was 19 and was seduced by his 16-year-old cousin at a family reunion. Nicole, well, she never attended college.

"You still planning to retire in a few years?" she cooed, changing the subject as she wrapped herself in a sheet and pulled away from Macon's body.

"Couple more years," he said. "I want that full government retirement package. I've got a few odd jobs I do that bring in some cash. And, I think I can qualify for a clergyman's pension if I fill out the right forms and tell enough lies."

Nicole laughed out loud when he mentioned the preacher's pay.

"I've heard you calling out to the Lord," she said, handing him a glass of straight bourbon she'd just poured from the wet bar in the condo. "But it's when you're in me, not in church," she said with a wicked laugh.

CHAPTER 48

S itting side by side on one of the largest limbs in the tree house, Holly and her mother dropped a pinch of Slave Weed into a water pipe, put fire in the hole, sucked deeply, shared it a few times, then lay back on pillows filled with Lowcountry moss and exhaled.

"That's really good shit," her mother said, letting the last organic wisps of smoke filter through her nose. "It has history and tragedy deep within it. Our customers will keep it in humidors in their libraries along Park Avenue. They'll love it with cognac in front of a fire in Aspen after a day on the slopes."

Holly's mother, despite being a humble high school teacher, possessed an amazing gift for marketing marijuana to the rich and famous. Her herbal journey began when they started throwing parties for seniors graduating from Erskine College, where her husband taught. Smoking weed with the professors became a ritual for a small group of enlightened students invited to the annual affair in the tree house, a few miles off campus.

One such student from Randy Holladay's first days of teaching was Benjamin Freid, son of a New York lawyer, who'd come to Erskine for a Southern experience. That he finished first in his class and went on to earn a master's degree from Harvard Business School was no surprise to those who knew him.

What might have shocked his peers, however, was the fact he'd run a very successful drug business from his dorm room for three years, and built on that model once he graduated.

"I'll send a sample to Ben in New York," Holly's mother said. "Once he smells it, he'll want a truckload for his Manhattan friends. They'll not only like its effect, they'll revel in the slave history behind it. They just love this kind of stuff."

Holly and her mother were of the same mind when it came to sex, pot, alcohol, and other things that should be used in moderation for recreational reasons. They even shared similar thoughts about politics, its usefulness, uselessness, its treachery and its talent for producing unexpected and unintended results.

But they had long ago agreed not to discuss religion.

When Holly was growing up, there was no mention of God or Jesus or the Bible. She didn't know how to pray. She'd never been to church. She was raised to believe in herself, her family, her friends and the good that lives inside each person she met.

Her parents explained the world in evolutionary terms, using the forest around them to make their point. The hawks, wildcats, turtles, black snakes, beetles, and ants all had a unique place on earth, as long as man didn't screw it up too much.

Holly understood and accepted their beliefs, but came to Christianity one Sunday morning while delivering honey to a friend's house. As she passed a small white church, tucked perfectly in a pine thicket, she heard organ music wafting down the dirt road that led to the open front door. She stopped briefly at the end of the road and listened as the congregation began singing an old Methodist hymn, "Church in the Wildwood."

There's a church in the valley in the wildwood,
No lovelier place in the dale.
No spot is so dear to my childhood,
As the little brown church in the vale.

Taking a few steps down the dirt road, she then heard the men of the choir come in with their bass voices.

Oh, come, come, come, come....

Then the rest of the Methodists would enter with the refrain over the continuing bass notes.

Oh, come to the church in the wildwood,
Oh come to the church in the dale.
No spot is so dear to my childhood
As the little brown church in the vale.

Mesmerized by the soft sounds and early morning light that filtered through the trees that April morning, Holly kept walking until she was at the open door, her morning shadow casting down the center aisle like an omen.

The country preacher, seeing the 16-year-old girl standing there, motioned for the congregation to keep singing and for Holly to walk to the front of the church.

Oh, come, come, come, come....

With each step she felt the warmth of the people, many of whom she knew by name, as they reached out and touched her, lovingly, without judgment, whispering kind things that fell upon her ears and kept her moving forward. That's when Jamie Norris, the minister, a man of 50, held out his arms at the altar.

Oh, come, come, come, come....

When she reached the railing, still clutching the jar of honey, she dropped to her knees on the purple velvet cushion and lifted her eyes to meet the simple wooden cross hanging from the ceiling behind the pulpit.

Without a word, the Rev. Norris laid his hands upon her flaxen hair and the choir fell silent except for three men whose voices filled the rarified air like a distant drum beat.

Oh, come, come, come, come....

"Take unto your bosom this child of God," Norris said, somehow knowing a lost soul had wandered into his church. "Let the spirit of the Lord warm her soul and replenish the love she has for mankind, granting her everlasting life in the name of the Father, the Son, and the Holy Ghost."

To which the congregation automatically responded, "Amen."

The very next Sunday, Holly was baptized and given a delicate gold cross and chain that hung around her beautiful neck, a sign of her surrender to Jesus Christ and his teachings.

Her parents did not attend. Her younger brother, Woody, stood at her side and was the first in line for the covered-dish meal following the simple ceremony.

CHAPTER 49

After lunch in the Senate Dining Room, Brumby walked with Donald Young to the Metro station where he said goodbye, still wondering about his orders to cover cow farts.

On his stroll back to the press gallery, he passed Henry Smalls on the sidewalk. His acquaintance from back home seemed preoccupied and, again, hardly noticed him.

"Henry," Brumby said, "Where you going?"

Henry Smalls was still steaming about Thomasina Lee Johnson's fleecing of the federal government when he looked up and saw Brumby.

"I'm so sick of this place I could just shit," Henry said, grateful to have somebody to whom he could bitch. "I can't believe this country has lasted as long as it has. God knows it will never make it another two hundred years. The money we throw away is un-fucking-believable...."

That's when Henry remembered he was talking to a reporter.

"What money?" Brumby asked, carefully slipping his notebook out of his back pocket.

"That bitch Thomasina Lee Johnson was just awarded more than a million bucks to retire," Henry said, his voice on edge.

"Can't wait to run that column," said Brumby, who had enjoyed writing Thomasina Lee Johnson out of office. But that was a rare victory for journalism in this town, and they both knew it. The system, they'd learned, was much bigger than they thought when they came to Washington thinking they could make a difference.

"How long have you been here?" Henry asked.

"Going on four years," Brumby said.

"Well I've been here 14, and believe me, it doesn't get any better. It just gets worse and worse. The rich get richer, and the blacks get blacker. I'm sick of it."

Brumby jotted Justin Lee Johnson's name in his notebook, stuck it back in his pocket, looked at his friend, and said, "You having a mid-career crisis, Henry? You thinking about leaving?"

The question caught Henry off guard. He'd never really thought about leaving Washington. It was his dream job. It's where he always wanted to be, near the center of gravity, the eye of the storm, and every other cliché that comes to mind.

As a young black man he'd seen Washington as a place of opportunity; a place where he could overcome prejudice, use his education, his charm, his wit, and be rewarded, appreciated, and above all, happy.

But now that he'd been through this meat grinder a few dozen times, he saw how things *really* worked. Granted, he might have been naïve when he arrived from South Carolina, but he knew politics wasn't for sissies. He thought he knew how bad it could get. But he was wrong. It's always worse than you think.

"Leaving? That's a good question," Henry said, taking a seat on a bench. "I don't know if I can do anything else. I might be ruined by this line of work. It taints you. It gets in your blood. I don't know."

Brumby said he knew how Henry felt, that his world was changing in ways he didn't like and might not be able to stomach. Then he sat down, his hand resting on Henry's arm.

"By the way," Brumby said, "you know anything about those dead cows back home?"

"You know about that already?" Henry asked.

Brumby, sensing Henry was ready to talk, nodded and pulled out his notebook.

"My boss at DOE says there's nothing wrong with the water in the Salkehatchie, and there's nothing to worry about," Henry said, rolling his eyes.

"That's funny," Brumby replied. "My new boss is saying the same thing."

As they sat there in the shadow of the Capitol, staring toward the Lincoln Memorial, they knew they were being set up.

"There's a line from an old Clint Eastwood movie," Brumby said, thinking through the situation. "I think it was called *True Crime,* or something like that. Anyway, Eastwood is this typical over-the-hill newspaper reporter — an alcoholic, burned out, a few weeks from retirement — when he gets assigned to cover an execution, and a rookie reporter is told to tag along.

"There's a point where they begin to believe the guy being executed might be innocent, so they're interviewing people, trying to get the story before he fries. Anyway, they're walking out of the room when the young reporter turns to Eastwood and says, 'You know that guy is lying, right?'

"That's when Eastwood, in his best cynical snarl, turns to the young reporter and says, 'They're all lying, son; we're just here to write it down.' That's how I feel about this fucking town. Everybody's lying, and I'm just here to write it down."

Henry nodded, and they sat for a full minute staring out across official Washington.

"Wanna go down to the Hawk and Dove, grab a beer, talk about it?" Brumby said, breaking the silence.

"Sure," Henry said. "Fuck this place and everybody in it."

Which is kind of what they had in mind.

CHAPTER 50

As Luke Thompson sat in the cramped offices of AARP, he opened an unmarked envelope that was on his desk when he arrived at work.

Inside he found a single sheet of paper, hand-typed, apparently on an old typewriter, which made it stand out in a world of computer-generated documents.

There were hardened White-Out smudges where mistakes had been covered up.

Quickly, he scanned through the list of names and dates under a typed heading, "Internal Internment Inventory: Savannah River Site," to see if anything rang a bell.

Weldon Kees, Poet, Communist, Drowned, San Francisco, 1955.
Michael Rockefeller, Suspected Spy, Stabbed, New Guinea, 1961.
Frank Morris, Clarence and John Anglin, Double Agents, Shot, Alcatraz, 1962.
Lt. J.P. Kennedy, U.S. Navy, England, plane crash, 1944.
Rocco Perri, Organized Crime, Canada, Strangled, 1944.
Flight 19 (21 Airmen), Bermuda Triangle, Drowned, 1945.
Lionel "Buster" Crabb, British Frogman, M-16 Mission, Shot, 1956.
Camilo Cienfuegos, Cuban Revolutionary, Shot Down, 1959.
Glenn Miller, Band Leader, English Channel, plane crash, 1944.

He remembered how much his mother loved Glenn Miller's band, the sound track of World War II, and stories about how he disappeared on a flight across the English Channel.

And there was a Kennedy, back during the war, in another plane crash. Why would their names be on this list? Luke tried making sense of the information but found himself lost in a graveyard filled with unfamiliar, abbreviated victims. Until his finger stopped on three names, and he trembled.

Spc4. Tatum Trinity, Cpl. Joseph Goodson, Spc4. Thomas O'Connor, Cambodia, Helicopter Crash, 1968.

He knew these men. Tatum Trinity served under his command in Vietnam, Bravo Company, 123rd Aviation Battalion, 23rd Infantry Division, where the beautiful young boy from South Carolina walked security for a group of Medevac helicopters and their pilots, of whom Luke was one.

While war was hell, it also had its wacky elements, like a company mascot named "Squeezy," a 10-foot Burmese Python that escaped when a drunken soldier opened its makeshift cage to show it off to visitors.

Tatum Trinity had been the unofficial snake charmer in camp and said he thought he knew where the reptile was likely holed up — in a clay bank near a river where they captured it. High on weed and hungover from a party the night before, he set out with two buddies to recapture Squeezy. Within the hour, they were lost in the jungle at the intersection of Genocide and Confusion at exactly the wrong moment.

Luke was flying recon that day when he came upon what would later be known as the My Lai Massacre. At the time, however, it was simply unmitigated rage and revenge. Below, in a small Vietnamese village, Luke saw American soldiers systematically executing hundreds of people — including women and children — letting them die where they fell. Outraged, he sat his chopper down between a group of fleeing villagers and a gang of soldiers hellbent on killing every last one of them.

That's when Luke came face to face with Lt. William Calley, leader of the squad, who threatened his life if he interfered.

"What's going on here, Lieutenant?" Luke shouted over the thump of his helicopter blades.

"This is my business," Calley screamed, trying to get around Luke who was guarded by his machine gunner at the helicopter door.

"What is this? Who are these people?"

"Just following orders."

"Orders? Whose orders?"

"Just following...."

"But these are human beings, unarmed civilians."

"Look, man, this is my show. I'm in charge here. It ain't your concern."

"Yeah, great job."

"You better get back in that chopper and mind your own business."

"You ain't heard the last of this."

Infuriated, Calley fired his weapon over Luke's head as he was herding panicked survivors onto his chopper. In retaliation, Luke had his door gunner spray the ground in front of Calley and his henchmen with 50-caliber rounds to scare them off.

Just as he was lifting off, he saw three soldiers come out of the brush a hundred yards to his right. It was Tatum Trinity and his buddies, lost and looking for a snake. That's when two of Calley's men instinctively turned and fired, not knowing or caring who or what they were shooting, and the three men fell like rucksacks to the ground.

Overloaded and under fire, Luke veered his chopper high and right, just clearing the trees that surrounded the killing field.

A year later, during a special closed hearing of the House Armed Services Committee, Chairman Mendel Rivers (D-S.C.), who was anxious to play down the massacre allegations, sharply criticized Luke Thompson and his crew, saying they were the ones who should be punished for turning their guns on American troops.

After an intense cover-up failed, Lt. Calley was court martialed, convicted of murder, and given a life sentence, but he served less than four years before being released.

Luke, for his part in saving the lives of numerous villagers and reporting the massacre to his superiors, was awarded the Distinguished Flying Cross, which he threw away.

He considered the entire episode a farce and the Army never accepted his story about Tatum Trinity and his two buddies, who were also murdered that day.

Officially, Spc4. Tatum Trinity, Cpl. Joey Goodson, and Spc4. Tommy O'Connor were listed as missing in action in Cambodia in a helicopter crash, which Luke knew was a lie. He told Tatum's father just that when they met a few years after the war, trying to rid his dreams of the nightmares that followed him home. The information only made Granville Trinity more irrational, and did nothing to make Luke sleep easier.

"Sarah," Luke Thompson shouted around the corner. "Where did this envelope come from? Did it come in the morning mail?"

Within seconds a young woman with bright red hair and a short, no-nonsense haircut appeared at this door.

"It was under the door when I came in this morning," she said. "Does it have a return address?"

Luke looked all over the manila envelope for any hint of origination, but it was clean except for a brown coffee cup ring on the back.

Luke sniffed the stained circle, using the only clue available.

"French press," he muttered to himself. "Colombian…possibly Ecuador."

CHAPTER 51

Butterbean fell in love with Holly the moment he heard her voice.

That was the fateful night she ended up in Orrie's bed and never left. And while many of the roustabouts that populated the encampment thought her presence would ignite a holy war with the sightless sidekick, they became instant friends when Holly knocked on his door the very next morning.

"I'm Holly," she said when Butterbean cracked open the door to his Embassy Suites room. "I'm going to be Orrie's wife. I know you have practically raised him and you're the closest thing he has to family, so I would like to ask your permission to marry him."

Butterbean stepped out of the room, closing the door quietly behind him so he didn't disturb the slumbering choir lady, and breathed deeply. Holly's essence was that of Ivory soap and summer rain.

Without saying a word, he raised the back of his right hand to her cheek, rubbing it softly, letting his fingers feel her nose and mouth before gently fingering her hair. Then his hand felt the cross that hung on her neck.

"You're a child of God," he said softly. "We don't get many of dem around here."

Holly, who was taller than Butterbean, took hold of his weathered hands, held them in hers, and said, "I am here to save your only son."

Butterbean smiled, opened his arms for a hug, and said, "What took you so long?"

CHAPTER 52

By late summer, Butterbean and Holly had initiated a supply-and-demand system that she tracked on her laptop computer. Under the old system, a lot of good weed went to waste.

But with Holly's organizational instincts and her mother's marketing connections, Slave Weed had become a booming boutique commodity selling for $1,000 an ounce in a test run in New York, where well-heeled ladies walked their pampered poodles and Wall Street wunderkinds escaped the pressures of peddling worthless paper to working people.

To date, Holly and Orrie had deposited $100,000 in each of 13 small banks in South Carolina and Georgia, all under the name Horton Smith, winner of the first Masters, carefully keeping each account within the boundaries of federal insurance coverage.

Orrie, having emerged from beneath the dark cloud of medication and madness, played the part of Mr. Smith, a well-dressed, clean-cut businessman who visited each bank, opened new accounts, and chit-chatted with pretty young tellers who whispered about him every time he walked out.

While Orrie had once been a familiar face in the area due to his early golfing lore, the fresh-faced teenager had taken on the look of a somewhat spacey, middle-aged man in a seersucker suit sporting a stylish haircut by the time Holly completed his makeover.

Granted, he was stoned to the gills, but nobody ever knew because that's the only way they ever saw him. When asked to fill out forms, he always listed his occupation as "farmer."

The wedding had been simple but elegant at the church in the wildwood on the first weekend in August, two days after Holly's 24th birthday. Her family sat on one side of the aisle. Butterbean sat on the other.

When asked who gave this woman to be wedded to this man, Holly's mother and father stood, kissed their daughter on each cheek, and responded, "We do."

The reception at the tree house was attended by a hundred people who seemed to come from everywhere and nowhere at once. No cars were allowed. Guests walked the last mile through the forest to the party and stayed until late in the evening when Holly's parents were sitting in the crow's nest, staring at the stars, sharing a hash pipe.

"I hope we're that happy," Orrie said, leaning his head on Holly's shoulder.

"Yeah," she said with a sigh. "They're so cute at that age."

That same afternoon, Granville Trinity poured Bourbon into his Cuban coffee at an outdoor café on South Beach when his cell phone rang.

"Yeah," Trinity answered, his left eye twitching behind a pair of Ray-Ban aviator sunglasses.

"Three copies," the voice on the phone said. "One delivered to the kid, one to the newspaper reporter, and one to the nuke guy in Washington."

"Good," Trinity said, looking left, then right, then left again before jamming the mini-bottle in his coat pocket. Not since he hired Roland Alstead, a private investigator, to dig deeper into the disappearance of his son had he been this close to slitting somebody's throat.

What Alstead uncovered, quite accidently, was a list the government never intended for anyone to see. In fact, he was pretty sure "official Washington" didn't know it existed.

Hired to find out what really happened to Trinity's son in Vietnam, Alstead came across an inventory of bodies buried at the Savannah River Plant. While nobody in their right mind would make such a list, the government was not always in its right mind.

By all appearances, the document was compiled by a low-level government accountant whose job it was to justify expenditures at SRS, including grave diggers. The list had been incorrectly filed along with other "Top Secret" reports from the Vietnam era that revealed how many civilians had been slaughtered by U.S. troops, mostly young soldiers shooting at anything that moved.

Of special interest was the name Spc4. Tatum Trinity. It included a report of how the young soldier was killed in a clandestine chopper crash, shot down over Cambodia, a place U.S. forces were not supposed to be.

Attached to the report was an addendum written in longhand, stating the men were actually killed by friendly fire at My Lai.

It proved everything Luke Thompson had told him years before. He still had a letter from Tatum written a few weeks before saying he was on recon duty and looking forward to his R&R in Hong Kong. A similar story checked out with one of Tatum's buddies, Joey Goodson, whose father confirmed he was told his son met the same fate.

Trinity, therefore, came to believe his son and his Army buddies had been sacrificed in a misguided cover-up, and, like many victims of the government's malfeasance, were secretly buried in a mass grave at the Savannah River Plant along with some other government mistakes.

Increasingly paranoid, Granville Trinity didn't trust the mainstream media to buy into this story. He'd met with Lee Bandy once in Washington, laid out his rambling conspiracy theory, but was given short shrift. Perhaps because his personal hygiene had been hit-and-miss lately. His drinking was out of control, he'd recently been arrested for vagrancy only three blocks from his luxury condo, and he couldn't stop crying.

Trinity was haunted by the coffin draped in an American flag that the government sent home. He remembered sitting graveside, distraught and sobbing, as a master sergeant in dress uniform handed him the burial flag, expertly folded by the seven-man Honor Guard that stood at strict attention and fired a 21-gun salute directly into his broken heart.

It wasn't until a year later that he learned the casket was empty. That's when Granville Trinity declared all-out war on his own government. That's when he picked three people to do his dirty work.

Luke Thompson was an obvious choice due to his interest in the bomb plant and his history with the massacre. Brumby McLean, he thought, already knew of his former boss' suspicions. If he connected the dots, Trinity thought, it might win the young reporter a Pulitzer Prize.

His long shot was Orrie Adger, grandson of the infamous state legislator Frank

Finklea, the man who sold the land to Nu-Chem and died with a closet crammed full of government misdeeds, mostly his own.

He didn't know if Adger knew anything about Tatum's death and disappearance, but he was the only living link to Finklea. To play this wild card, however, Trinity needed to approach young Adger carefully, knowing he was living outside the law and likely to spook easily. That's when Alstead found Leon Feinbaum, the family lawyer.

"Good, good," said Trinity, who hadn't shaved in two weeks. "The wheels are turning."

"Yes, sir, Mr. Trinity," Alstead said. "Anything else?"

"Yeah," Trinity said, grimacing between sips of his bourbon-enhanced Cuban brew. "Send a copy to that son of a bitch Robert McNamara. Tell him we're coming after his ass, too."

CHAPTER 53

Holly drove Butterbean even farther into the deep recesses behind the Pine Curtain to see a doctor. But not just any doctor.

He'd been complaining of headaches. But when Holly suggested they go into town to see a medical doctor, Butterbean's only response was, "Don't need no doctor, Miss Holly. I done seen too many of 'em in my day, and dey can't help me none. I believe in *natural* healing."

Holly, knowing that "natural healing" could only help so much, sought the advice of LeeBelle, who told them about the root doctor who lived so deep in the woods that even the most avid hunters never ventured near his abode. She said the magic man might help him control Butterbean's "absences." That's what she called those times when he slipped off into other places and times.

"I ain't know if he do dat kind of thing," LeeBelle told him. "But Miss Dora from church was having fevers and fits after her second baby, and nobody knew what to do wid her. Finally, her husband took her to da root doctor. That old man gave her something to rub on her stomach and the fevers and fits went away. I'm jus' sayin'."

So Holly drove Butterbean in her VW convertible, top down, over the concrete bridge that spanned one branch of the Salkehatchie. They both enjoyed the coolness that swept over them while they dipped closer to the water on that sweltering summer day.

Then, without warning, Butterbean dove to the floorboard and screamed as he tried to push himself deep into the small car.

"What?" Holly shouted. "What's wrong? What's wrong?"

As she pulled the car to the roadside, she tried in vain to get Butterbean's attention but he was somewhere else, eyes clinched closed, fear etched on his face. Then, out of nowhere, clutching his right leg, he let loose a blood-curdling scream.

"I'm hit!" Butterbean shouted. "I'm hit! Gawdalmighty, I'm hit!"

Orrie had told Holly about Butterbean's involuntary channeling, but she had not seen it. Now she was a witness, and totally terrified, as Butterbean became a young black boy caught in a crossfire up to his knees in swamp water, wounded in the right thigh by a Confederate bullet fired from a 4-foot-long Enfield, 58-caliber musket in the South's last-gasp effort to stop Sherman's army on its march from Savannah to Columbia.

Unable to see inside his nightmare, Holly tried to touch him, only to be rebuked by a boy who said his name was Elijah, that he'd recently fled Butterfield Plantation, but was rounded up by the soldiers in blue. Along with other escapees, Elijah was forced into a service as a tree cutter for the Yankee troops on the march.

Criticized by abolitionists for turning thousands of freed slaves away as his army marched through Georgia, Sherman changed tactics. As he pushed north, he gathered up the poor souls in his wake, fed them, handed them an axe, and sent them into battle.

What Elijah thought was freedom turned into a nightmare as he and 50 other able-bodied slaves were herded to the front lines and told to cut their way through the Salkehatchie Swamp.

To Butterbean, it was suddenly Feb. 3, 1865, the temperature had dropped overnight to just above freezing, and a steady, slanting, sleet-filled rain fell as he cowered behind a tree. That's when a hail of bullets and cannon fire from Rebel earthworks turned his world into a living hell.

It was, as one old man put it, the point of no return for cutters, who were unceremoniously marched into withering fire, axes in hand, swinging at tupelo and cypress trees as bullets ripped through the cold, wet air.

That's because there was no turning back. If they refused to go forward, Sherman's troops would shoot them. Their only hope was to cut their way through and hope to survive, if only by God's grace.

That's when the bullet tore into Elijah's leg, splattering blood in his face. He was, despite being in the safety of a bright red convertible on a clear August day, wounded, crying and begging for help. In the confusion, his cousin Quentin, two years older, tried to pull him behind a tree for protection.

"We gone make it...." Quentin shouted, trying to figure out which way to go with his wounded friend. But the options were few. Smoke from the guns hung low in the swamp and visibility was zero. The only option was straight ahead, chopping trees and hiding behind them as they fell into knee-deep water.

But just as those words left his mouth, a bullet ripped through Quentin's neck, and he fell across Elijah like a sack of wet meal. Elijah, panicked, shoved the dead weight off his legs and crawled across submerged cypress knees to escape the hailstorm of bullets.

If Elijah had lived, he might have told his grandchildren the rifle shots sounded like angry hornets as they passed above his head, most landing with a thud in the soft wood of the water-soaked swamp trees. While history has romanticized the Civil War, its skirmishes were mostly occasions of atrocious attrition. Neither side had accurate weapons or time for target practice. One Confederate officer said of these battles, "If you are a beetle on the ground or a squirrel in a tree, you are in mortal danger."

But 19th century soldiers compensated inaccuracy with volume, as both sides fed a continuous barrage of bullets that was bound to hit somebody, sooner or later. This reality was made worse by the day-to-day conditions suffered on the battlefield. Especially what was left behind by the Confederacy: barefoot, dirty, hungry, unpaid, wounded men who'd been conscripted into an unwinnable war.

It was almost as bad on the other side of the lines. Just before the first shots of this battle were fired, Union officers encouraged their men to fight, saying, "There's food on the other side of that river," which, of course, there was not.

Unable to console or control Butterbean, Holly began to cry as he howled in pain and sorrow, rubbing his head in agony. A pawn in what would be called the Battle of River's Bridge, Elijah and Butterbean were sacrificed in a senseless attempt by Southern troops to stop Sherman's troops as they sliced their way through the southwest corner of South Carolina like a cold knife of revenge.

Behind Elijah came 6,000 Yankee troops, working left and right to flank 1,600 Rebels, whose last-gasp was announced with four 10-pound parrot cannons, a few 12-pound smooth-bore Napoleon guns, and two howitzers.

Bleeding badly, Elijah dragged himself close up behind a bigger man who'd fallen across a log. There he breathed deeply, not knowing if it would be his last, and tried to decide what to do as wood chips burst from trees around him, and he heard the disgusting sound of lead slapping into already dead flesh.

Ahead were the Confederate guns, perfectly placed. While Elijah's short life as a slave was unbearable, it only became worse under Sherman.

Freezing, shivering, injured, and afraid to move, the young boy could hear the shouting sergeants sloshing through the swamp water behind him, hitching mules to fallen trees they were dragging out to construct corduroy roads for wagons and artillery to advance.

Without choice, Elijah leapt from his position, dragging his right leg, using his axe as a crutch. As he turned toward the Confederate lines, a shell ripped off his right arm, spinning him around. Stunned, he stared in stark terror at his severed hand as it sank slowly into the bloody water. Then three bullets tore into his chest as he staggered and fell, splashing in the mud, finally falling onto the sharpened abatis as others ran past him in panic and ultimately, despair.

Holly, trembling with horror, could only wait and watch as Butterbean's body experienced the pain and suffering on the side of a quiet country highway. When it was finally over, Butterbean was drenched in a sweat, his arms and legs pulled tight into the fetal position, crying uncontrollably.

CHAPTER 54

As Holly maneuvered the little convertible slowly down a weed-choked lane, she could hear tree branches snapping under her tires. She gripped the wheel tightly in both hands out of fear and concern for Butterbean. The old dirt road once led from one Indian village to another, but now was in danger of disappearing beneath a canopy of leaning sweet gums, kudzu, and Spanish moss.

"It's spooky in here," Holly said to Butterbean as she carefully steered around a rotten log. "I just hope this guy can help you."

The top was still down on the car as Butterbean sat motionless in the bucket seat, cocking his head to the right as he listened to crickets chirping deep in the dense swamp that surrounded them. He was suspicious of the claim that the root doctor could help him, but he could no longer bear the intense headaches that preceded his absences, or the total exhaustion that followed.

"Maybe we took a bad turn," Butterbean said to Holly as the jungle tightened around them. "You see anybody?"

"No," Holly said, using her left hand to flip on the car's headlights. "Maybe we should come back in the morning, you know, when there's more daylight."

As those words left her lips, a figure appeared before them in a Chicago Bulls jersey, No. 23. It hung from his shoulders to below his knobby knees. On his head sat a blue jay, and in his right hand, he held a wriggling black snake.

Holly hit the brakes and the Beetle jerked to a stop a foot or two in front of the man. Holly screamed, but the sound of her voice dissolved into the black forest like a fist in a punching bag. Before she could catch her breath to scream again, the old man leaned down, let the snake slither off into the underbrush, and raised a gnarly finger to his lips.

"Shhhhhhh!" the old man said, in a voice just loud enough to be heard over the VW's idling engine. "Da Indians are coming back."

Holly and Butterbean were completely puzzled. They could hear, smell, and taste the primal forest around them. They were deep in the swamp, where nobody goes unless they're hunting alligators or root doctors. If something happened out here, they'd never be found.

Butterbean somehow summoned the courage to say, "Dere ain't no mo' Injuns 'round here. Dey run 'em all off."

"Shhhhhhhhhhh!!" the old man insisted once more, his eyes glancing side to side as Holly killed the car engine and he stood silently in a grotto of honeysuckle and Carolina creeper. Lifting his right hand, the root doctor adjusted an earpiece in his right ear, scrunched up his face as he strained to hear, then frowned and said, "Shit! Double play. Detroit over Cleveland in da tenth. Who da hell are you?"

Holly was speechless. Butterbean was not.

"You da root man?" Butterbean asked, climbing up in the bucket seat to get his mouth over the sun visor.

"Dat what dey calls me," the old man said, removing the wire from his ear and stuffing it into the right-hand pocket of his extra-droopy North Carolina Tar Heel basketball shorts. "Whatchall need? Spirit juice? Wart removal? How's 'bout some hair of the dog?"

"What dat do?" Butterbean asked innocently.

"Nuttin' for you," the old man said with a snort. "But it sho nuff pisses off a dog."

With that the doctor turned and started walking down an ill-defined path towards what appeared to be a Winnebago covered in vines. Reluctantly, Holly and Butterbean got out of the car and followed. When they climbed up two shaky steps into the camper, what they found took their breath away.

"Dat's monkey meat," the old man said, slowly stirring a small pot over a can of Sterno. "You know dat island down 'round Beaufort? Dey brings 'em from there to the bomb plant for experimentashum. I ain't know what dey do to 'em. But da monkeys 'scapes and I catches 'em in my fox traps. Dey ain't as smart as people think."

By now Butterbean was sniffing the foul-smelling air trying to discern what the old man was having with his monkey meat entrée. He was about to say something about his diet when the blue jay on the old man's head screeched, flew off, and landed on Butterbean's hat.

"He don't like monkey meat," the old man laughed. "Makes him irregular."

Butterbean hated blue jays. They were mean and loud. But he sat perfectly still as this one nested in his old straw hat. Normally, he'd swat the obnoxious bird away. But something told him not to.

"Dey descended from da dinosaurs, you know," the old man said as he chewed and sucked the chicken bone clean. "Da longer you looks at 'em, da mo' you'll see it, plain as day."

Nothing was as plain as day to Holly, who was still getting accustomed to the gloom in the room. The more she saw, however, the more she wanted to turn and run. But, she thought, this might be Butterbean's only hope.

"Mr. Butterbean Green here needs help," she said haltingly, being careful where she stepped between pizza boxes, half a rusty wheel barrow, and some smelly old clothes. "Miss LeeBelle sent us. Said you might help cure him."

"From what, Missy?" the doctor asked. "Has he got the heeby-jeebies? Da holy-moleys? Da Runs? Da squirts? Da willies? Da red ass? Da dead eye? Or you just wants to put sumpin' down on da Braves game tonight?"

Holly looked at the old man sideways, then slowly asked, "You're, like, a bookie?"

The old man stared back at her for a considerable moment, turned his head slightly to meet hers, and said, "Root doctoring ain't covered by Medicare, Missy. A man's gotta eat."

With that the doctor sat down on a nasty sofa, snagged a chicken leg from a bucket of Church's Fried Chicken sitting beside him, sniffed it, looked at Butterbean and said, "What's wrong wich you anyway?"

"I goes off," Butterbean said, dropping his head. "Dey comes and gets me, takes me, and I ain't know why. Nobody know dat I know where I go. But I know. Mostly it's awful. But it ain't always bad. I just don't say nuttin' 'bout it 'cause, well, I just ain't got the words to tell it."

196

The old man stood up, moved closer to Butterbean, letting his eyes flutter as he reached out and touched his arm. When he did, static electricity sparked between them and Butterbean jumped back in surprise.

"I gots whatcha need, boy," the old man said, holding the chicken leg in his mouth as he looked around the room. Then he stretched to the end of the sofa and grabbed an empty Mountain Dew can that hadn't been properly recycled. Looking up at his visitors, the doctor spit three times into the can, plucked a hair from his right eyebrow, stuffed it in, chewed a fingernail off his right thumb, stuffed it in, then licked the drumstick clean, pushed it down in the can, then capped it with a wad of tobacco from under his lower lip.

Holly watched all this in disgust as the old man tied a stray shoestring around the top of the can and walked slowly toward Butterbean.

"Just wear dis magic bone 'round yo neck and dey won't take you nowhere no more," he said in a hoarse whisper. "Dey scared of dat bone. Dey knows da power. Keep it wicha, all da time. When dey comes to gitcha, you just tell 'em you ain't going and dat's all dere is to it. Dat's all you gotta do. Just tell 'em. Dey'll listen, 'cause dat bone could be deres, and dey knows it, dey fear it, and you's got it."

Butterbean felt the old man drape the shoestring over his head and clutched the can to his chest like a cross. He'd seen voodoo back as young boy on Butler Island, but wasn't sure he believed in it. Then one day, Butterbean laughed at a man wearing a cat's paw around his neck to cure the shakes. Without missing a lick, his mother swatted him with a broom and told him to never taunt the spirits or his grave would be robbed.

Recollecting the fear on his mother's face, Butterbean believed the chicken bone would help him exorcise his demons, just like he came to learn how that cat's paw cured that man's palsy, and he began to cry.

"Dere ain't no crying in voodoo," the old man said with some disgust. "Now get on outa here and tell dem spirits you ain't going next time. You just tell 'em they can't come in 'less you invites 'em in. It's all 'bout love. Dey can't go where love is. Dat's da God-spoken truth. Now get on outta here. I got a C-note on da Padres tonight on da West Coast."

Thinking the unholy ceremony was over, Holly put her arm around Butterbean and started inching toward the door. That's when the good doctor held out his hand.

"Oh," Holly said, fumbling for her purse. "How much, um, do we owe you?"

"It ain't up to me, Missy," the old man said. "Da spirits control da co-pay. But 50 dollars is reasonable and customary for a house call."

"But you ain't come to us," Butterbean broke in. "We's come to you."

"You done come to my house," the doctor said with a grim smile. "Dat a house call."

After Holly found some cash and handed it to the old man, he shooed them out the door, replaced the wire in his ear and settled back on the sofa to finish off his bucket of fried chicken.

On the ride home from the swamp, Holly looked over at Butterbean as he fingered the Mountain Dew can, kissed it, then clutched it with both hands.

"I'm sure that will help," she said, knowing the old man had prescribed the equivalent of a root doctor's placebo. "He's supposed to be one of the best root doctors around, you know."

Butterbean looked straight ahead, wiped his nose on his sleeve, and said, "I hopes so, Miss Holly. I sho hopes so."

CHAPTER 55

C harlie Wong skipped up the front steps of the U.S. Custom House on East Bay Street in Charleston, pushed open the front door, and heard his footsteps echo as he stepped into the cavernous building's hollow interior.

On the outside, the Custom House looks like the Supreme Court, the kind of 18th century architecture designed to impress regardless of functionality.

But Wong was not interested in any of the many offices that ringed the three-story interior walls where federal bureaucrats fiddled with foreign forms that flooded their in-box every day.

Instead, he walked briskly through the marbled lobby and out the back door facing the waterfront where a parking lot full of BMWs awaited shipment through the Columbus Street terminal.

The identical stone stairs on the front and back of the building bore witness to its once prominent role in the port city. Started before the Civil War, the Custom House was completed in 1879 and sat directly on the waterfront so that ships could pull in and be inspected before gaining entry or leaving Charleston.

Today, sitting on the back steps, shielding his eyes from a glinting summer sun over the Cooper River, was Doug Barnes, a CIA operative dressed like a homeless person, chewing on a sausage biscuit and sipping coffee from a Hardee's cup.

Recognizing his contact, Charlie Wong sat down and snatched a crispy hash brown from the bag at Barnes' feet.

"You're late," Barnes said without turning his head in Wong's direction.

"There was a weck on the bwidge," Charlie said, reaching for another hash brown.

"Which bridge?" Barnes fired back.

"I don't know," Charlie said. "There are bwidges everywhere awond here,"

"It's always something with you people," Barnes said, swatting Charlie's hand away from the hash browns. "Plan ahead next time. Whad'ya bring?"

"The usual," Charlie said. "Some tubing. Some metal wods. Nothing gweat."

Barnes nodded, tossed the biscuit wrappers into the brown paper bag and crushed it in his hands, then said, "Okay, log it, tag it, then get rid of it."

Charlie stared at the wadded bag, wishing there were more hash browns, letting the smell of fresh brewed coffee waft under his nose and asked, "You don't want it?"

"Hell no," Barnes said. "That stuff's hot."

"So what you want me to do with it?" Charlie asked.

"Just throw it in the river."

"Which wiver?"

"I don't know," the aging agent said with some exasperation. "Like you said, we've got rivers everywhere around here."

Then Barnes turned to Charlie, lifted his sunglasses to expose his intense eyes and asked, "Where's Moses?"

"Shacked up in Savannah," Charlie reported.

"With that woman?"

"Same one," Charlie said. "I think we weady to take her, don't you, boss?"

Barnes, who spent four years flying Marine helicopters before joining the Bureau, turned slowly toward Charlie and said, "You're not paid to think, Chink. You're paid to spy."

Charlie bristled slightly at this retort, feeling he'd earned Barnes's respect after five years of passing him clandestine information on the Custom House steps, behind Italian restaurants in West Ashley, and in plain sight along The Battery.

Indeed, his name was not even Charlie Wong. That was the name the CIA gave him to set up his restaurant in Barnwell because it sounded more Chinese than his real name, Melvin Maxwell, which they didn't know was also an alias for his given name, Wo Ja Ching.

But none of that really mattered to Charlie. As long as the bills in the bottom of the crushed up Hardee's bag had pictures of Benjamin Franklin on them.

"Is he doing anything else?" Barnes pressed, wanting to know everything about Macon Moses, his whereabouts, and his love life.

"I think he woves her," Charlie said, his words almost obscured by the horn blast of a passing container ship. "But I don't think she woves him. Charlie think she's twouble."

"No shit, Sherlock," Barnes said, looking left and right. "That's why we're following them. They're up to something, we just don't know what. Not yet, anyway. Now get outa here before I decide to have you shipped back to Beijing on one of these Chinese bathtubs."

Barnes always treated Charlie like this because that's the way he was taught to treat foreign informers. Never get to know them, his instructors preached in the old days, because sooner or later you'll start to like them, and that's never good; sooner or later you might have to kill them.

Barnes was in his late-40s and saw action in the first Gulf War, the one we won in a few weeks against a pitiful Iraqi army. He'd strafed a few columns of Iraqi troops as his squadron followed Gen. Norman Schwartzkopf's swift-moving tank corps across the desert toward Kuwait. Figured he killed a few hundred along the way.

But he'd never strangled a man and watched his eyes roll back in his head the way some of his ground-pounding buddies did. Sometimes he wished he'd pulled out his service revolver and fired a shot directly into somebody's heart so he could be sure he'd snuffed out a life. Only three more months to a retirement without a kill.

"Get the hell outa here, Charlie," he said abruptly. "Meet me next month behind the Bojangles on Savannah Highway. They've got better biscuits."

Charlie picked up the Hardee's bag as if he were gathering trash and walked back up the steps where he tossed the brown paper into a garbage can, making sure he slipped the wad of crisp hundred-dollar bills into his jacket pocket.

Next stop, Mamma Fu's Asian House restaurant in Goose Creek, also known as the Chinese Embassy of the Lowcountry, where he would deliver the bag of radiated material he always told Barnes went into the river.

In a small dark room in a non-descript cinder-block building at the Naval Weapons Station along the Cooper River, Seaman Ron Walker had been watching the two men on a screen that linked with an overhead satellite. Afterwards, he walked briskly toward the center of the room and handed a printout to Lt. J.G. Keith Namm, who studied it briefly and snarled, "Send an S.O.S. message to Langley, same old shit."

After Charlie Wong walked away, Doug Barnes spit on the sidewalk, strolled a few blocks south to Waterfront Park, leaned against a railing, looked out over the harbor, then pulled a cigarette from his sock.

"Need a light?" a man said, as he thumbed a well-worn Zippo lighter and produced a flame.

"Thanks," Barnes said, leaning in with the tip of the cigarette, hardly looking at the man who appeared at his side. As he exhaled a plume of smoke, Barnes glanced up and down the jogging paths that wound their way along the waterfront and said, "Anything new, Bernie?"

The stranger slowly removed the jacket to his blue-striped seersucker suit, draped it over the railing, looked both ways, then down at the ground, and said, "I'm supposed to ask you that question, remember?"

"Oh yeah," Barnes said, knocking some ash off the end of his smoke. "But what's this I hear about your daughter running for governor?"

Bernie Aiken was not amused by the question. His only child, Berkeley, a state legislator, had been mentioned as a candidate for governor in the next race. He advised her to stay out of politics. But she didn't listen, as usual.

"Stick to business," Bernie said, trying not to let his aggravation show. As Director of Field Operations, he'd seen guys like Barnes come and go. Double-dippers who'd slipped into the Company when it needed bodies to fight the War on Communism. Barnes was a poster child for all that was wrong with the modern spy game. Oh, how Bernie longed for the old days when agents were educated Ivy Leaguers like himself, steeled to the mission, steeped in tradition, willing to do whatever necessary, whenever necessary, without emotion, or whining.

"You're a sorry excuse for a spy," Bernie said, covering his mouth with a handkerchief he'd pulled from his back pocket. "In the old days, we'd shoot you on suspicion."

Barnes laughed a little, turned to the elder statesman of secrecy and said, "Suspicion of what?"

"Suspicion of suspicion," Bernie said, folding and refolding the handkerchief. "Didn't need much reason back then."

Barnes instinctively edged a half-foot away from Aiken, knowing the old man with the grey hair was armed and had killed more people than he dared imagine. Bernie Aiken was a legend in the Company. Old school. The kind that overthrew governments. Made people disappear. James Bond in a summer suit.

"Um, we're still getting regular reports of Chinese activity around nuclear facilities," Barnes began, suddenly doing his job. "Mostly the same players doing the same stuff. One of our guys speaks Russian. He picked up some chatter about Cuba, but he couldn't connect any dots."

Bernie Aiken listened but appeared more interested in a tour boat heading out towards Fort Sumter.

"I'm supposed to tell you we got this case we're running on a couple of guys from here who live in Washington," Barnes said. "One's a reporter for some weekly rags around here. The other works for DOE, or DOD, one of those. One of our agents gave some cash to this crazy chick who said she could tape their conversations. She's supposedly the sister to the one that works for the DOE or whatever. But she disappeared. Go figure. Anyway, it's way below your pay grade, sir, but somebody thinks they're fags, and we can use them somehow. I'll keep you posted."

Aiken had, in fact, found the tour boat more interesting than this briefing from a wino. The boat filled with chatty tourists was just the kind of target terrorists could easily attack, kill a lot of innocent people, and scare the hell out of everybody.

Then Barnes started talking again.

"Oh, and I've got this paperwork the office wanted me to give to you," he said, hoping to impress his superior. "Some kind of list. We got it off an informant who said he got it from a double agent named Alstead. We can't figure out what it means."

Barnes handed Bernie Aiken the same list of names that had been showing up in some strange places. Looking over his shoulder, the master spy scanned the page and frowned.

"Do you know what it is?" Barnes asked. "The only name I recognized was Glenn Miller, the band leader. My mom loved that guy. And I think that J.P. Kennedy might be a real Kennedy. You know, a Kennedy Kennedy. Like JFK's older brother. I thought he was killed when his plane blew up on a secret mission in World War II. Why would those guys be on this list?"

"Don't ask," Aiken said, folding the paper into his pocket then flipping the seersucker jacket back over his shoulder. "Any mention of the Middle East? Any unusual activity?"

"No, why?"

"Because your bosses are still fighting a Cold War that doesn't exist," Aiken said, dabbing the early-morning sweat forming on his brow. "While we're waiting for the Russians to attack, the terrorists are coming in through the sewer pipes."

"You mean like Arabs?" Barnes said, fingering the last inch of his smoke. "I ain't seen no towel heads around here."

"Of course not," Bernie Aiken said with disdain. "You wouldn't know a terrorist if he walked up and lit your cigarette."

Doug Barnes took a final drag and flicked the butt into the river before saying, "You mean like…."

But when Barnes turned to talk to the ageless Bernie Aiken, he was gone.

CHAPTER 56

H olly Holladay knew when she woke up that morning she was pregnant and couldn't wait to tell Orrie when she returned to Jesus Saves the next day.

For now, however, she would try to keep her secret, even from her mother, as they discussed logistics in a small café in downtown Greenwood.

"It's not about quantity; it's about quality," Holly said, knowing she was parroting the lesson she learned at her mother's side. "A pound of this stuff is easily moved and worth more than a cargo van filled with pedestrian product."

Her mother, still blonde and beautiful despite some streaks of gray in her hair, sipped on a cup of herbal tea, looked up at her daughter and said, "I'm very proud of you, Holly. I knew one day you'd turn out to be a fine judge of the bud, as well as a stealthy and wealthy distributor."

Holly let a smile spread across her face, knowing she had pleased her mother, the second most important person in her life. While she'd always been a kindred spirit with her father, she and her mother had to work harder to reach nirvana in their relationship.

Whereas her father was a wispy dreamer of golf in the kingdom, her mom was a realist, the kind who could pin-prick a party balloon before it left the ground.

"It's really quality, heirloom stuff," her mother said. "It'll bring big bucks, so you'll have to use the off-shore accounts. It's wonderful in the Caymans this time of year."

The Cayman Islands had become the vacation spot of choice for the Holladay family for the past 15 years, mainly as a depository of cash.

Like clockwork, after her parents finished their school year, she and the rest of the clan would pack up and fly to the Caribbean for vacation, always pretending to be a Mormon family from Minnesota instead of drug smugglers from South Carolina.

This meant Holly and her siblings were swaddled in heavy clothes to hide the cash strapped to their bellies beneath Mormon underwear, and they would say things like, "You betcha," and "Anyhoo," when passing through customs.

Once on the island, they'd make their rounds of momma's favorite banks, download their cargo, then hit the beaches for a week before returning to the tree house.

"This is going to be yours by yourself," her mother said. "So I'm going to call Ben in New York and tell him you're coming up with a sample. If that goes well, which I'm sure it will, you can begin shipments before Christmas."

Holly beamed as she and her mother discussed the logistics of a dope deal that would not only increase the family business, but bring them closer together as mother and daughter.

"So," her mother said, smiling as she put down her tea cup. "When's the big day?"

"Big day?" Holly asked, feigning innocence.

"You know, when's the baby coming?" she asked. "What's your due date?"

"How did you know?" Holly asked.

"Mothers know," her mother said, allowing a laugh. "I think it was last month, on a Tuesday night, when I woke up knowing my first grandchild had just been conceived."

"Really?" Holly said, totally impressed and completely exasperated.

"No," her mother said laughing. "I saw you throwing up in a barf bag in the car before you came in this morning. Dead giveaway, darling."

With that, Holly reached her hands across the table, lacing her fingers in with her mother's dirt-stained digits, and replied, "Actually, Mom, I think it's twins."

Two weeks later Holly would fly to New York to meet Ben Freid. He would handle the details of marketing this new strain of Slave Weed to his richest and most influential clients in the Big Apple.

CHAPTER 57

Back in camp, Orrie awakened with the usual sense of dread, waiting for the pain to strike when he swung his legs out of bed onto the floor. Every morning of his life began this way.

First he would slowly roll his head from left to right to see how much collateral damage had been done by the Jack Daniel's he chugged the night before. If it hurt too much, he'd roll over and try to go back to sleep.

But this morning was different. Holly had left the day before to meet with her mother in Greenwood. The room was quiet, but he could still smell her softness in the pillow and the scent of "Love Potion Number Nine" that she kept by the bedside for him to apply to his leg while she was gone.

In recent weeks, after he told Holly about the night he saw Butterbean and the choir lady naked in the Salkehatchie, his therapy had included daily walks down to the black river where he'd soak his withered leg in the cool waters that flowed slowly by the Healing Springs Baptist Church and Country Club.

Orrie, of course, was skeptical. He and the boys around the campsite had always figured Healing Springs was a myth the black folk latched onto when there was little else to believe in. Thus it was with some astonishment that the first touch of his left foot was not followed by a jab of pain that usually ran up his leg and laid him back in bed, sweating for a moment, before trying it again. This time, almost without noticing, he placed his foot on the floor and it touched without igniting the forest fire.

Unconvinced, he lifted his leg and replaced his foot on the floor, feeling the same thing. Nothing.

Then with a quick roll, Orrie swung his entire body around on the bed, placing both feet on the floor, stood carefully, wobbling a bit, and felt that strange and long-forgotten memory of stability.

Unsure how to react, he walked slowly but surely into the next room and back, ending his stroll by sitting back on the bed, waiting for the pain train.

But it did not come. Maybe it was just late. Got held up somewhere in dreamland. It had been tardy before.

He recalled being hungover and stumbling out of bed without thinking, striding steadfastly toward the bathroom to take an enormous and urgent piss, when suddenly the leg would give way and send him crashing to the floor, where he pissed anyway, while screaming in pain.

But this was different. The longer he waited for the train to show up, the more he began to think it might not. Testing the floor with his bare foot again, he stood up and took a few steps, stopped, took a few more, stopped, then turned quickly like a gunslinger and walked back to the bed and sat down.

He did this three more times before he felt the distant vibration of the train's steel wheels on the tracks, warning him of danger, and he fell back into bed with a silly grin beginning to spread across his face.

CHAPTER 58

It was becoming increasingly obvious to the forlorn and forgotten that things around the campsite were changing. Holly chased off some of the most repulsive characters, and canceled Nigger Night, much to no one's dismay. She planted a long row of marigolds and mums around the first tee, daisies down the walkways, and tulips around the perimeter to spruce the place up.

It came to pass, therefore, that a brave and refreshed Orrie Adger emerged one fateful Saturday morning from his Embassy Suites room dressed in a fresh Polo golf shirt, a pair of plaid plus-fours, knee-high socks, pure white FootJoys, and a tweed snap-cap that Holly had purchased for him at a golf shop in Atlanta.

Amid the laughter of a few hung-over halfwits, Orrie retrieved the long-maligned 1-iron from its lofty position above the pulpit bar, and walked steadfastly toward the first tee.

There were only three people still stirring around the smoldering campfire at this time of the morning: Dicky Dingle, a plumber from Snelling; Little Larry Bloodworth, an accountant with Farm Bureau; and Carl Gooding, the venerable voice of Big Dog Radio who had partied too hard the night before and slept in the hammock strung between two pine trees.

When they saw Orrie walking slowly toward the tee box, golf club in hand, they snuck up behind him as quietly as they could and waited for him to collapse as he always had before. But this time Orrie just kept walking, one steady foot in front of the other, making his way along the gravel path, feeling the first rays of a sun-splashed morning spread across his face like the hand of God brushing away the grime of years gone by.

Standing on the tee box, looking down at the small green nestled near the trickling river, Orrie took a practice swing that barely clipped the ground, causing early-morning dew to jump and dance in the brilliant sunlight.

Then, without thinking, Carl Gooding did what any good radio announcer would do in a situation like this. He started doing play-by-play, straight from the "Caddyshack" script, so quietly only he, Dicky Dingle, and Little Larry Bloodworth could hear his commentary.

"What an incredible Cinderella story," Carl began to whisper. "This unknown comes out of nowhere to lead the pack, at Augusta, on the final hole…he's about 455 yards away. He's going to hit about a 2-iron, I think."

With that, Orrie placed the face of his infamous 1-iron in front of an innocent marigold, drew the club back in a rhythmic plane to the top of the swing, moved his hips forward, rolled his feet the way Mr. Picard taught him long ago, then clipped the top of the plant as pretty yellow petals fluttered down like confetti.

"Boy, he got all of that," Carl related in a voice that mimicked the drug-laced commentary comedian Bill Murray provided in the flick.

"The crowd is standing on its feet here at Augusta. The normally reserved Augusta crowd…going wild."

As Orrie held his follow through, he sensed a new beginning within the basic cells of his body. So he stepped up to the next unsuspecting flower and took his stance.

"For this young Cinderella, coming out of nowhere, he's got about 350 yards, so he's going to hit about a 5-iron, don't you think?" Carl continued, trying not to laugh.

At that moment Orrie swung and topped another flower, spewing petals into the air as Carl said, "Oh, he got all of that one…he's gotta be pleased with that… the crowd is just on its feet here…he's the Cinderella Boy…as he lines up this last shot…he's got about 195 yards left…looks like he's got about an 8-iron."

As Orrie prepared to destroy another of God's beautiful plants, Carl whispered, "This crowd has gone deathly silent…a Cinderella Story…outa nowhere…a former greenskeeper, about to become the Masters champion."

Then the air exploded with more flowery remnants as Carl jumped up and screamed, "It looks like a mirac…It's in the hole! It's in the hole!"

While Carl had correctly quoted the lines Murray adlibbed in the movie, his punctuated pronouncement scared the hell out of Orrie, who turned a bit too quickly and felt the point of the knife deep down in his leg.

"Shit, Carl," he said, wincing and grabbing his knee. "Where the fuck did you come from?"

"Same shit hole you did, Puddles," Gooding said, standing up while brushing soot from his pant legs. "Hey, that was great, man. I haven't seen you swing a club like that since you were a kid."

Orrie took those words in like water making its way down a dying man's throat and said, "Neither have I, Carl. Neither have I."

CHAPTER 59

In the Hawk and Dove, Brumby and Henry were into their fifth beer and beginning to believe they both knew something the other didn't know about the seriousness of nuclear waste disposal.

They also began to fall into a comfort zone with each other. They'd both ordered Heinekens. They munched assorted nuts out of a bowl on the table, leaving the nigger toes until they noticed the similarity and started giggling.

"That was all I ever heard them called, too." Henry said, stifling his laughter. "I don't even know their real name."

Brumby was just as amused, holding his mouth to keep from spewing his beer across the table. "They're Brazil nuts," he said, choking back tears. "I didn't know that until last year. Guess we're both victims of our times."

In more ways than one. They were having fun, something a pudgy white boy and a mixed-race mulatto could not do back in their home state. And it gave them a chance to reflect on that moment they met when they were kids.

"You remember that time I saw you in the shower?" Brumby said, shyly. "I never forgot that moment."

Henry blushed, took a swig of his beer, and looked at Brumby cautiously.

"Me either," Henry said, looking down at his beer. "You know how it is."

The two men were about to face that moment when they heard a noisy confrontation at the front door. From the gloom of the booth beyond the bar they could see the silhouette of a woman poking her finger into the chest of a man twice her size who was trying to control her rage.

"I don't need no fucking ID to get into no fucking bar," the woman said, the words sliding awkwardly out of her mouth. "I'm a goddamn veteran, a fucking Marine, man. If this is the Hawk and Dove, then you're the sorry-ass dove and I'm the motherfucking hawk. Semper Fucking Fi, dickhead!"

Grabbing the woman by the throat, the bouncer pinned her against the wall, lifted her off the ground, and said with a discernible hint of malice, "Look, lady. I don't give a shit who you are or where you've been. You ain't getting in here acting like that. This is a respectable joint. Now shut up, or I'll call the cops."

The woman squirmed but couldn't remove herself from the man's grip and quickly settled down, almost.

"I'm looking for my brother," she rasped, as he slowly loosened his grip on her throat. "He's a big shot with the DOE. I saw him come in here. He's sitting in the back somewhere. I've gotta tell him something important."

The bouncer felt the muscles in the woman's scrawny body relax a little and said, "If you can walk back there like a lady, I'll let you go. But you better behave."

With that, Hannah Jane gathered her tits back into their bra cups, ran her right hand through her kinky hair, threw her head back, and walked to where Brumby and Henry sat.

"Oh, shit," Henry said, realizing the unpleasantness headed their way was his besotted sister. "Here," he said, handing Brumby a few 20s. "Take care of the tab. We've gotta get out of here, quick."

While Brumby signaled to the waitress for a bill, Henry stood up to head off Hurricane Hannah Jane.

"Hey there, big brother," Hannah Jane said so loudly everybody in the bustling bar could hear her. "I've been trying to call you all fucking week. You ain't returned any of my calls, you sorry sumbitch."

By then Hannah Jane had reached their table, picked up Brumby's half-empty mug of beer and downed it in a single gulp, then reached for Henry's.

"We're leaving," Henry said sternly as he gathered his things and motioned for Brumby to follow.

"Oh," Hannah Jane exclaimed, noticing Brumby. "Is this the homo they were talking about? The one nobody back home knows about? Are you boys playing footsie under the table? Getting ready for a redneck rendezvous in the bushes somewhere?"

Brumby, attempting to give the waitress the money and a tip, froze when he heard Hannah Jane's pointed assumption, looked over at Henry and said, "We're not gay. We're just friends."

"Yeah," Hannah Jane said with a snort. "And I'm not a drunk, I'm a social worker."

"You mean social drinker," Henry panned.

"Yeah," Hannah Jane said, picking up an unfinished drink from another table. "What you said."

With that Henry hurried his sister back out the door onto Pennsylvania Avenue where young congressional bureaucrats brushed by in a late-summer rain.

"What the hell are you doing up here?" Henry snarled, dragging Hannah Jane along by the sleeve of her coat. "I thought I left you in Augusta, at the VA."

"What a bunch a pansies," Hannah Jane said as she recoiled from her brother. "Say the right things and you're outa there like a church monkey checking out of a whore house."

Henry understood none of what his sister was saying, but was sure he didn't want anyone else to hear it, so he slapped her once across the face and said, "Look, bitch. I've bailed your ass out of every sewer you've fallen into because you're my sister and I'm supposed to love you. But that's down there, and this is up here. It's different up here. I live here. Now what do you want?"

Hannah Jane squinted hard at her upstanding brother, snorted, sniffled, swallowed a hunk of mucus, then said, "They're out to get you, Henry."

"What?" Henry said incredulously. "Who?"

"They. Them. The Assholes who run the world. You know, the sumbitches that screw us all. They've got a plan to use you and your friend to cover something up, blame it on you, I don't know, it's confusing. Some shit about where the bodies are buried. I just thought I better warn you, that's all."

With that Hannah Jane slumped over, and Henry let her slide ungracefully down the wall.

"But we're not gay," Henry said, looking cautiously over at Brumby. "Are we?"

CHAPTER 60

I t was mid-morning on Monday when Holly parked the red Volkswagen convertible in front of the doctor's office in Groton, set the brake, then looked both ways before opening the door. Now that she was carrying what she believed were two new lives in her womb, she was being more cautious than ever.

The idea of living the rest of her life with Orrie Adger was like a dream come true. Granted, the dream needed a little tidying up before it was perfect, but it was coming into focus, and she'd never been happier.

Despite Orrie's troubled past and medical issues, she knew his heart was good.

They had, in fact, discussed the need for Jesus in her life. How He had come to her in the church that Sunday morning. How important faith was to her, to Orrie, and now their children.

Orrie had been inside a real church maybe a dozen times in his life and didn't understand all the fuss. But if Holly wanted him to be a Christian, by God he'd be a good one.

On his birthday, Holly gave him a small gold cross on a chain, just like the one she wore around her neck. When she presented it to Orrie, he broke down and cried.

Putting his life in the hands of this beautiful woman and the Holy Spirit was a no-brainer for a guy like Orrie, who had very little brain left. The more he listened to Holly's sincere conversion, the more he longed for that kind of peace and serenity in his life.

With every passing day he felt closer to God, started reading the Bible, turning his destiny over to Jesus, putting his faith above his personal pleasures, and feeling as if he'd finally found a home for his lost soul.

So, yeah, if Holly wanted him to be a Christian, a faithful follower, a child of God, he was more than willing to be born again.

And so too, thought Holly, might his golf game.

As she approached the doctor's office, she noticed the symmetrical handicap ramps running up each side. It was balanced, stable-looking, and she mused, just right for twins.

While she'd avoided most of the morning sickness that comes with pregnancy, she needed a prescription for nausea before she flew to New York to seal the carefully crafted distribution deal.

Although she'd seen her mother work these deals with the devil, this was the first time she'd been dispatched to do the negotiating alone. It was, she thought, a major step in her mother's effort to establish an heir apparent to the family business.

So she stepped gingerly up the right-hand steps, opened the door to the waiting room, saw an open seat, and sat down.

It wasn't until the door closed behind her, squeezing out the blinding late summer sun, that she looked around the room and made eye contact with those sitting in folding chairs along the wall.

"Good morning," she said, breaking the silence. "What a great day to be alive."

That's when her eyes adjusted to the inside light, and she noticed all the other people in the waiting room were black.

Not that there was anything wrong with that, she thought to herself. She was a modern woman, raised by enlightened parents who taught her to respect all people of all races, genders, religions, and creeds.

But, even though she knew the population in the lower part of South Carolina was much higher in African-Americans than the Upstate, she was often struck by just how much higher it was.

"Everybody doing all right?" she asked out loud, trying to make conversation and reduce the stares she was getting. "Guess not, huh? I mean, we are at the doctor's office, right?"

She thought that would break the ice, but it didn't. The four old black men and three women shuffled a bit in their seats, began to whisper, and seemed relieved when the door opened and a white nurse appeared.

"Abraham Middleton," the nurse called out, not looking up from her clipboard. "Abraham Middleton."

Mr. Middleton, an elderly gentleman, reached out for his walker and slowly pulled himself up. That's when the nurse lifted her eyes and saw Holly sitting in the corner.

"What are you doing over here?" the nurse asked.

"Who, me?" Holly asked.

"Yes," the nurse answered. "What are you doing over here?"

"Over where?"

"Over here."

"Where should I be?"

"Over there," the nurse said, pointing to the other side of the building.

"What's over there?" Holly asked.

"The other waiting room," the nurse said curtly.

"Really?"

"Really." The nurse answered.

With that Mr. Middleton shuffled awkwardly across the room, and Holly gathered her things. She'd heard stories about segregation, when water fountains, theaters and doctors' offices were separated by signs for "White" and "Colored." But that was a long, long time ago.

"They took the signs down, Missy," one black lady said as Holly turned to leave, "but old ways die hard around here."

CHAPTER 61

Macon Moses had just crossed the Bluff County line back into South Carolina after a weekend of sex and drugs that left him feeling like a man who had all the answers.

As he watched the endless rows of perfectly planted pine trees go by on Highway 3, he counted his blessings: a good government job with a nice pension; a sex maniac for a girlfriend, who just happened to share his devious desire for money; a congregation of devoted disciples who provided him with even more sex and even more disposable and untaxed income; a revenue stream from more than one government, run by idiot agents who didn't know their asses from holes in the ground; and a big dick, even if it took a few prescription pills to maintain his prowess.

When he pulled into the check point at Nu-Chem to begin a day-shift rotation, he handed his ID card to the security guard at the gate.

"Good weekend, Macon?" Jesse Stewart asked, knowing the Reverend had a lively and interesting sex life.

"The Lord has blessed me," Macon said as he clipped his badge onto his shirt pocket. "The Good Lord has blessed me, indeed."

"Well," Jesse said with a snorting laugh. "All I know is that when I come back in the next life, I want to come back as you."

Macon Moses smiled at his white friend and said, "It don't work like that, Jesse. You gotta be black first, then you come back as whitey."

"How come?"

"Because that way," Moses said, "you know what you missed."

Jesse laughed as Moses drove slowly into the most dangerous compound in South Carolina with no intentions of protecting anything but his own ass.

CHAPTER 62

Henry Smalls dragged Hannah Jane around the corner to a doorway on Third Street Southeast to get out of the rain and asked Brumby to leave them alone for a while.

"Sorry about this, Brumby," he huffed. "I've got to deal with her."

"All right," Brumby said, starting to walk off toward his apartment. "But call me later, okay?"

"Yeah, sure," Henry said. "I'll call you, and we'll talk."

"About what she said?" Brumby said, fumbling with an umbrella.

"You mean the conspiracy theory?" Henry asked, catching his breath.

"Well, yeah, that, and you know, the other thing."

"Yes, that too," Henry said, turning his attention back to his derelict sister who was throwing up on the sidewalk.

"What are you doing in Washington?" he asked her as he wiped vomit from Hannah Jane's mouth.

"The VA in Augusta," she said, trying to stand up. "They transferred me to Walter Reed, you know, for extensive detox. I bribed a guard, and he let me out if I promised to come back."

"What did you bribe him with?" Henry asked without thinking.

"A blow job," she said proudly. "The universal currency."

"Okay," Henry said with some disgust. "Well, I'm taking you back to the hospital. But first you've gotta tell me about this conspiracy shit you're talking about. Where did you hear that?"

Hannah Jane stood up, dragged a sleeve across her mouth, burped, and said, "There was this guy at the VA, said he was some kind of special agent for somebody, former Green Beret, you know, the place is full of 'em."

"What did he say?"

"Well, he beat around the bush a lot, talked real loud, trying to act real important like he was big shit, you know. But when I told him you were my brother he got real quiet, said you better watch out, that you are the bait."

"Bait?" Henry said. "What kind of bait?"

"How the fuck should I know?" Hannah Jane said. "That's all he said. Maybe if I had blown him he'd woulda told me. But he wasn't my type."

"What do you mean he wasn't your type?" Henry said incredulously.

"He was one of them damn Arabic fuckers," she said, screwing her mouth up. "There's something about them sumbitches. They don't taste right."

CHAPTER 63

Brumby's hand was shaking when he tried to unlock the door to his small apartment.

As he entered the overheated room, he grabbed some mail from the box outside his door, glanced through it, noticed a plain envelope, threw it all on his desk, flipped on the air conditioner, then felt something drip on his hand. He walked into the tiny bathroom to get a towel, looked into the mirror, and realized he was crying.

Why, he thought, did she have to say gay? Why couldn't she have said that he was a murderer, or a child molester, or a spy, or a pony fucker. Anything but gay. It was a word he'd been afraid of since the first time he heard it. Because, he feared, he was.

All those nights he'd rolled around in the Murphy bed with Charlotte McKennon. Two people trying their best not to have sex for totally different reasons. She because she didn't love him. He because he didn't love himself.

Brumby went to his desk drawer and pulled out a pack of Marlboros. He hated smoking more than he hated gay people, but it was the only thing that satiated his soul at times like this, which was increasingly more often.

Moving the pile of mail, he put his feet up on the desk, lit a cigarette, and inhaled deeply, letting the smoke linger in his lungs longer than usual, allowing its poisons to penetrate the pink and perfect inlets of his respiratory system, the one part of his body he could destroy on his own without help from his father.

That Marlboro was followed by another, then another, until the sun set on Capitol Hill and he sat alone, the red glow of the cigarette the only thing distinguishing him from total darkness.

CHAPTER 64

Butterbean Green kissed the choir lady on the cheek as he always did when they finished having sex and listened as she stuffed her bra and panties with wads of cash.

"I appreciate you toting for me," he said. "We's just got so much, ain't got no place to put no mo'."

The choir lady smiled, bent down and hugged Butterbean as she put on her dress and arranged her bosoms and bustle so the bills wouldn't make noise when she walked.

"You just lay back and relax, baby," LeeBelle said sweetly. "I'll keep this for you down at the Head Start office. Nobody ever knows where money comes from or where it goes down there."

"'Course, you can keep some of it for yoseff," Butterbean said with a smile.

"I will, sweetie," she said. "I'll buy the grandbabies some clothes and get my hair done the way you like it, maybe spend a little on a new dress, you know, so you can see what you're getting for your money."

Butterbean just lay back in the bed and smiled. Ever since he and the choir lady had been doing midnight benedictions down at Healing Springs, he'd come to believe the powers of the holy water were bringing his sight back.

Whereas before he had only seen shapes and blobs and shadows, he was beginning to see colors and flashes of light, beauty where none had previously existed, except in his dreams.

"It's a miracle, I tell you," he said with a spiritual flare. "I've talked Puddles into putting some holy water on dat leg of his. Between dat and da potion Miss Holly be rubbing on him, he just might return to the land of the living 'fo long."

The choir lady chuckled as she rustled out the door.

"There wadn't nuttin wrong with you two boys that the love of some good women couldn't cure," she said.

"Praise the Lord," Butterbean said to himself. "Hallelujah."

CHAPTER 65

Jack Cantey stood at his fireplace, poured three fingers of Jack Daniel's into a glass, lifted it to his nose, inhaled the essence of the sour mash bourbon, then slugged it down in one gulp.

"You can't trust anybody but family," he said matter-of-factly to his grandson, Trey, who was sitting in a leather chair behind him. "The government will fuck you. Your friends will fuck you. Your business associates will fuck you. You can't trust any of them, you hear me?"

Trey was now 31 years old, overweight, the divorced father of three, living in a trailer house with a 23-year-old waitress, a sorry-ass coon dog, and a huffing habit that cost him $50 dollars a day for cheap canned heat.

"I hear you, Boss," Trey said, using the term of endearment everybody employed around the farm. "But what about Autry? She's family."

Jack Cantey glared at his grandson, his blood pressure rising, and said, "She ain't nothing to nobody no more, you hear me, boy? She's trash. Nothing but nigger-loving trash. Shacking up with that Macon Moses motherfucker."

Trey didn't answer that one. He'd seen his grandfather lose his temper before, retrieve a deer rifle from the gun cabinet, load and lower it, his right eye twitching as he stared through the scope and said, "Just one shot, one fucking shot. I'd bring that damn nigger preacher down with one shot."

Then he'd walk back over to the bar, pour another slug of Jack Daniel's and slump in his favorite chair.

"I'd offer you a drink, Trey, but I know you can't have none," the elder Cantey said. "I admire the way you've stayed off the stuff. More self-control than I'd have, I can tell you that."

Trey nodded, having smoked a joint and huffed a can of Sterno just before coming up to the big house for his weekly visit with the lord and master. After losing his job at the bomb plant for drug use and his marriage going to hell, Trey survived off his granddaddy's largesse and what money he could make selling drugs to workers on the farm.

The only real inconvenience was not being able to drink, at least publicly, a stipulation in the plea bargain two years prior that allowed him to walk away from a felony DUI where a black teenager was killed in a hit-and-run.

That was common justice for rich white folks in these parts. And Jack Cantey fit that category, although he didn't start out rich. He built the family ranch up from 40 acres he bought with a GI loan after the war and raised prize-winning beef while eventually expanding his farm to a 3,000-acre ranch.

Having grown up the son of a traveling and often-unemployed shoe salesman, Cantey was determined to own as much land as he could, believing it to be the only thing on which a man could depend.

And while the locals knew he owned a lot of land between the Savannah and Salkehatchie, few knew of the thousands of acres in Utah and Nevada where he produced Big Macs on the hoof for the McDonald's Corporation.

"One of these days all this is going to be yours," Cantey continued, as Trey picked at a scab on his right hand. "Unfortunately, your daddy ain't worth the bullet it would take to shoot him, so it's going to fall on you to hold all this together. You up to it, son?"

Trey squirmed in the big leather chair, knowing exactly how to handle his grandfather. All he wanted to hear was how great he was and how it would be hard to follow in his footsteps, but he'd try.

For most of his life he'd followed his grandfather around the ranch learning how to clear pastureland, raise cows, cheat the help, screw a few black women on the side, and never, ever, let anybody take away the land.

He joined the Marines to be more like the Boss, but instead of heroic stories from the Ho Chi Min Trail, he got a nasty drug habit from Camp Lejeune, North Carolina.

"Oo-rah," he would say sarcastically whenever granddaddy Cantey would mention his service to his country.

"But here's what you have to know, Trey," Cantey said, putting his drink down and opening the gun cabinet. "There will always be people trying to screw you out of what you've got. It's just the way things are in this world. So you have to be on guard."

With that he slid the big deer rifle out of its slot in the cabinet, pressed the coolness of the gun barrel against his cheek, and said, "And it ain't always the ones you think. There's the run-of-the-mill crooks and garden-variety swindlers out there, but you usually know who they are and how they operate. No, it's the Jews and the Catholics, even those goddamned Mormon fuckers, and, of course, the niggers."

Trey nodded in agreement, pretending to care. He heard it all before. All he really cared about was getting high today and how he could get high again tomorrow. To him, the family ranch was a pot of gold he would someday inherit and sell off, acre by acre, just to piss off his grandfather.

"I heard Autry was pregnant, again," Trey said, knowing he was throwing gasoline on Jack Cantey's already overheated temper. "Probably Macon Moses, again."

The old man turned toward his grandson, lowered his glass to the coffee table, thought about his mulatto granddaughter, then slipped the strap of the deer rifle over his shoulder.

"I'm gonna get that black sumbitch," he said, starting to slur his words, and aiming the powerful gun around the room.

"Um, that's not loaded, is it, Boss?" his grandson asked.

"Not yet," the Boss said, almost to himself.

"Oo-rah," Trey said, halfheartedly.

"Oo-fucking-rah!" Cantey said breathlessly, clicking the trigger.

CHAPTER 66

On any given weekday morning more than half the people in this part of the South Carolina swamp turned on their radios to listen to Carl Gooding, King of the Cooter Festival.

"I didn't sleep too well last night," Carl said into the microphone that hung down in front of his easy chair in the back room of the Big Dog radio station. "I was tossing and turning and thinking about Ellie Johnston.

"I got to remembering when Ellie Johnston was Ellie Dunbar before that no-count rascal Jimmy Johnston knocked her up when she was in the tenth grade. Well, they got married, and the baby was a pretty little girl who grew up to work over yonder at the highway department giving driver's license tests to people who couldn't read or write and had no business on the highways endangering everybody's lives.

"Word is that Bobbie Jo Johnston, the aforementioned offspring, never flunked anybody on the driver's test, whether they could parallel park or speak English, didn't matter.

"Which got me to thinking…and I wish it hadn't because I need my beauty sleep…but that got me to thinking about how random life is and how the sexual activity of one horny-little high school kid can impact the South Carolina highway death rate many years down the road.

"So, I woke up this morning wondering exactly how many of you were awarded driver's licenses by Miss Bobbie Jo Johnston who wasn't exactly the best driver's license examiner the Palmetto State ever employed, and quite frankly, I got scared and walked to work."

With that the lights on the control board lit up with callers, Carl smiled, leaned back in his chair, and said, "So let's hear a little traveling music with old Bob Mitchum singing about that Thunder Road…."

Let me tell the story, I can tell it all
About the mountain boy who ran illegal alcohol,
His daddy make the whiskey, son, and he drove the load
When his engine roared they called the highway Thunder Road.

And there was thunder, thunder, over Thunder Road,
Thunder was his engine and white lightning was his load,
And it was moonshine, moonshine, quenched the devil's thirst,
The law, they swore they'd get him, but the devil got him first.

"See there," Carl said breaking into the song, "you can blame it all on that no-good Jimmy Johnston boy who couldn't keep his thing in his pants where it belonged."

Joe Moskos was driving his Ford Taurus into work while listening to Carl Gooding, knowing full well what was waiting for him on his desk.

"I wish moonshine and bad drivers were the biggest threat to our lives in this neck of the woods," he mumbled as he slowed for the security check and geared up for another day's work at the bomb plant.

CHAPTER 67

"We have two official reports on ground-water contamination and nei-ther one mentions any foreign matter in local streams," Moskos said over the phone. "Who's doing these studies, the Mickey Mouse Club?"

Henry Smalls was still in bed, nursing a hangover, rubbing his forehead with his left hand while he held his cell phone in his right. Hannah Jane was passed out on the floor of his apartment in Foggy Bottom.

There was a slight pause before he finally answered, "One was done by DOE, the other by Westinghouse, Joe."

"That figures," Moskos said. "They're the same ones who did the cancer studies and found nobody from the plant ever died of cancer! Ever!"

"I know, I know," Smalls said, switching the phone to his other ear. "It's all bullshit, Joe. You know that. The agency will never let an independent firm con-duct a study. And, hey, what if they did and it came back with the truth, that we're poisoning the planet? What do you think we're going to do about it? All it would do is set off a panic that would put us all out of work."

Joe Moskos was seven months from retirement eligibility with the federal gov-ernment and already had a job offer from Westinghouse paying almost twice what he was making to do the same job. When Westinghouse made the offer, it came in a plain manila envelope marked "Top Secret." As if double-dipping to maintain a continuum of lies was a secret in this part of the world.

"Do you know where I live?" Moskos asked Henry in a slow, but deliberate tone.

"No," Henry said, rolling back onto his pillow. "Not exactly. Somewhere around North Augusta, I suppose."

"That's right," Moskos replied. "I live in a subdivision called Atomic Acres, built in the '50s, expanded in the '60s. Nice houses, big lots. It's where all the scientists and engineers live. I'm surrounded by nuclear nerds. You know why?"

"No," Henry sighed. "Tell me why, Joe."

"Because all the smart people live upwind and upstream from this fucking place," he said, trying to contain his rage. "The poor, dumb bastards living downwind and downstream are the ditch diggers, welders and rivet counters who don't know any better."

There was another pause on the line as Henry let Joe calm down a little before saying, "Joe, we both know what's going on, and we both know we can't do a damn thing about it. So what exactly do you want me to say?"

Moskos swiveled in his chair, almost knocking over a photo of his family on the edge of his desk, then said, "Just do the press release and send it down here, Henry. No, better yet, I'll boot up the last one you did, change the date, and send it out. Same shit, different day."

"That's our motto," Henry said, trying to make Joe Moskos laugh.

It didn't work.

CHAPTER 68

Potency appeared unannounced, like a prisoner of war, almost unrecognizable, slope-shouldered and half-forgotten, on the doorstep of a weeping widow-in-waiting, who didn't know what to say, how to act, or exactly what to do after going so long without hope.

It was almost a year after the accident before Orrie even knew he was impotent. Other areas of his body screamed louder, demanding morphine, oozing blood, doubling him over in pain, night after night.

That moment of recognition finally came when Camille, his physical therapist, wore a particularly low-cut T-shirt one day, bent down in front of him, showed her magnificent breasts to the world, including Orrie, and nothing happened.

It just so happened he wasn't racked with pain at that particular instant and had a chance to stare at her cleavage the way a puppy is hypnotized by a handkerchief.

He remembered that every part of his body responded to that stimulus except the part that was supposed to respond. Visually, he noticed it. Mentally, he wanted it. But physically, there was nothing. Nothing at all.

Over time, the prescription pills and Slave Weed, combined with lots of booze, erased all memory of what was missing. And, eventually, when there were no signs of life, the emotional search was called off.

But suddenly there it was, shaken like a corpse, awakened from a deep sleep, stiff and erect, standing at attention, ready for action, all because of Holly and her magic potion.

Or was it just because of Holly?

Orrie didn't know or care how or why his penis had suddenly risen from the grave, but it had since become his best long-lost friend. It happened that night when Holly brought him home drunk and wasted, sponged him off, washed his nasty tangled hair, laid him down on the clean white sheets, and made love to a man who didn't know he could.

Since that fateful night, Holly upgraded his therapy to include weekly baths in warm waters from Healing Springs, a regular regimen of Love Potion No. 9, and a prescription for Viagra.

"Better living through chemistry," he said as he pulled her close and let her feel his erection against her body.

"And a little bit of voodoo," she said with a girlish laugh.

With that he rolled on top of her, pulling the sheet up high like a cape and letting it billow over their naked bodies. As it fell like a silken tent, Orrie lowered himself as he kissed her softly, darting his tongue between her lips, then thrusting it downward as his chest touched the tips of her breasts.

"I never thought this would happen again," Orrie said, breathing deeply after they fell sideways, exhausted, in the bed. "I had blocked it out of my mind. Golfers are good at that, you know."

It was the first time in almost 20 years that Orrie had referred to himself as a golfer, and it kind of caught him by surprise. "When I was playing," he said softly. "I could block out pain, noise, distraction, people, weather, everything, and just focus on the target and striking the golf ball at the exact moment with every swing."

Holly wrapped the top sheet around her curvy body, snuggled up next to him and said, "You're still the best there ever was or ever will be."

Orrie thought about that for a moment, kissed her on the nose, and added, "Was…maybe the best there ever was."

Although his love life had experienced an unexplained and miraculous renaissance, he doubted such a miracle could bring his golf game back to where it had been at its peak.

"I murdered a few mums the other day," he said softly in her ear.

"I noticed," she purred as she slid down and kissed his chest.

"And I didn't fall down," he added shyly.

"I noticed that too," she said, as her head disappeared beneath the sheet.

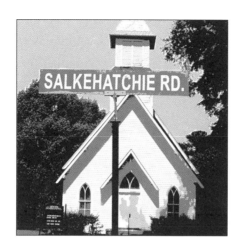

CHAPTER 69

Despite the "No Trespassing" sign that had been run over by some kids on an ATV, strangers occasionally showed up at the Healing Springs Baptist Church and Country Club, where the smell of a beer-soaked campfire always languished in the pines.

Usually the intruders were lost and could be rerouted by the end of a shotgun. But sometimes it was some outlaw lawman looking for a payoff, which he usually received.

One dreadfully hot August afternoon, Orrie was reading the Gideon Bible he found in his Embassy Suites hotel room when a dark blue Audi turned off the blacktop, onto the dirt road, leaving dust behind it like the contrails of jetliners that streaked across the southern sky.

"I heard 'em a mile back," Butterbean said, leaning over to where Orrie was sitting in a lawn chair, wearing a purple Furman Golf Team shirt, "Sounds like one of dem foreign cars. Whatcha think?"

Orrie lifted his head, then squinted into slanting sunlight.

"Cops don't drive Audis," he said, slowly standing, marking his place in Genesis with his thumb. "Better get the gun, just in case."

By the time those words left Orrie's mouth, Butterbean had already slipped back into the clubhouse and retrieved a 12-gauge Remington that he loaded and let hang by his side. By then the car pulled up under some elm trees, parked in the shade, and a man in a tan Haspel suit stepped from the driver's side.

Because it was still early in the day, there weren't many vermin hanging out, just Orrie, Butterbean and Kenneth Hunter, an electrician who was sleeping in the hammock for a few weeks because his third wife threw him out. Away from the clubhouse, two roofers were playing badminton with a lit cherry bomb, but stopped when they saw the car.

"I'll handle it," Orrie said, out of character. For years he'd never handled anything, allowing the world to come and go without any personal involvement. Partly because he didn't give a damn, and partly because it hurt too much to stand up.

As he walked slowly toward the man and the car, he noticed both were well-polished. The man, tall with thinning hair and a gray goatee, was wearing sunglasses, the loose-fitting khaki suit, a Grateful Dead T-shirt, and loafers with no socks. Before saying hello, Orrie observed another man in the passenger seat who did not get out.

"Sorry for the intrusion, Mr. Adger," the driver said calmly, raising his hands slightly to show he meant no harm. "I would have called ahead, but you weren't listed in the book."

"No phone," Orrie said politely, knowing Butterbean was holding the shotgun behind him.

"Allow me to introduce myself," the driver said. "My name is Leon Feinbaum. I'm an attorney from Charleston. I've been trying to track you down for a few months."

"Been right here the whole time," Orrie said cautiously, having little use for lawyers. "What can I do for you...Mr. Feinbaum, is it?"

"Does my name sound familiar to you?" the driver asked, removing his sunglasses to reveal a pair of piercing brown eyes.

"Sorta."

"Maybe not," Leon said, folding the glasses into his top coat pocket. "Your father and I attended the same institution."

"My father's dead," Orrie said matter-of-factly.

"I know," Leon said. "He was a friend of mine. So was your mother."

"She's dead, too."

"A very sad ending for both, I'm afraid."

"What do you want?" Orrie asked, getting to the point.

"I, um, have something for you," Leon said. "And I brought a friend along who would like to meet you."

"Who?"

With that Leon motioned to the man in the car who slowly opened the door and stepped out. He, too, was lean and gawky, not nearly as well dressed, with unruly gray hair and a stupid grin on his face.

"Orrie, say hello to Bill Murray."

There was a silence that seemed to last for eight or nine days as Orrie examined the man who stood before him, Carl Spackler himself, dressed in a RiverDogs baseball cap, a dark blue T-shirt, cut-off fatigue pants, and combat boots.

"I heard you guys were growing some really wicked shit out here," Murray said, dropping his lower lip the way his character, Carl Spackler, did in the movie. "Thought maybe you might spare a little. I've got money. I've got a part-time job."

"Yeah, I know," Orrie said, stifling an impromptu laugh. "You're a famous actor."

"No, no, not that," Murray said, staying in character. "I'm working with Mike Williams, you know, the groundskeeper down at Joe Riley Park. He lets me cut the grass, water down the infield before games, pull the tarp, stuff like that."

"Bill's also part owner of the team," Leon added modestly.

"So, you live in Charleston?" Orrie asked. "I used to live there."

"Well, sorta," Murray said, shuffling his feet. "I'm kind of a drifter. My kids and my ex-wife live in Charleston. I commute between there and the planet Zenon."

"Then you've come to the right place," Orrie said, pulling out a joint he had stuck behind his ear. "We're kind of extraterrestrial around here, too."

"So I've heard," Murray said, looking around the place. "So I've heard."

CHAPTER 70

For the next three hours, Orrie, Butterbean, Leon, and Carl Spackler sat around on paint buckets smoking Slave Weed and laughing their asses off as they used the front of the Bible to roll joints.

"You know I never liked Chevy Chase," Murray said, letting the smoke from a toke drift from his mouth up into his nose. "We had an argument back during the Saturday Night Live days. It got kinda ugly."

"What about?" Orrie asked.

"Seems like Chevy threw a pissed-off ferret into my dressing room," Murray said, trying to recall. "Or it might have been the other way around. I forget shit, you know. Seems like we were both pretty high at the time."

"In fact," Murray continued. "The only time the two of us are in the same scene in 'Caddyshack' is when he comes into the cave where Carl lives, and we smoke this humongous Robert Marley joint. It was all adlibbed. The whole movie was a joke. Everybody was stoned except Ted Knight, who got pretty tired of our shit after a while."

Butterbean had been quiet during all these rowdy remembrances, but after a while he spoke up saying, "Mr. Murray, Mr. Murray, I really like 'Caddyshack' and all dat, man, but I gots to aks you one question."

"What's that, Mr. Bean?" Murray slurred. "Or may I call you Butter?"

"How comes deys only one black man in dat whole damn movie? The only time you see a brother is when Rodney Dangerfield runs over dis Steppen-Fetchit character with his damn big yacht. How come dat is?"

Murray screwed up his mouth, thought about it, then said, "I thought you were blind, man. How do you know there was only one black man in the movie?"

"I just knows," Butterbean said, straightening his sunglasses.

"Well," Murray said, crossing his eyes after another monster hit, "It's because we're a bunch of rich, racist, white crackers."

Butterbean thought about that before saying, "Dat's what I figured. Kinda like dat turd floating in the swimming pool."

"Exactly like that," Murray said, blowing a smoke ring.

As that punch line rippled through the group, Orrie took the joint from Murray, pulled a huge hit, let it soak into his soul, then added, "It's still a fucking classic, man. Every golfer in the world knows every line in it. Even Tiger Woods. It's his favorite movie."

"Yeah, he told me that when we were playing together in the Bob Hope," Murray said, shaking off a shiver from the potent weed. "In fact, I'm teeing it up with him and Freddie next week at Augusta. We need a fourth. I heard you were pretty good. Wanna play?"

Orrie gagged so hard he was rendered speechless.

Here it was again, finally, an invitation to play the most revered golf course in the world. And even though he hadn't actually played in years, his beer-soaked brain suddenly connected with his marijuana mouth and said, "When?"

"Next Tuesday morning," Murray replied.

"Are you serious?" Orrie asked.

"I'm dead serious," Murray replied.

"You swear?" Orrie asked again, suddenly noticing the unopened Bible.

"I swear," Murray said, raising his left hand and placing his right hand on the Good Book.

"It's the other way around," Butterbean said without skipping a beat.

"Oh," Murray said, switching hands, then adding, "I swear to God."

To which Orrie just smiled and said, "Well, thank you, sir. Thank you very little."

And the whole group cracked up laughing again.

CHAPTER 71

By dusk a harvest moon was rising over the pine tops and Bill Murray was snoring in the hammock. Leon Feinbaum had secured a bag of Slave Weed to take back to Charleston, no charge. But there was still something he needed to discuss with Orrie.

"Can we walk down by the river and chat?" he asked Orrie, putting a fatherly arm around his shoulder. "I've got something to give you."

Having accepted the invitation to play Augusta, Orrie didn't want his crippled leg to reveal his actual inabilities.

"Maybe we can just sit on the porch," he said, leading Leon away from the campfire.

Seated in two wicker rocking chairs somebody stole from a plantation nearby, Leon Feinbaum told Orrie how he and Tom Adger met when they were patients at Hancock Hall, about the adventures they shared, how he loved his mother Jeannie, and how sad he was when the entire family fell apart.

"I started the ACLU Chapter in Charleston and helped a lot of people," Leon said. "I was a rebel back then. Now I'm in private practice and helping myself, mostly. Murray's a client. So is Pat Conroy, the author. Dan Marino, the quarterback. We all hang out in Charleston and get away with murder."

Orrie shifted in his wicker chair, trying to find a comfortable position. He vaguely remembered his father's funny Jewish friend from his childhood days at Butler Bay. But it all seemed so very long ago.

"What did you come to tell me?" Orrie asked.

"Well," Leon said, fidgeting with his wedding ring. "Personally, I wanted you to know your father loved you very much. He just had trouble showing it. He said golf stole you away every time he tried to do something fatherly with you. And then, he said, the distance became too much for him to span."

Orrie felt a tear rising in his eye and turned to wipe it away. Everything about his father was a tender topic. His mother, too. Money and madness put them at odds with a world they never understood. They were perhaps the most ill-suited couple to ever bear a child, and he was cursed with being that child.

"Okay, so you guys were buddies in the old days," Orrie said. "What's that got to do with me now?"

"Nothing really," Leon said. "I just thought you might like to know something about your dad. He wasn't a bad guy, just a man who lost his way."

There was a brief silence as Orrie absorbed this flashback into his misunderstood childhood, then said, "Is that why you came out here? To tell me that?"

"Yeah, well, that and something else," Leon said, digging into his coat pocket. "A man brought some paperwork to my law office recently and told me to deliver it to you. He said he worked for someone who hoped you might know something about it."

"Who's it from?"

"I don't know, exactly. The man wouldn't say."

"So, what's it about?"

"It took me a while to figure it out," Feinbaum said, unfolding a piece of paper. "It's weird, actually. It seems to be a list of names, you know, people from the past, who disappeared for one reason or another."

Orrie had no idea what this had to do with him, and Leon Feinbaum could tell he was confused. With good reason. So was Leon.

"So what is it?" Orrie asked. "A hit list or something? I heard old Frank Finklea was a pretty ruthless fucker."

"Actually, you're pretty close," Leon said. "It looks like a list of missing persons, you know, the kind that go missing and are never found."

"Like Jimmy Hoffa?" Orrie said, thinking he was being funny.

"Exactly," Leon said with a straight face.

"Oh," Orrie said, suddenly looking more closely at the piece of paper and the names on the list.

"It really does say Jimmy Hoffa," he said, his left hand starting to shake as he bit his lip.

"Which makes it even more interesting," Leon said, raising an eyebrow.

"How come?" Orrie asked.

"Because Jimmy Hoffa disappeared in 1975, seven years after your grandfather's death."

CHAPTER 72

Holly was shocked when she pulled up the long dirt road to the campsite and saw Orrie hitting balls on the tee box.

"Are you all right?" she asked, leaping from the convertible, running toward him.

"Almost made a hole-in-one," he said without looking her way. "Would have made it but you were talking in my backswing."

She slapped him on the shoulder, spun him around and kissed him hard on the lips.

"Does it hurt?" she asked.

"Only when I swing the club," he deadpanned. "No, actually, I've almost found a way to work around my left leg. But I think we need to go shopping. I need new clubs. These don't work anymore."

"You got a tee time?" she asked, punching him on the arm.

"Yeah, as a matter of fact I do," he said, saving the best for last. "Next Tuesday, with Bill Murray, Fred Couples, and a guy named Tiger. We're playing some goat track called Augusta National."

Holly shrieked with excitement.

"You're going to play Augusta with Tiger Woods…and Bill Murray?"

"Yep," he said, casually lining up a wedge shot to the green below. "I hear it's a pretty nice place."

"Damn," she said, stomping her foot. "That's the day I have to be in New York to meet with our new distributor."

"That's okay," Orrie said. "They don't allow women in there anyway."

With that he hit a knock-down wedge shot that skipped onto the green, took one hop, and checked up right next to the hole.

"I'm going to have to work on my short game," he said nonchalantly. "I hear the greens over there are like putting in your bathtub."

CHAPTER 73

I t wasn't until that night when they were in bed that Orrie pulled out the envelope Leon Feinbaum had delivered to him earlier that day.

"What's that?" Holly asked.

"Not sure," Orrie said. "Something that lawyer gave me. Said it might involve my grandfather and the nuke site."

"I thought you didn't know your grandfather," Holly said, staring at the paperwork.

"I didn't," Orrie said. "All I ever heard was he was a mean son of a bitch with a lot of power until he was killed by an unsatisfied constituent."

"So what's it say?" Holly asked, inching closer.

"Just some names and dates, 20 or so," Orrie said, handing the list to Holly. "I don't really understand it, but it's kinda scary."

"Your grandfather had some sneaky connections to the bomb plant, didn't he?" Holly asked.

"Yeah, something like that," Orrie said. "It was all kind of weird, hush-hush stuff. My parents never talked about it."

As she continued to study the list, a strange look came over Holly's face.

"This is a list of people buried at the Savannah River Site," she said, her voice cracking slightly as she spoke. "These people were foreign dictators, political enemies, spies, counterspies, mobsters, like Hoffa, and Communist sympathizers."

"Our government killed them?" Orrie asked, innocently.

"Somebody did," Holly said, crossing her legs.

"But why make a list? Seems kinda stupid," Orrie said, beginning to see some fear in Holly's eyes.

"I…don't…know," Holly answered, halfheartedly. "But you know that old saying about where all the bodies are buried? Apparently there's more buried at the

242

bomb plant than nuclear waste."

Orrie thought about that for a moment then remembered the truckers at the campsite talking about a place where the government was going to move all that nuke stuff, eventually.

"But wasn't all that junk supposed to go to that mountain place, Yucca Something, out west?" he asked.

"Yeah, right," Holly said, still poring over the list. "This is why they'll never move it."

Orrie looked at Holly's ashen face and asked what was wrong.

"Who knows about this?" she asked with some trepidation in her voice. "Who knows we have this list?"

CHAPTER 74

L uke Thompson also had it, but he didn't know what to do with it.

As a watchdog agency supported by grant money, his first allegiance was to his underwriters, that endless list of contributors who are usually satisfied if you attend their annual foundation fundraiser and let them show you off to their liberal friends.

But Luke knew they weren't what they seemed. Despite the façade of private money left by dead altruists hoping to change the world, they were agenda factories, filled with number crunchers and hand shakers and mind benders who played to a coveted audience of financial inbreds woven so deeply into the fabric of the government one could not exist without the other.

And in the media, he thought, what a story this would have been 20 years earlier when there was still a semblance of independent news reporting. That evaporated in the '80s and '90s. Now success only answers to a single parent, money.

Perhaps, he thought, the police. But which police? Local, state, federal, CIA, FBI, Secret Service, National Security? They hate each other, spy on each other, infiltrate each other.

After all these years, Luke had something on these bastards. After digging though tons of documents, talking to disgruntled scientists, investigating politicians, bribing interns to find out what was really going on behind the walls of government facilities, this needle simply fell out of the haystack. An unmarked envelope slid under the door.

And now that he had it, he was scared to death to use it.

CHAPTER 75

D exter and Donald Young sat like mirror images at a table in the Capitol Club on K Street, an $8-dollar cab ride from the White House.

"Is everything taken care of?" Dexter asked his brother, looking around the crowded dining room.

"Of course," said Donald, the eldest by two minutes. "We've made the financial arrangements, we've codified the deal by fax, we've even talked to the new employees and assured them everything is on schedule."

"Well," Dexter said, beginning to twist his napkin, "I just hope it doesn't turn out like the last time you made the arrangements."

Donald Young didn't appreciate his sibling's dig and let him know it by kicking him under the table with a well-placed wing tip. Then he said, "Look, little brother. None of this would be happening if it weren't for me. You'd still be sitting at home in Utah fiddling around with an editorial about recycling if I hadn't brought you along with me. So straighten your tie, sit up straight, and try to act like you're not from where you're really from."

Indeed, neither man was from where he said he was from. While the brothers presented a spiritual heritage, both had homes in Las Vegas, where their land holdings included thousands of acres outside Alamo, Nevada, within driving distance of a government project called Yucca Mountain.

While politicians in the Silver State battled over the well-being of their constituents, the Young brothers saw nothing but opportunity. They'd already bought up land where they expected towns like Alamo to expand. When Yucca Mountain ramped up for business, they planned on being the first to profit.

"Everything's going just as planned, little brother," Donald said as the twins clinked glasses of Pellegrino in a gesture of unity. "Ah, I see our business associates from Vegas have arrived."

Waving his hand towards the front of the restaurant, Donald motioned four gorgeous hookers to come to their table.

"But, but, why are there four of them?" Dexter asked tentatively.

"Two each," his brother replied. "Unless you want me to take three."

CHAPTER 76

Back on the job, Macon Moses used his cell phone to call the car lot and make sure Hoon Calhoun, his lot manager, was sober.

"You sold any cars today, Hoon?" Macon asked without saying who he was or why he was calling.

"Oh, hey, Mose, good to hear from you, you must be back from the beach already?" Hoon said, lighting up a cigar. "Hell, yeah, man, we're wheeling and dealing down here, you know that!"

"But have you made me any money?" Macon asked, wanting to know the details. "How about that Yukon, you sold that yet? That's a damn house payment for both of us if you move that sucker."

Macon Moses didn't have to explain the used car business to Hoon Calhoun, who used to sell paint thinner and hand grenades in high school. His bread and butter on this rung of the car-buying food chain was young black men with no job and no credit. They had nowhere to go except Bubba's Used Cars, where Hoon Calhoun's business cards read, "Buy Here Or We Both Walk."

When explaining his sales strategy, Hoon always used the example of a black man named Cadillac Jack who lived in a shack, but always has a shiny new car parked outside.

"It's the law of the jungle," Hoon says, waving his arms around for effect. "Every nigger knows that you can live in your car, but you can't drive your house."

With a credit line from Commercial Car Loans, Inc., which ran about 45 percent per annum, a man could drive off with almost anything on the lot. And if it came back in three months for lack of payment, even better, Hoon said. He'd make money off the repo man, the tow truck and the impoundment lot. He couldn't lose.

"We doing just fine, Mose," Hoon said. "We running a new radio commercial for the Labor Day weekend."

"What's it say?" Moses asked, impatiently.

"Let your neighbor do the labor," Hoon crowed as he did in the radio commercials. "You just enjoy the ride! We got them pretty Volvos the ladies like, and we got real American wheels like that Monte Carlo that you gents are so jiggy on these days. So come on down to Bubba's Used Cars where we can *save you money*!"

"That's all fine and dandy," Moses said to Hoon. "You just make sure my thousand dollars a month is ready next week, and you can croon all you want on the radio. And if you steal from me…."

"I know," Hoon said, raising his right hand and repeating the company slogan, "the man that steals from Macon Moses will have his manhood removed."

"That's right," Moses said. "It don't rhyme, but it's effective, ain't it?"

"Yessir, it sho is," Hoon said, hanging up before his boss could ask about the missing Buick.

Standing in front of him were two IRS agents who'd been looking over the car lot's books, Macon Moses' bank accounts, and his sometimes suspicious inventory.

"Local cops say that Buick Riviera was here yesterday morning," the taller agent said.

"I just don't recall that car at all," Hoon said. "Was it red, you say?"

"Red, with a white top, big shiny wheels, spinners, the kind you people like, and it's as hot as a branding iron, and you know it," the shorter man said.

"Maybe, just maybe, one of our associates simply parked a car here while in transit," Hoon lied. "And if that's the case, I couldn't really be held responsible if it happened to be stolen, could I?"

"Look, asshole, we don't really give a shit about the Buick," the tall man said, leaning close to Hoon's face. "We want your boss. He's dirty. Agencies are falling all over themselves trying to piece his network together. So, you either cooperate, help us nail his ass, or we start caring about that red-hot Riviera."

CHAPTER 77

Macon Moses hung up the phone, stared into the dark Carolina night, and thought he heard something. It was on nights like this he thought he saw Jack Cantey sneaking around the perimeter with his deer rifle. But mostly it was the unearthly sounds he and the other guards at Nu-Chem reported hearing from the nuclear burial ground.

One time Tuggy Johnson said he heard a woman singing. Rufus Montaigne said he saw a man, clear as day, walking across the field holding his head in his hands. Bunky Odom swore he heard a man begging for his life.

When their supervisors heard these stories, they wrote it off to wind in the sycamores, or swamp gas. So nothing official was ever recorded. Which was a good thing.

Moses, after all, was pretty sure a few of his customers ended up in this dump, mixed in with the radioactive generators, pipes, and assorted pieces of America's nuclear machinery.

The running joke among the guards was that the place was a burial ground for more than nuclear junk. Some referred to the western end of the cemetery as 'Hoffa's Corner." They even said Amelia Earhart might have landed in between rows F and G.

One of the older guys used to say that on stormy nights he could hear Glenn Miller's band playing in the distance. Another retired guard said he heard President John Kennedy had orchestrated a clandestine dig back in the '60s, looking for his long-lost brother.

Moses, a man of God, was edgy when it came to spooks and things that went bump in the night. All black people were. It was in their DNA to be afraid of the supernatural.

Especially when he went to what he and his buddies called "terrorist camp" at Fort Meade in Maryland. Every four years the Nu-Chem Security guards were required to undergo riot training, some pretty intense crowd-control procedures that seemed to apply more to the '60s rather than the '90s. But hey, they got paid for it.

It was eight years earlier when Moses was approached by a female instructor who took notice of his passionate delivery of a neck crunch to a fellow guard. While the mock fight was simply a training exercise, Moses's eyes narrowed, his lips pursed, and his strength multiplied tenfold when he came to what the instructors called the "time to kill."

Some people, Moses realized, were squeamish about killing, even if it was only simulated. He, on the other hand, told an instructor he wished it were real, like the Wrath of God coming down on evil-doers.

That's all it took for him to get an interview with a Marine colonel who decided to hold him over for a few more weeks of training. Thus Macon Moses was quietly transferred to Langley headquarters in Virginia where he was taught the art of elimination without detection, also known as Assassination 101.

Two months later, as an initiation, he whacked a guy outside a gay bar in Atlanta. His handlers told him wrap the body in a sheet, put it in the back of his pick-up truck, and bring it to work, which he did. When he finished his shift the next day, his truck was empty and wiped clean.

In eight years, Moses killed 15 people, which he didn't consider a big deal considering how many bad people there are in the world. And he was serving his country. At least he assumed he was serving his country. The money always came in a box delivered by UPS – $15,000 in unmarked bills. Nice and clean.

Over the years he'd gotten inventive on the job. They never told him how, just who and when, leaving room for creativity.

One guy he strangled behind a Baptist church. Another one he ran off a mountain road. A few years ago there was this woman, a beautiful bitch from Budapest or Beirut somewhere, who he kidnapped, raped, and left in a hotel room for the cleanup crew.

But sometimes he thought he heard her whimpering, you know, with that faint foreign accent. Then the wind would whisk the sound away into the swaying sycamore trees where he thought he saw Jack Cantey toting his deer rifle through the scrub brush.

CHAPTER 78

Henry threw Hannah Jane into a D.C. cab, held her down with one hand and ran the other through his hair, holding back a scream.

"Why me, why now, why ever?" he asked himself, looking over at his nasty-ass sister, passed out against the window. "And why did she have to say what she said? Where does she get this stuff?"

"Where to, pal?" the cabbie asked, not really caring about the answer.

"Walter Reed, emergency entrance," he said.

"If it's an emergency you shoulda called 911," the cabbie said.

"No, it's not an emergency, just an everyday thing," Henry said with exasperation in his voice. "She's drunk. Just get us there so I can get rid of her."

Secretly Henry wished he could get rid of his sister for good, but no matter how much she drank and whored around and got into fights, she wouldn't die. Once, he had to retrieve her from some hell-hole hotel in Edgefield where she was beaten half to death. Another time he had to go get her in Greenwood, where she had taken up with some bikers who were renting her out by the hour.

So why, he asked himself, could someone with so little credibility say something that would sting so deeply?

Just before Hannah Jane entered the Hawk and Dove, Henry had found himself staring at Brumby's hands, the way they swung from his shirt sleeve like succulent hams in a smokehouse, browned and tough on the outside, no doubt soft and tender underneath.

And, of course, he remembered that day in the showers when they seemed to have an unspoken understanding.

But Henry had always been labeled a ladies' man. Despite being somewhat short, he was popular with women because he had wavy hair, rakish dark eyes and a nice, athletic body.

The only problem was, Henry didn't know what to do with them when he got them. Sort of like the dog that chases cars. To what end?

To cover his inability to consummate a love affair, Henry would win the girls over with his charm, bring them to the boiling point, then pull the pot off the stove, sometimes saying he wanted to save himself for marriage because that's what it said to do in the Bible. This only made the girls love him more.

But he remembered Brumby, the plump melancholy loner who didn't fit into any one clique, just seemed to bounce like a pinball from one marginal group to another. And he didn't look a bit older than that day in the high school shower, when the stood naked and speechless, unable to explain what they felt.

Since then, there was always something about the way Brumby walked that made Henry take note. It was nothing terribly noticeable, just a hitch in his stride, a clever little quirk that made him look interesting from afar.

Henry was brought quickly back to reality when Hannah Jane barfed on his leg.

"Goddamnit, Hannah Jane!" Henry shouted, "What the hell am I going to do with you?'

"Hey," the cabbie yelled back through the plastic partition. "You gotta clean that up or it's an extra 50 bucks for the detailing."

"Don't worry," Henry said with irritation ripping through his voice. "It's on me, not on your seat. I'll take care of it."

But as he moved Hannah Jane over to wipe his leg with his handkerchief, he felt something in her coat pocket. Reaching in cautiously, he found a wad of hundred-dollar bills. Maybe fifty, maybe more.

"What are you doing with money?" Henry demanded in a whispering rage, trying to get Hannah Jane to wake up. "You never have money! Where'd you get this money?"

Hannah Jane rolled her eyes, finally focusing on Henry, considered the question and said, "Same place you get yours, little brother. The gubment," then passed out in his lap.

That's when Henry noticed a wire hanging out of Hannah Jane's shirt. Pulling on it, he walked it down to a tape recorder wedged in her pants.

"Shit," Henry said. "What the hell is going on here?"

When they got to Walter Reed, the nurse in the emergency room checked the computer and said Hannah Jane was not and had never been a patient there.

Disgusted, tired, and extremely irritable, Henry took a hundred dollar bill out of Hannah Jane's pocket, handed it to the waiting cabbie and said, "Take her outside the Beltway and leave her at a truck stop."

"Which one?" the startled cabbie asked.

"Doesn't matter," Henry said. "She'll get a ride home. She always does."

CHAPTER 79

Every other Wednesday, Macon Moses strolled into the Barnwell Post Office and checked Box 66, officially assigned to his mother, who'd been dead for 12 years. To cover himself, he always bought a few stamps before glancing at the little window to see if he had mail. Usually he did not. Only about twice a year did something show up. And the letters were always the same: his name typed on the outside, no postage, no return address, just an envelope, a name, an address, and a deadline.

Moses assumed the letters came from someone deep in the bowels of the intelligence community. He never knew who, nor did he care. At first he spent the money on wine, women and new trucks. But that was drawing attention. He decided to invest the cash in the stock market, which was earning him some nice returns for his early retirement.

On a recent Wednesday, however, he walked into the post office, spoke to Eunice behind the counter, bought some stamps, then glanced at the rented box on his way out. There, lying slightly slanted, was another envelope.

Without breaking stride, he walked casually over to the box, turned the dial – nine left, six right, two left, and it clicked open.

Moses casually stuffed it into his back pocket and walked to his truck in the parking lot where he slowly slit open the top with his thumb, then reached in to retrieve the paperwork.

As he unfolded the paper, he had to look twice before he could believe what it said:

Name: Orrin Adger
Address: Jesus Saves, SC
Deadline: ASAP

Moses read it three times before laying it on the seat, firing up the Dodge Ram, and squealing out of the strip mall parking lot, almost hitting a little old lady pushing a grocery cart.

CHAPTER 80

After dropping off a trash bag filled with useless low-level radioactive waste at the back door of Mama Fu's Asian House in Goose Creek, Charlie Wong went in the front door, paid $6.95 for the lunch buffet, filled his plate with egg fu yung and spring rolls, then grabbed a seat in the corner of the former bowling alley where he watched the restaurant crowd with intensity.

Mostly middle-class people, he concluded, much like his business crowd in Barnwell, albeit 20 times bigger. Bet they haul in a bunch of money, he thought. He must be doing something wrong. He worked his ass off six days a week in his Chinese restaurant back home and barely got by, even with his spy money.

That's because his clientele was mostly black folk, the kind who come in with six kids under 12, sit for an hour and a half, and clean out the buffet.

If it wasn't such a good cover, he'd switch to the pre-paid cell phone business, or the car title loan game. That's where the real money was. Same clientele, just more profit. They never pay those things off. They just keep coming back for extensions. And, eventually, you own them, their car, their house, everything.

Charlie was starting to think about these things because his daughter was getting close to college age. And while many young Asian students were headed off to Harvard and Stanford on scholarships, his wispy young waif of a daughter was going to be lucky to graduate from Barnwell High School.

Still, his wife wanted her to go to college, perhaps a small school like Coker in Hartsville, or Newberry, or Francis Marion, where she wouldn't be overwhelmed by the size and where the admission standards were friendlier.

"Everybody thinks our kids are computer geniuses," he complained to his wife recently. "She can't even find the Internet."

So, at 44 years old, Charlie Wong was worried about his future. His restaurant recently got a "C" rating from the Department of Health and Environmental Control. Rat droppings in the kitchen. Uncooked fish left out of the refrigerator. Hot water not hot enough. An undocumented worker. The list went on. Pretty soon, Charlie told himself, he was going to close the door on his restaurant and get a job at the bomb plant like everybody else or sell insurance. Start a less labor-intensive business. Something.

It's expensive being a spy in America, he complained to his contacts, always to no avail, which made Charlie mad. Let somebody else chop suey, he would say. Find another sucker to sell you Swanson's chicken broth for won ton soup. Charlie had a little something going with Doug Barnes and the FBI, another little something from the Chinese Embassy via Mama Fu's, but he wanted more. Much more.

And then, between bites of egg fu yung, he figured out how to get it.

CHAPTER 81

At exactly 9 a.m. the next day, Nicole Davis entered the First National Bank of Statesboro, flirted with the security guard, walked over to Bert Hawkins, the branch manager, and said she needed to finish up some paperwork on a loan and close her account because she was moving to California.

Hawkins, 26, a former offensive lineman and business major from Georgia Southern, was smitten with Nichole's long legs, husky voice, and sexual innuendos.

"How you doing, big boy?" she always said when sliding into the chair in his office. "Having any fun lately?"

Bert Hawkins always tried to act like he'd just returned from an orgy in Las Vegas when, in fact, he spent the weekend mowing his grass and renting the latest "Star Wars" movie.

"Never a dull moment," he'd say, unable to take his eyes off Nicole's well-displayed cleavage. "You know how it is."

Nicole would always lean over his desk, motion with her long fingers and painted fingernails for him to come closer, and she'd say, "Yes, baby, I do know how it is. You're not so shy when you're on the phone."

That kind of talk made Bert nervous, but he loved it.

For six months he'd been calling Nicole on the special cell phone number she'd given him. He would only dial the number when he was out in his workshop, behind his house, where he told his wife he was doing some wood work.

The wood, however, was his.

Just the sound of Nicole's voice on the other end of the phone drove him crazy. She would tell him things she wanted to do to him and he would moan, slowly driving his right hand into his pants, beneath his underwear, grabbing himself and rubbing in simulated agony.

"You want me to suck it?" she would say softly. "You want to slide it into Nichole's hot pussy, baby? I'm not sure I can handle a man like you. That's why you have so many kids, Bertram. Your wife simply can't resist you."

Bert always closed his eyes when she called him Bertram. It reminded him of his seventh-grade teacher in Valdosta, Miss Whitney, who was also black, beautiful and beyond his reach.

"Do that other thing," Bert would say quietly into the cell phone as he hid behind the lawn mower and fertilizer spreader.

"What other thing?" Nicole would purr.

"You know."

"Oh," Nichole would say in mock surprise. "You want me to roll over, is that what you want, Bertram?"

At this point Bert would close his eyes and envision Nichole's beautiful ass in his hands, her hands reaching back for him, her groans and moans filling his mind where once there was the image of his wife, Rachael, and their three children.

"Yes," he would respond with a raspy voice, getting a firmer grip. "Then, please say…it."

Nicole would light a cigarette, exhale away from the receiver, and begin, "You know how I like it, Bertram. You know where to put it, baby. Just give it to me. I'm so wet. I'm so hot. Please, Bertram, baby, please, baby, please…."

And then there would be silence, followed by deep breathing, and Bert would sigh, "Oh, my God…oh, my *God*."

After a while, Nicole would come back on the line and say, "You okay, baby? You were so, so good. Was it good for you, baby?"

"Oh, yeah," Bert would say, zipping up his pants. "That was wonderful. Thank you."

"No problem, baby," Nicole would always respond. "No charge. You're special."

Which is why she was able convince Bert that Macon Moses was a soldier on yet another deployment, forge his signature on a second mortgage on the condo, and walk out of the First National Bank of Statesboro with a certified check for $200,000.

CHAPTER 82

M acon Moses pulled up to the Healing Springs Baptist Church and Country Club and parked in the spot reserved for clergy, even though no one else was around on a Tuesday morning.

Looking around the corner, he noticed the campsite was quiet, a single wisp of smoke rising from the ashes before being swept away by a southwesterly breeze.

It was so quiet, in fact, that Moses could hear the water burbling below at the curve of the Salkehatchie, where his congregation filled their water jugs and waited for miracles to pour forth from the forgiving and formidable God he preached about on Sunday mornings.

On the seat beside him was a pistol, a rope and a knife, his weapons of choice. And while he never thought he'd be working this close to home, he didn't flinch when the assignment came. Nor did he question why.

A soldier, he reminded himself, never asks why, just when, and who, and he knew the answer to that question already. And somewhere deep within his soulless self he was saddened. He'd seen Orrie come back to life in recent months. He'd met and liked Holly, Orrie's new wife, a knockout he hardly deserved.

But business was business. He'd make it look like an accident. Everybody would be heartbroken when they found Orrie's shirt downstream, caught on a log. What a waste, he would say when asked to preach at Orrie's service. One of God's lambs had survived the darkness of drink and smoke and the devil's laughter, only to slip and fall victim to the very waters that brought him back to the light.

Of course, there would be no body to bury. Gators probably got him, Moses would say.

But before he could pray over Orrie Adger, he had to find him.

"You be late for church or early for choir practice," a voice behind him said, causing him to turn and crouch by training and instinct. It was, somewhat to his embarrassment, one of the young boys, Willy, who worked for Orrie and Butterbean.

"I, um, was just looking for Mr. Orrie," Macon said. "You seen him?"

"Guess you didn't hear," the boy said. "He and Mr. Butterbean left early dis morning for Augusta, says they was going to play golf at that fancy course."

"Augusta National?" Moses asked.

"Yeah, that's it," the boy said.

"Well," Moses replied, regaining his composure and walking casually back to his truck. "They say everybody should play it once before they die."

CHAPTER 83

At exactly 7:26 that morning, Orrie turned left off Washington Road into the driveway where guards in starched uniforms protect the world's greatest golf course from the world.

On this beautiful September morning, he and Butterbean had risen early, dressed in their new golf duds, hopped in Holly's red convertible, and pulled out of the campsite just as the sun was breaking over the eastern stand of pines, for the 45-minute drive across the Savannah River into Georgia.

"Dey gone let me in?" Butterbean asked, not realizing the guard was standing next to him.

"That depends," the guard said, startling the old caddie who didn't know he was so close. "If you are one Mr. Orrie Adger and you are one Mr. Butterbean Green, then we're going to let you in because your names are on this list. If you are not these two gentlemen, we're going to invite you to leave. Identification please. "

Orrie dug in his pocket for his McDonald's Fun Card that gave him a free Big Mac for every nine he purchased. As he handed it over to the guard, the VW puttered in the early-morning silence.

"You got a driver's license, Mr. Adger? Something with your picture on it?" the guard asked.

"Not really," Orrie said. "You know, in all the excitement."

The guard handed the card back to Orrie, looked at Butterbean and said, "And you, Mr. Green?"

Butterbean didn't move.

"Um, sir, if I might," Orrie injected. "You see, Mr. Green is my caddie, always has been. Unfortunately, he's never actually had a driver's license because, you see, sir, he's blind."

The guard thought about that for a moment, looked down at the small black man and said, "A blind caddie? How's that?"

"I can't explain it, sir. It just is," Orrie said.

The guard looked the two over good, then said, "Wait here."

With that he stepped back into the guard shack, picked up a telephone, hit two numbers, and started speaking.

"I tolds you dey ain't gone let me in," Butterbean whispered.

"Shut up," Orrie said. "We're invited guests."

About that time the guard emerged from the shack, looked at the two vagabonds and said, "Mr. Woods said he would meet you at the clubhouse. Have a nice day, gentlemen."

With a sigh of relief, Orrie pushed the little red car into first gear, revved the engine, popped the clutch, and began what would be the most emotional ride of his life, down Magnolia Lane.

"We're really here, Butterbean," Orrie said, trying not to drive too fast. "Augusta National, and it looks even better than it does on television, if that's possible."

"Smells real pretty," Butterbean said, lifting his nose to the scent of new-mown grass and polished brass. Smells like money."

Orrie laughed as they drove a quarter mile down the gravel-packed avenue of hundred-year-old magnolias that opened to a courtyard with a circular drive around a fountain where the statue of a boy with a golf club stood in a state of eternal play.

Behind him was the real image of golf: a tall, almost skinny, light-skinned African-American who was known to the world by only one name.

"It's Tiger," Orrie whispered out the side of his mouth to Butterbean. "He's right there, man. So don't do or say anything stupid, okay?"

"Who me?" Butterbean replied.

"Yeah, you," Orrie said. "Just be cool."

"Good morning, gentlemen, and welcome to Augusta National," Woods said as they crunched to a stop in the pebbled driveway in front of the white, low-slung clubhouse.

"Hello, Orrie, I'm Eldrick Woods," he said, extending his hand. "But you can call me Tiger."

Orrie swallowed hard, pumped the hand of the famous golfer and said, "I'm Orrin Adger, but you can call me Puddles."

"I've heard all about you," Woods said, motioning for someone to come take Orrie's golf bag from the back of the convertible. "And you must be Butterbean."

"Dat's me," Butterbean said, suddenly nervous when he heard someone grabbing Orrie's clubs behind him. "Hey, where you going wid dem clubs?"

"It's okay," Woods assured him. "They're just going to take them over to the range. We'll get you a caddie suit and meet you there. Why don't you go with Herbert. He'll take good care of you. I hear there are doughnuts in the caddie shack."

Butterbean climbed out of the car and was led by a handsome young man named Herbert toward the practice range while another man who looked just like him opened Orrie's car door and said, "I'll park your vehicle, Mr. Adger."

Orrie stepped out, already wearing golf shoes, and handed the man his keys, then said, "Be real careful; it's my wife's car."

"I'll take excellent care of your vehicle, Mr. Adger," the man said. "Just one small problem, Mr. Adger."

"What's that?"

"Your shoes, sir."

"What about my shoes?"

"They're spikes, sir. We prefer that guests wear soft spikes."

"Oh, shit," Orrie slipped, forgetting that he hadn't properly updated his footwear.

"Don't worry, Mr. Adger," the man said. "We'll have them changed out, shined and waiting for you when you get to the range, if you'd like."

Orrie reluctantly took off his golf shoes and handed them over.

"Enjoy your day here at Augusta National," the man said.

"I'm sure I will," Orrie said, wide-eyed in his stocking feet, then started up the steps into the clubhouse where golf immortals live forever.

CHAPTER 84

Twenty minutes later, Holly stepped from the subway in lower Manhattan, walked into the massive lobby of the office complex, punched the button for the 94th floor, and experienced what felt like a ride at the state fair as it whisked her upward without a sound.

She'd worn a carefully chosen taupe suit, just boxy enough to hide the baby bump. Dead give-aways of her Southern Belle roots were her color-matched pumps and Coach handbag.

As she looked at the other people on the elevator, she tried not to appear as out of place as she felt. All the others were clearly New Yorkers, dressed in black, heads down into their cell phones or staring blankly at the floor numbers as they blinked by on the display screen above their heads. Indeed, there was not a sound except when a man in the rear turned the page of his *Wall Street Journal*.

"How's everybody doing?" she said suddenly, trying out a little Southern hospitality on the unsuspecting group.

Stunned, 11 heads turned immediately in her direction, but none spoke.

"It's a great day to be us, isn't it?" she said, but got nothing in return.

Undaunted, she was about to continue to embarrass them into answering when the doors opened, and she stepped off on the 94th floor.

"Nice talking to y'all,' she said, waving to the silent statues as the doors closed.

Then she studied the list of company names on the wall, and found what she was looking for: Benjamin Freid, Import-Export Inc., Suite 9406.

With 15 minutes to spare before her 8:30 appointment, Holly stepped quickly down the hallway to the ladies' room where she entered a stall, locked it behind her, hung her purse on the door, and threw up in the toilet.

CHAPTER 85

O rrie walked through the old clubhouse at Augusta National wearing no shoes and the look of awe that overcomes every first-timer who enters the building.

First there is the feeling that, hey, this is just a normal place, kind of dated, actually, like you just stepped back into the 1960s. The halls are narrow, the ceiling is low, and it smells a tad musty at first. Through the window, he saw the grand oak that stands beside the first tee, like an official starter for the ages.

Then Orrie noticed the oil painting of Bobby Jones, the grand-slam amateur who built this historic club from a former nursery with his dear friend Clifford Roberts.

Jones, it's said, was the inspiration behind Augusta National, but Roberts, a businessman, was the brains that made it all work. Together they created one of the most beautiful golf courses in the world and cleverly crafted a mystique to go along with it.

While Augusta, Ga., was a relatively unknown and uninspiring river village far removed from the beaten path, these men lured the national press to their fledgling golf tournament by calling it "The Masters" and treating the baseball-minded scribes from New York and New England like kings when they arrived by train en route home from spring training in Florida.

It was these writers, this band of gypsy storytellers including Grantland Rice and Red Smith, who built the legend of Augusta National in the nation's imagination. It was their words that transformed a routine golf tournament into golfing lore.

All by design, the historians say. It was Bobby Jones who realized lore was just a mixture of truth and fantasy stitched together by wordsmiths infatuated with themselves and their ability to exaggerate.

"I owe everything I've done in golf to E.B. Keelor and his magic typewriter," Jones once said of an Atlanta newspaperman who made his exploits famous.

Across the hallway was a similar portrait of Clifford Roberts, a stately gentleman, who, unfortunately, took his own life with a pistol down by a pond near the par-3 course that slopes gently down the eastern side of the clubhouse. Even in paradise, Orrie thought, not every story has a happy ending.

As Tiger explained the lineage and antiquity of the club and its members, Orrie realized how selfish he'd been when he was playing the game, and how little he really knew about its history. At the age of 32 and finally entering the shrine of his boyhood, he was suddenly humbled by the past his youth had ignored and what fate had stolen from his promising future.

"Thirty minutes on the range, then we'll tee it up," Tiger said. "Bill and Freddie are already out there. I'll join you shortly."

Looking around, Orrie innocently asked if that would be enough time to make their tee time, to which their starter answered, "Mr. Adger, the group playing ahead of you teed off yesterday, and the group behind you tees off tomorrow. Enjoy your round."

When Orrie was led to the immaculate driving range, he imagined what it would be like to step onto that hallowed ground with people studying every move you made.

Then he saw Butterbean, standing beside his golf bag, resplendent in the pure white jumpsuit every caddie at Augusta wore. But something distinguished Butterbean. Instead of wearing tennis shoes, like the rest of the caddies, Butterbean was barefoot. Tucked into the neckline of his white jumpsuit a green Mountain Dew can glittered in the sparkling sunlight.

"I think dey done changed from Bermuda to some kind of hybrid," Butterbean said, wiggling his toes. "I remember it was thicker before."

Orrie always listened closely to what Butterbean had to say about golf because he was always right. And, he'd actually been here before.

When Butterbean was a teenager, before the accident blinded him, he came to Augusta with his uncle Trellis, a looper at Charleston Country Club back when Mr. Piccard was there and before they converted to golf carts. It was Mr. Piccard who brought Trellis to Augusta to caddie for him, and on one such occasion he brought along his young nephew, Butterbean Green.

So it came to pass that Butterbean caddied for Cary Middlecoff, winner of the 1955 Masters, who was a very nice man who loved to talk about the golf course he was playing. That proved to be a valuable lesson to Butterbean, who soaked up every nuance of Augusta National that day, storing the memories in a place where his vision used to be.

"Don't try to stay up with dees guys," Butterbean said, handing Orrie his wedge and tossing a few range balls on the ground. "Just plays yo own game."

To Orrie's left was Bill Murray, who was striping his 3-wood down the left side of the practice range with a power fade.

"Hey, Puddles," he said, pushing a ball into place with the head of his club. "Glad you could make it. You know Freddie, don't you?"

"We've met," Orrie said, extending his hand to Fred Couples as he walked over from another hitting station on the range.

"It's been a long time," Couples said, shaking Orrie's hand. "I kinda lost track of you after your mom and dad passed. Those were some fun times at Butler Bay. I remember you won a junior title, then what happened? An accident or something, I heard. "

"Yeah," Orrie said. "It's been a while. I was in a car wreck. Sorta got off track for a bit."

"But, hey, you look great, man," Couples lied. "Where you been playing?"

"Healing Springs," Orrie said without thinking. "You probably wouldn't know it."

"It's got a signature hole," Murray butted in. "In fact, it's the only hole."

"Really?" Couples asked.

"Really," Orrie answered with a laugh. "You should come play it sometime. You'd like it."

"Yeah," Couples said, sagging back towards his hitting station. "Next time I'm down that way."

"For sure," Orrie said, swinging his new Callaway wedge to loosen up.

"You're on the tee in 10 minutes, Mr. Woods," a man in a green jacket said, and Orrie dropped the wedge and reached for his driver.

CHAPTER 86

At precisely 8:30 Holly entered Ben Freid's outer office, was greeted by his secretary Sandra, who instinctively brought Holly's favorite herbal tea and said her boss was looking forward to meeting her.

While Holly had been around the nickel-bag dope business all her life, this was her first venture into the real world of drug smuggling. While most people perceive it to be handled by a bunch of roughnecks down at a loading dock in the middle of the night, the real business of illegal drugs was conducted in high-rise office buildings where they served herbal tea, Passion Fruit, to be exact.

At 8:35 Sandra showed Holly into Freid's inner office, where he was standing next to a floor-to-ceiling window that looked out over the Manhattan skyline.

Turning, he saw the angelic figure that was Holly Holladay, extended his hand, and said, "As beautiful as your mother. So nice to meet you. Please have a seat."

He wore a double-breasted blue suit with a pale, robin's-egg blue button-down shirt that served as a perfect nest for his power-red tie that fell exactly to his belt buckle, not an inch too short, not an inch too long.

Somewhere between 40 and 50, Freid had silvery hair, kind eyes and soft hands, exactly the look you want if you're smuggling tons of illicit drugs around the world.

"A pleasure to meet you," Holly said. "My mother has told me so much about you that I feel like I know you."

"Not too much, I hope," he said with a smile. "There are aspects of our relationship that should go unmentioned in polite company."

By that Holly assumed he meant the drugs, but for a fleeting, uncomfortable moment she wondered if there was something else going on between this man and her mother.

"You've been friends for a long time, right?" she said, crossing her legs as she took her seat facing the window.

"Yes," Freid said, taking a seat at his desk, facing her. "We met at a Grateful Dead concert while I was at Erskine."

"Really?" Holly said. "She never told me that."

"It was the semester before I took your father's class. But that was a long time ago, and…."

Ben Freid stopped mid-sentence when he saw a puzzled look on Holly's face that caused him to turn quickly toward the window behind him.

In the distance, closing fast, he suddenly saw what she saw: a jet airliner, flying low, squeezing between two buildings, banking slightly.

Before either could react, American Airlines Flight 11 from Boston en route to Los Angeles, grew larger until they could see the faces of three men in the cockpit, screaming.

CHAPTER 87

A t Augusta National, everybody is treated like golf royalty, even on Tuesdays. "Now, ladies and gentlemen, in the 8:40 group, please welcome the winner of the 1997 Masters and the current 2001 Masters champion, Tiger Woods," a man in a green jacket said to a small crowd of members gathered to watch the foursome tee off.

Like a machine, Woods stuck his tee in the ground, steadied the ball atop the peg, stepped back, took dead aim with the shaft of his driver, strode forward, addressed the ball, then sent it sailing down the first fairway, over the pedestrian crosswalk to the top of the hill, just left of the gaping sand trap, an easy wedge to the green.

"And now, the 1992 Masters champion, Mr. Fred Couples," the man announced.

That's when Freddie teed up his ball, took two lazy practice swings, hitched his pants, then unleashed a graceful arc that sent his ball singing straight down the fairway, 30 yards behind Tiger.

"Now teeing off, Mr. William Murray," the man said.

Bill Murray, ever the clown, pretended to trip over his driver, which made the small crowd laugh. Then he teed it up, waggled his club, and snapped one dead left into the pine trees.

"Don't worry," he said to the audience. "I can still make triple from there."

The laughter barely subsided when the starter said calmly, "Now teeing off, former South Carolina Junior Amateur Champion, Orrin Adger."

Orrie, appreciating the fact the starter did not mention the year of his youthful triumph, stepped carefully forward, teed up his ball, looked over at Butterbean, and tried to take in all that was Augusta National on a sun-splashed September morning. Orrie noted the clock beside the first tee read 8:46, then swung with all his might, sending the ball straight down the right side where it began to draw left and landed in the fairway, just past the crosswalk.

That's when Orrie let out a sigh of utter relief, and somewhere in the lost canyons of his mind, he heard Mr. Picard simply say, "Thank you."

CHAPTER 88

At precisely 8:46 Eastern Standard Time, a fully-fueled Boeing 767 entered the North Tower of the World Trade Center at 466 miles per hour, 1,400 feet above street level, piercing deep into the infrastructure of the building before exploding in a massive ball of fire and flames.

Ben Freid, Holly Holladay, and her unborn children were vaporized an instant after they were crushed to death by the plane's impact, the first of more than 3,000 souls who would perish in the minutes and hours to follow.

By the time Orrie and Butterbean walked down the slope and up the incline on the first hole to reach his tee shot, a second plane, United Airlines Flight 175, slammed into the South Tower.

Just before both towers dramatically disintegrated, Orrie had accepted his double-bogey on the first hole after a four-putt. Then, after reaching the second green in regulation, had a reasonable putt for birdie.

That's when they all turned to watch two grim-faced men in green jackets headed their way from the clubhouse in a golf cart.

Butterbean, who had walked the green barefooted and determined Orrie's putt broke two feet to the right, suddenly perked his head up, listened to the whir of the golf cart coming fast across the grass toward them, and said simply said, "Uh-oh…dis ain't good."

"No problem," Orrie said, studying the left-to-right, downhill putt. "We've had worse, old pal."

"I don't think so, Mr. Orrie," Butterbean said. "I don't think so."

CHAPTER 89

September 12, 2001

As news of the terrorist attacks on the World Trade Center and the Pentagon continued to hold the country in a frightful and disturbing grip, Orrie, distraught and enraged over the news of Holly's death, waded knee-deep into the downstream tug of the Salkehatchie River, a bottle of Wild Turkey in one hand, a 1-iron in the other.

When the cold water engulfed his testicles he screamed skyward, cursing God in heaven for everything that came to mind.

"You do-nothing, holier-than-thou, beyond-understanding, life-everlasting, son-of-a-bitch," he swore, swaying as his golf shoes sank in the mucky matter that stirred up the silt when he staggered, one foot in front of the other, trying to keep his balance.

"Where have you fucking been? What can...I do...now? How could you...?"

An unearthly darkness swept away the slip of fading sunlight that seeped through the canopy of tree branches hugging the narrow stream, the temperature dropped dramatically, and a deep, far-away rumble vibrated through Orrie's spine.

That's when Orrie felt a presence and turned quickly to see if anyone was standing behind him. Assured that he was alone, he unleashed another unholy tirade.

"I don't care what they say about you," he screamed, taking another slug from the bottle and waving the 1-iron for effect. "I think you're a fucking phony. A figment of everybody's frightened imagination. A Goddamned...."

The lightning struck so fast it ionized the electrons in the air, sucking the words out of Orrie's mouth, making him gasp for air as he fell back on his butt in the water.

"Shit,' he said, using the golf club as a cane to regain his footing, still managing to keep the whiskey bottle above water. This was, after all, the worst day of his life, an existence that had seen more than its share of highs and lows.

Stunned by the shock wave from the lightning strike, Orrie struggled to his feet, still ankle deep in mud, with fresh rain slapping his face. Orrie looked up and shouted, "You missed me, you overrated sumbitch! You missed me! Trevino was right; even you can't hit a fucking 1-iron!"

Thus he never heard Macon Moses step into the stream with a length of rope in his hands, slip it over Orrie's neck, twist and pull it tight, before holding the once-beautiful boy's head under water in a murderous baptismal.

"In the name of the Father," he said, pulling Orrie's head up as the body spasmed. "The Son," he continued, dunking him deeper into the depths. "And the Holy Ghost," he said, as Orrie's body fell limp.

"Amen." Moses said sadly, without remorse, as raindrops dappled the slow-moving swamp water.

EPILOGUE

For three months after the terrorist attacks, the nation was in a constant state of mourning and madness.

Charlie Wong closed his failing restaurant in Barnwell and moved to Charleston so his daughter could enroll at Trident Technical College. There he opened a Subway restaurant with his new partner, Doug Barnes, who'd taken his retirement and invested the bribe money he'd collected over the years from various snitches and snoops.

Dexter Young rethought the family's plans of a newspaper empire after his twin brother Donald was found dead in a hotel room with three hookers.

Jack Cantey finally convinced the federal government to approve an independent water-quality survey on the Salkehatchie watershed, but died of a heart attack before it was completed.

Luke Thompson was found dead in his Subaru, parked outside the Department of Energy with his hands bound and two bullets in his brain. The D.C. Police never found a scrap of evidence, but left the case open.

Brumby McLean and Henry Smalls quit their jobs in Washington and joined the Peace Corps where they served a year together bringing fresh water to a village in Uganda before realizing they were not gay after all, simply insecure.

The envelope Brumby received was lost among some junk mail and thrown away, unopened.

Hannah Jane returned to South Carolina, lived for a while in a doublewide with an ex-con who beat her savagely, then drove them both into a bridge abutment after a New Year's Eve party.

Butterbean Green moved in with the choir lady. He quit growing Slave Weed, became a deacon in the Healing Springs Baptist Church, and watched the weeds and seedlings slowly overtake the one-hole golf course. But he was quieter now, a quality that stemmed from his heartbreak over Orrie's death. He stopped wearing the bone the root doctor gave him in the hopes of channeling Orrie's restless soul. And on occasion, when late summer storms approached, Butterbean welcomed the unsettled spirit of his best friend into his haunted world. He and Orrie would walk the sun-splashed fairways of eternity, together again, if only for a little while.

On a cold, rainy Sunday morning, Park Police found Granville Trinity's body leaning back against the Vietnam Memorial wall, just below the name of his son, a self-inflicted bullet wound to his head, a soggy, unreadable copy of the list in his right hand.

Eventually, the Confederate flag was taken down by the men of the Healing Springs Baptist Church and Country Club. They placed a wreath on the door in remembrance of Orrie Adger's unexplained disappearance.

Carl Gooding spent a month telling his devoted audience that Osama Bin Laden was hiding out in the Salkehatchie Swamp. He said that Harvey Womack had seen him coming out of Tucker's General Store in Seigling, and Harvey was going to personally lead a group of coon hunters and their dogs in there to get him, as soon as the weather warmed up and he got his shotgun back from his ex-wife.

The Yucca Mountain Project cost the U.S. Government $15 billion to prepare a place where the nation's nuclear waste could be safely stored in Nevada. However, it was put on indefinite hold in 2008 when President Barack Obama needed a favor from Senate Majority Leader Harry Reid of Nevada in order to pass important financial legislation to save the economy from the financial fiasco.

Macon Moses, knowing he'd made too many enemies, stayed on full alert, guarding against a terrorist attack that would never come, waiting for Nicole Davis to return his calls, and keeping an eye on a freshly tossed mound of soil in the nuclear cemetery as it settled ever so slowly in with the rest of South Carolina's buried lies.

THE END

Dum Spiro Spero
(While I Breathe, I Hope)